ONCE BURNED

"Why didn't you tell me there was a catch to drinking your blood? Maximus said that doing it made me, ah . . ."

"Mine," Vlad finished without hesitation.

My temper rose at his complete self-assuredness. "I didn't agree to that, so forget it."

He sat on the edge of the bed and leaned down, setting his arms on either side of my face.

"You think my blood is the only tie between us?"

His voice was low, yet edged with palpable hunger. It seemed to rub me in places I'd only ever touched before, making my anger fade under a flash of desire. Vlad was so close that his hair was a shadowy veil all around me, and when he began to caress my face with light, sure strokes, it was all I could do not to close my eyes in bliss.

"This is our true tie," he whispered, his breath falling hotly onto my lips. "You're meant for me, and I *will* have you."

By Jeaniene Frost

Jeaniene Frost

ONCE BURNED

A NIGHT PRINCE NOVEL

AVON

An Imprint of HarperCollins Publishers

This is a work of fiction. Names, characters, places, and incidents are products of the author's imagination or are used fictitiously and are not to be construed as real. Any resemblance to actual events, locales, organizations, or persons, living or dead, is entirely coincidental.

AVON BOOKS
An Imprint of HarperCollins*Publishers*
10 East 53rd Street
New York, New York 10022-5299

Copyright © 2012 by Jeaniene Frost
Excerpts from *Halfway to the Grave*; *One Foot in the Grave*; *At Grave's End*; *Destined for an Early Grave*; *This Side of the Grave*; *One Grave at a Time* copyright © 2007, 2008, 2009, 2011 by Jeaniene Frost
ISBN 978-0-06-178320-3
www.avonbooks.com

First Avon Books mass market printing: July 2012

Avon Trademark Reg. U.S. Pat. Off. and in Other Countries, Marca Registrada, Hecho en U.S.A.
HarperCollins® is a registered trademark of HarperCollins Publishers.

Printed in the U.S.A.

10 9 8 7 6 5

To JBA, for everything.

Acknowledgments

For once, I really *am* going to keep this short. Thanks to God, who carries me through all things; to my husband, who is my rock; to my agent and publishing house, who help make these books possible; to readers, for buying and recommending them; and to my family and friends, for their love and support.

Finally, to Dracula fans who, like me, always wanted him to win at the end instead of Van Helsing—this one's for you! *wink*

Chapter 1

 I parked my bike in front of the restaurant, wiping the perspiration from my upper lip. It was unseasonably warm this January, but sweating during a Florida winter was better than freezing in a Northern one. I twisted my hair into a knot, my neck cooler once the long black swath was off it. With a final swipe at my forehead, I entered the restaurant, ignoring the tables in favor of the patrons seated at the bar.

It only took a glance to see that most of them were average height, with a few extremely tall exceptions. Damn. If Marty wasn't here, then I had to ride to his next favorite hangout, and it looked like it was going to rain. I threaded through the tables, making sure to keep my right hand affixed to my thigh so it wouldn't accidentally brush anyone. It was that or wear the bulky electrical glove that inspired questions from nosy strangers. When I got to the bar, I smiled at the pierced, tattooed man who scooted enough to give me space at the countertop.

"Seen Marty?" I asked him.

Dean shook his head, rustling the chains that led from his nostrils to his ears. "Not yet, but I just got here."

"Raquel?" I called out. The bartender turned around, revealing a beautiful but bearded face that tourists surreptitiously or openly stared at.

"The usual, Frankie?" she asked, reaching for a wineglass.

That wasn't my real name, but it was what I went by nowadays. "Not this time. I'm looking for Marty."

"Hasn't been in yet," she stated.

Raquel didn't ask why I'd come in person instead of calling to ask that same question. Even though all the carnies that wintered in Gibsonton pretended they didn't know about my condition, none of them except Marty ever attempted to touch me, and no matter the weather, they didn't offer me a ride when they saw me on my bicycle.

I sighed. "If he comes in, tell him I'm looking for him?" We were supposed to start practice two hours ago. The off season turned Marty from a rigidly disciplined partner into a frequent slacker. If I didn't find him soon, he'd pass the point of being reasoned with and would stay out all night drinking and telling stories about the old carnival glory days.

Raquel smiled, revealing pretty white teeth in stark contrast to her dark, bristly beard. "Sure thing."

I started to walk away, but Dean tapped his beer with his fork, directing my attention back to him with the sound. "Want me to call the Tropicana and ask if Marty's there?"

He had correctly guessed the next place I was headed to, but then again, Dean had known Marty longer than I had.

"It's only a mile and I need to keep my legs in shape."

"They look fine to me," Dean said huskily, his gaze lingering on the limbs in question before moving over the rest of my body. Due to the heat, I only wore shorts and a tank top, so his view was pretty unrestricted. Then Dean shook his head as if to remind himself why checking me out was a bad idea. "See you around, Frankie," he finished in a brisker tone.

My chest tightened with an ache that was as familiar as it was useless. Yeah, Dean knew why fantasizing about my legs—or any other part of me—was pointless, and I'd long ago accepted that there were some things I'd never have. Yet in a flash of weakness, I found myself looking at a couple who were seated at a nearby table. Their fingers were interlaced as they whispered to each other. That simple touch was something they hardly seemed aware of, but it caught my attention like a spotlight beamed onto it, turning that ache in my chest into something closer to a burn.

The couple glanced at me, perhaps sensing my stare, but then their gaze quickly passed me by. Either they hadn't noticed the scar that ran from my temple to my right hand, or they didn't find it as interesting as the lizard-scale tattoos covering Dean's entire body, Raquel's beard, J.D.'s eight-foot height, or Katie's fourteen-inch waist that looked even tinier compared to her ample hips and double-D chest. It was still early, too. Most of Showtown USA's regulars didn't get here until after nine.

The couple continued to stare at the group by the bar without any attempt at subtlety, and the annoyance I felt over my friends being gawked at shook me from my brief melancholy. Some tourists came to Gibsonton to marvel at the carnival remains decorating many streets, or to see the occasional trained bear, elephant, or other exotic animal on someone's lawn, but most of them came to stare at the "freaks." The locals were immune to it, or played up their peculiarities for tips, but I still couldn't shake my anger over the rudeness so often displayed. Different didn't equal subhuman, yet that's exactly how many of Gibsonton's residents were treated by passersby.

Still, it wasn't my place to lecture people on their lack of manners, not to mention Raquel wouldn't take kindly to me chastising her customers. With my lips compressed together, I headed to the door, startled when it flung open as I reached for it. I jumped back in time to avoid being plowed over by a man who strode through as though he owned the place, but I wasn't fast enough to prevent his hand from grazing my arm.

"Ouch"! he snapped at the contact, giving me an accusing glance. "What the hell?"

He didn't know it, but he was lucky. If I hadn't learned to harness some of the currents in me, or released the worst of them into lightning rods only an hour before, his experience would've been much worse.

"Static electricity," I lied. "It's bad around this area."

His expression said he didn't believe me, but I had nothing in my hands, and my outfit wouldn't conceal much, either. After another glare, he turned his back on me.

"Which exit do I take to get to Tampa?" he called out to the bar at large. "My damn nav system isn't working here."

That wasn't unusual around these parts and I knew the answer, but I stayed silent, not wanting to risk another inadvertent touch by talking to him again.

I went out the bar door—and a harried-looking blonde ran right into me. She let out a yelp that I mentally echoed out of sheer frustration. After months of a spotless record, now I'd zapped two people in less than five minutes. At least Rude Dude had taken some of the extra voltage out of me so hers probably *did* feel like static electricity instead of mild electrocution.

"I'm sorry," I said, backing away at once.

"It's my fault." She laughed, patting me in an apologetic way. "I wasn't looking—"

I didn't hear the rest of what she said. Images seared across my mind in varying shades of black, white, and gray.

I was in bed with my lover, our heavy breathing the only sound in the room. Afterward, I whispered that I was going to tell my husband I was leaving him the following weekend.

That wasn't what made me stiffen, however. It was the next images that filled my mind, in full color this time, only hazy, as though seen through a fog.

I was in a thick, swampish area, staring in

horror as my husband's hands clamped around my throat. Pain exploded in my neck, blurring his image as I futilely scratched and clawed at his gloved hands. He increased the pressure while telling me he'd found out about my affair and exactly how he'd dispose of my body. The pain intensified until it seared its way down my entire body. Then, mercifully, it stopped, and I felt like I was floating away. My murderer stayed where he was, his hands still clamped around my throat, unaware that I was now looking down at him from outside my body. Finally, he let go. Then he walked over to where he'd parked the car, opened the trunk, and took out several items as though musing over which one to start with first . . .

"Frankie!"

I blinked, back in my own consciousness, the hazy images fading into the familiar, crystal-clear surroundings of the bar. Dean stood between me and the woman who'd unwittingly triggered my abilities by touching my right hand. He didn't make that same mistake, but Dean was close enough that I had to look over his shoulder to see her. She clutched her hand as though it hurt, her brown eyes wide as she babbled something to the man I now knew was her husband. The same man who'd murder her tonight, if I didn't stop him.

"I didn't do anything!" she kept saying. "She just started screaming . . ."

Her husband grabbed her arm. "Screw this creep show, Jackie, we'll get directions somewhere else."

"Stop them," I gasped to Dean, still feeling the phantom effect of fingers on my throat. "He's going to kill her."

If anyone in the bar had been minding their business before, that statement directed their attention to me better than a gunshot. Jackie gaped at me, but her husband's eyes narrowed. He began to push his way past the small crowd that gathered around us, dragging her along.

Dean stood in their path, blocking the way to the exit. "You're not leaving yet," he said calmly.

The husband paused, looking Dean up and down. If Dean's expression wasn't intimidating enough, the scaly green tattoos covering his skin rippled when he crossed his arms, showing bulky muscles.

"Come on," the husband muttered. "I don't want trouble—"

"Look in his trunk," I interrupted, my voice stronger. "You'll find work gloves, duct tape, and leaf and lawn bags."

The surrounding patrons had begun to stare at the husband. He laughed uneasily. "I don't have to listen to this shit—"

"Plus he has an axe, a shovel, flashlights, bleach, rope, pliers, and a book on forensics," I cut him off again. "You found out she was leaving you and you couldn't handle it. So you were going to strangle her, pull out all her teeth, and cut off the ends of her fingers so even if her body *was* found, no one would be able to identify her."

He looked stunned. Jackie began to shake while tears spurted from her eyes. "Phil, is—is that true?"

"No!" he thundered. "The crazy bitch is lying!"

And then he made a huge mistake and whirled around, grabbing my shoulders. Dean went to haul him back, but I was faster. The memory of experiencing everything he intended for Jackie made me merciless, and I laid my right hand on his arm, releasing the hold I had over those unwanted currents in me.

Another series of images exploded in my mind, colorless from age, but that wasn't why I touched him. My vision dimmed as I felt the current surge from me into Phil in less than the time it took Dean to yank him away. Phil fell onto the floor, and after several blinks I saw with satisfaction that he was still convulsing. A few tourists screamed. Jackie sobbed. I felt bad about that, but a few tears now were a far better fate than what Phil had planned for her.

"What happened?" one of the unfamiliar onlookers demanded.

"He grabbed her, so she Tasered him," Dean said gruffly.

I didn't have a Taser, but J.D. moved in front of me, blocking that from view with his huge eight-foot frame.

Jackie recovered herself and, with shaking hands, pulled a set of car keys from Phil's pocket. He didn't seem to notice, being too busy twitching and pissing himself. No one stopped her as she went out to the parking lot, but Dean followed her after tossing me a grim look.

Jackie's scream moments later made several people walk out, some throwing money on their tables, some not. Jackie must have seen that I was spot-on about what was in the trunk.

Raquel came up to me and wearily rubbed her beard. "You're in for it now, Frankie."

I thought she meant I had to cover the lost revenue from the tourists who were beating a hasty retreat. It was my fault that they stiffed their tabs, so I couldn't blame Raquel, but covering those expenses was worth saving a woman's life.

It was only later, after Jackie sobbingly explained to the police what happened, that I realized the full extent of what Raquel meant. By then, it was too late.

Chapter 2

Marty stared in silence as I jumped on the trampoline with more force than was needed. With his four-foot, one-inch height, he was barely as tall as the edge of the trampoline, but his sideburns, wrinkles, and stoutly muscled frame showed he was no child. I looked away from him and focused my attention inward, barely noticing the landscape rising and falling with every jump. When I was high enough, I clasped my knees to my chest in a classic tuck, then quickly twisted into a pike before my feet hit the flexible surface and bounced me upward again.

Not tight enough in the tuck! I could almost hear my old trainer shout. *That's a full point deduction, Leila! You'll never make the team with scores that low.*

I pushed those memories aside and concentrated on my next move—a barani ball-out. This maneuver was even sloppier than the last, my foot doing an embarrassing slip backward upon landing. *Another deduction*, I thought automatically, but powered through the last set of somersaults and turntables. No self-respecting judge would give me high marks for those, but they looked impressive so the carnival spectators loved them.

This time, instead of landing on the trampoline, I changed direction at the last second and both my feet slammed down on Marty's shoulders. The velocity plus my weight should've brought him to his knees and broken several bones, but Marty stood ramrod-straight. He grabbed my ankles, steadying me with a grip that was firm enough to allow me to stretch to my full height of five-six, arms triumphantly extended over my head.

"And the crowd goes wild," Marty said ironically as I bowed.

I jumped down once he let go of my ankles. "Not as many crowds these days. People have too many other things to do than go to traveling carnivals."

He grunted. "If Stan had his way, you'd use your newfound celebrity status to help with that."

I grimaced at the mention of our boss's delight over what happened with Jackie two weeks ago. At least no one was gathered by our fence today. Just my luck that Jackie's sister had been a reporter who blasted the news of my "premonition" across every media avenue available to her. Phil pled not guilty and there wasn't enough evidence to prove he'd intended to murder his wife, but my knowledge of Jackie's plan to leave him combined with my flawless description of what was in his trunk was enough to draw the curious these past couple weeks. If not for my unfortunate tendency to electrocute everyone I touched, I could've made a nice stash doing palm readings, but as it was, I couldn't wait for my fifteen minutes of fame to be over.

"I need people to forget what I can do. You know why."

Marty stared at me almost sadly. "Yeah, kid. I do."

Then he patted my arm, not flinching at the current that shot into him with the contact. He was used to it, and besides, Marty wasn't human so it didn't affect him the same way.

"Come inside and I'll make you a shake," he said with a final fatherly pat.

I turned away so he wouldn't see my grimace. Marty was so proud of his blended concoctions that I drank at least one a week, but they tasted vile. If I hadn't noticed that they *did* seem to improve my health, I'd have secretly dumped most of them into potted plants instead of drinking them.

"Um, in a little bit. I need to work the kinks out of that last set of flips."

His snort told me what a bad liar I was, but he didn't argue. I heard the trailer door shut moments later.

Once he was gone, I returned my attention to practicing my part of our routine. Marty's part involved escaping out of several exploding objects in time to catch me for certain jumps or trapeze swings, but since he wasn't human, he didn't need to practice as much as I did. Good thing, too, or it would cost us a fortune in props and incendiary devices, not to mention the damage it would do to the lawn. We rented the land this trailer sat on, so if we trashed it, we paid for it.

Being a member of a circus sideshow wasn't what I'd dreamed of doing when I was a kid, but that was before I started frying the circuits of every electrical device I touched, not to mention shocking people by casual contact. With my condition, I was lucky to have a job at all. The only other occupation I'd be good for was government guinea pig, as I reminded my father whenever he lamented over my career choice.

I made my jumps smooth and measured, building a rhythm that allowed me to push away other concerns. Concentration was critical to success, my old coach used to remind us, and he was right. Soon I barely noticed the collage of fence-yard-roof that repeated with every jump until they blurred together in one indistinguishable mass of colors. Then I executed my series of somersaults, flips, and twists, landing with my feet planted apart and knees slightly bent to lessen the impact. The trampoline trembled, but I remained rigid, not taking that points-killing step backward. Then I raised my arms before sweeping into a low bow, the final touch of the routine.

"Bravo," a voice said mockingly.

I straightened, everything in me tensing. When I'd begun my bow, I'd been alone, but in the scant seconds since then, four men stood at each corner of the trampoline.

They looked like normal tourists, with their T-shirts and jeans, but only Marty could move that fast, which meant these men weren't human. Even if I didn't know to be wary of alternate species, the cold smile I glimpsed on the auburn-haired member of the quartet told me they weren't here to ask for directions. I tried to rein in my now-galloping heartbeat. If I was lucky, these creatures would think it came from my recent exertions, though the scent of my fear probably gave me away.

"This is private property," I said.

"You must be the Fantastic Frankie," the tall, auburn-haired one said, ignoring that. His voice caressed my stage name in a way that sounded sinister.

"Who wants to know?" I replied while wondering where the hell Marty was. He had to have heard these guys even if he didn't sense that a group of nonhumans were here.

I'd been on the trampoline when I asked the question, but was on the ground in the next instant, the auburn-haired stranger's grip bruising me. He grunted in pain as currents pulsed into him from his contact with my skin, but like Marty, those currents didn't debilitate him. His grip only tightened.

"How the fuck did you do that?" he demanded, his gaze turning from blue to bright, unearthly green.

I didn't answer. My mind was awash in grayish images as soon as my right hand came into contact with his body. Just like I couldn't prevent those currents from flowing into him, I also couldn't stop seeing the worst of his sins through that single touch.

Blood. So much blood . . .

Through the panicked memory of another person's murder, I heard him curse me for screaming, and then a sharp pain preceded everything going black.

I faced my captors in what looked to be a hotel room, my hands folded in my lap as if I was placing a dinner order and they were waiters. *If you ever meet another vampire, don't panic. You'll only smell like prey*, Marty had warned me. I knew what my kidnappers were after seeing their eyes glow green. That was why I didn't bother lying when they asked me how I doubled as an electric eel and had the ability to siphon information through touch. If I lied, they'd only use the power in their gaze to make me tell the truth—or do whatever else they wanted—and I didn't want to give them any more control over me than they already had.

I also didn't try to run even though they hadn't tied me up. Most people didn't know vampires existed, let alone what they could do, but with my abilities, I'd known about vampires before I met Marty. My unwanted talents meant I knew all sorts of things I wished I didn't.

Like the fact that my captors had every intention of killing me; that topped the list of things I wished I didn't know at the moment. I'd seen my death after being forced to touch the auburn-haired vampire again, and it was an image that made me want to clutch my neck while backing away screaming.

I didn't. Guess I should be grateful that my unwanted abilities meant I'd experienced so many horrible deaths, I could look at my impending execution with a morbid sort of relief. Getting my throat ripped out would hurt—I'd relived that through other people enough times to know. Still, it wasn't the worst way to die. Besides, nothing was set in stone. I'd seen a glimpse of my *possible* future, but I'd managed to prevent Jackie's murder. Maybe I could find a way to prevent my own.

"So let me get this straight," Auburn Hair said, drawing the words out. "You touched a downed power line when you were thirteen, nearly died, and then later, your body began giving off electric voltage and your right hand divined psychic impressions from whatever you touched?"

More had happened, but it wasn't information I wanted to reveal and he wouldn't care about those details anyway.

"You experienced the voltage part yourself," I said with a shrug. "As for the other, yeah, if I touch something, I get impressions off it." *Whether I want to or not*, I silently added.

He smiled then, his gaze roving over the thin, jagged scar that was the visible remains of my brush with death. "What did you see when you touched me?"

"Past or future?" I asked, grimacing at either memory.

He exchanged an interested look with his buddies. "Both."

How I would love to lie, but I didn't need psychometric abilities to know if they doubted me, I'd be dead in moments.

"You like eating children." The words made bile rise in my throat that I swallowed before continuing. "And you're intending to drink me to death if I don't prove useful to you."

His smile widened, showing the tips of his fangs as he didn't deny either charge. If I hadn't seen similar menacing, fanged grins through the eyes of people I'd been psychically linked to, I would have been pants-pissing terrified, but a jaded part of me simply acknowledged him for what he was: evil. And I was no stranger to evil, much as I wished otherwise.

"If she's the real deal like we heard, it could give us the edge we've been looking for," his brunet companion muttered.

"I think you're right," Auburn Hair drawled.

I didn't want to die, but there were some things I wouldn't do even if it cost me my life. "Ask me to help you kidnap children, and you may as well start in on my neck now."

Auburn Hair laughed. "I can do that on my own," he assured me, making my stomach lurch with revulsion. "What I want from you is more . . . complicated. If I bring you objects to touch, can you tell me about their owner? Such as what he's doing, where he is, and most importantly, where he *will* be?"

I didn't want to do anything to help this disgusting, murderous group, but my choices were grim. If I refused, I'd get mesmerized into doing it anyway, or get tortured into doing it, or die choking on my own blood because I was of no use to them. Maybe this was my chance to change the fate they intended for me.

Why do you want to? a dark inner voice whispered. *Aren't you sick of drowning in other people's sins? Isn't death your only way out?*

I glanced at my wrist, the faint scars that had nothing to do with my electrocution marking my skin. Once, I'd listened to that despairing inner voice, and I'd be lying if I didn't admit part of me was still tempted by it. Then I thought of Marty, how I hadn't told my dad I loved him the last time we spoke, how I hadn't talked to my sister in months, and finally, how I didn't want to give these bastards the satisfaction of killing me.

My head came up and I met the leader's gaze. "My abilities are tied to my emotions. Abuse me mentally or physically, and you'll have better luck calling a psychic hotline to find out what you want to know. That means no murdering anyone while I'm getting information for you, and no touching me at all."

That last part I said because of the lustful look the scraggly brunet had been giving me. My skin-tight body suit and boxer shorts didn't leave much to the imagination, but it was what I trained in. I hadn't expected to be kidnapped today or I'd have worn something more conservative.

"Don't think you can mesmerize me into forgetting whatever you do, either," I added, waving my right hand. "Psychic impressions, remember? I'll touch you or an object nearby and find out, and then your human crystal ball will be broken."

All the above was bullshit. They could do anything they wanted and I'd still pull impressions from whatever my right hand touched, but I'd used my most convincing tone while praying that, for once, I'd prove to be a good liar.

Auburn Hair flashed his fangs at me in another scary smile. "We can manage that, *if* you deliver what you say you can."

I smiled back with nothing close to humor. "Oh, I can deliver, all right."

Then I glanced at the light socket behind him. *And that's not all I can do.*

Chapter 3

 Auburn Hair's name was Jackal, according to what his friends called him. Their names sounded equally made up, so I mentally referred to them as Pervert, Psycho, and Twitchy since the last couldn't seem to stay still. Twitchy and Pervert had gone out over an hour ago to get some things for me to touch. I'd spent that time sitting on the edge of the hotel's lumpy mattress, listening to Jackal talk on his cell phone in a language I didn't recognize. I was getting chilly in my leotard, but I didn't pull the covers over me. All my instincts were urging me to stay still and not attract any attention to myself, as if that mattered. The predators in this room were very aware of me even if they didn't glance in my direction.

When Pervert and Twitchy came back, I looked at the duffel bag they carried with a mixture of dread and optimism. What was inside might lead to more grisly images blasting across my mind, but it would also ensure my survival.

"Put the objects in a row on the bed," I directed Twitchy, ignoring the startled look he gave me. If

I acted like a pitiful damsel in distress, then that's how they'd treat me. But if I acted like a vital tool in their search for whomever they wanted these objects to lead them to, I upped my chances for survival.

At least, I hoped I did.

"Do it," Jackal said, folding his arms across his chest. His stare felt like weights dropping onto me, but I took in several deep breaths and tried to ignore him. Seeing what Twitchy took out of the duffel bag helped with that.

A charred piece of fabric, a partially melted watch, a ring, something that looked like a belt, and a knife that shone with a distinct silvery gleam.

That last item made my heart skip a beat, something I hoped the others chalked up to nervousness instead of what it was. *Excitement.* The movies had it all wrong when it came to vampires. Wooden stakes wouldn't harm them, nor would sunlight, crosses, or holy water. But silver through the heart meant the party was over, and now I had a silver knife within grabbing distance.

Not yet, I warned myself. I'd wait until they were so convinced I was helpless that they wouldn't think twice about leaving a silver knife within easy reach. Or until at least two of them left again, whichever came first.

"All right, Frankie," Jackal said, snapping my gaze back to him. He nodded at the objects. "Do your thing."

I mentally braced myself and then picked up the charred piece of fabric first.

Smoke was everywhere. Twin beams of light cut through it, landing on where I was half concealed by the forklift. Terror flooded me as I realized I'd been spotted. My attempt to run was stopped short, and rough hands hauled me back.

At first the smoke was so thick I couldn't see past the bright gaze lasered on me. Then I saw dark hair framing a lean face that had the shadow of stubble around the jaw and mouth. That mouth stretched into a smile that wasn't cruel, as I'd expected, but looked surprisingly good-humored.

"Raziel," the dark-haired stranger said in a chiding tone. "You shouldn't have."

I'd heard parents scold their children more harshly, but that didn't stop the torrent of fear that flooded over me.

"Please," I gasped.

"Please?" The stranger laughed, revealing white teeth with two distinct upper fangs. "How unoriginal."

Then he let me go, turning around and waving farewell in a friendly manner. Relief overwhelmed me to the point that my knees trembled, but I didn't let that stop me. I lunged toward the warehouse door.

That's when the fire swarmed me, forming out of nowhere. It climbed up my legs in coiling, merciless bands, making me scream from the sudden blast of agony. I tried to run faster, but that only made the fire climb higher. I flung myself onto the floor next, rolling, every nerve ending howling with anguish, but the fire still didn't extinguish. It kept growing, covering me with ruthless, hungry waves, until a roaring blackness rushed up and consumed me. The last thing I saw as I floated above my lifeless body was the dark-haired vam-

pire still walking away, his hands now lit up by
flames that somehow didn't scorch his skin.

I blinked in disbelief. When my eyes opened, I
was back in the hotel room curled into the fetal
position, much like Raziel had been when he died.
I must have instinctively mimicked his actions with
the memory of those phantom flames.

"Well?" Jackal's demanding voice was a relief
because it centered me in reality instead of the
nightmare I'd been forced to relive. "What did you
see?"

I righted myself on the bed and threw the charred
piece of fabric at him.

"I saw someone named Raziel get Krispy
Kremed by a vampire who apparently can control
fire," I said, still trying to shake off the echoes of
that gruesome death.

The four of them exchanged a look that could
only be described as delighted. "Jackpot!" Psycho
exclaimed, pumping his fists into the air.

From how happy they were, I guessed that either
Raziel hadn't been a friend or they already knew
what had happened to him and this had been a test.

"Let's be a hundred percent sure," Jackal said,
his grin fading. "Frankie, touch the ring next."

I picked it up, tensing in grim expectation, but
a scattershot of images I'd already seen filled my
mind. They were still revolting enough to make me
want to vomit, but in addition to being in the grayish colors of the past, they felt fainter, like I was
watching a movie instead of experiencing them
firsthand. With a shake of my head to clear it, I set
the ring back down by Jackal.

"Maybe you made a mistake. The only impressions I'm picking up off this are yours, and they don't tell me anything new."

His hazel eyes gleamed emerald for a second, and then he let out a loud whoop that made me flinch.

"It's not a fluke, she's for fucking real!"

Anything that thrilled a sadistic child murderer freaked me out, but I tried not to let it show. *Don't panic*, Marty had said. *Prey panics, and then prey gets* eaten.

"On to the next one?" I asked, trying to sound as cool as I could under the circumstances.

They stopped their high fiving to look at me. "Yeah," Jackal said, pushing the knife toward me. His excitement was almost palpable. "Only this time, I want you to concentrate on the fire starter. Try to see where the bastard is, not just what happened when he butchered Neddy."

That told me the knife would make me relive someone else's murder, but that wasn't what made me pause before reaching for it.

"The fire starter?" I repeated. "*He's* the one you want me to find through these objects?"

Are you out of your minds? I almost added, but didn't because even if they were, I wasn't.

"You can do it, right?" Jackal asked, all mirth wiping from his expression.

Sure I could, but I didn't want to. I doubted the fire starter was a friend; Jackal calling him a bastard in that contemptuous tone plus wanting me to find where he was smacked of nefarious intentions. Anyone smart would avoid being on the same *continent* as that creature if they were at odds, yet Jackal and the others must be trying to ambush him. The memory of the fire starter's charming smile right before he burned Raziel to a heap of smoldering ruins was something I wanted to forget. But if I refused to look for him, I wouldn't live long enough to worry about forgetting anything.

Any way you cut it, I was stuck between a rock and a hard place. Or, more accurately, between a fang and a sharp place.

I reached for the silver knife. With that single touch, the grayish images from Neddy's death invaded my consciousness as though everything were happening to me. No surprise that the fire starter was the one who killed Neddy, using the knife after some preliminary toasting. Also no shock was that he did it with the same sort of detached geniality he'd shown while executing Raziel. I pushed past the searing pain I felt, past the feeling of floating into whatever awaited people after death, and focused on the fire starter, trying to see him *now* instead of only *then*.

This part was harder. In highly emotional situations, everyone leaves a piece of their essence onto objects, but the fire starter hadn't been worked up over killing Neddy, so only a smidgeon of his remained on the knife. Still, detached or not, nothing tied two people closer together than death. Something about the door to the other world cracking open made essences merge and imprint more strongly, so once I pushed past the seething remains of Neddy's rage and fear, I felt the fire starter's distinct essence. It was only as big as a thread, but I wrapped all my concentration around it and pulled.

Black and white images were replaced with full color clarity. Instead of the grimy riverfront setting where Neddy had met his end, I saw opulent drapes surrounding me. At first I thought I was in a small room, but then I realized the midnight-green drapes hung around a large bed, cocooning it. The fire starter lay in the center, fully clothed, his eyes closed as though he were asleep.

Gotcha, I thought, torn between relief and dismay at finding him in what I knew was the present.

I'd only seen him before through the grayish tones of past memories, but spying on him in the present was different. No one else was in my head but me. Free from other people's perspectives, I took my time studying the fire starter.

At first, he looked like a normal, well-built man in his thirties, but then hints of his uniqueness showed. His espresso-colored hair was past his shoulders—longer than most men dared, but on him it somehow looked supremely masculine. Black pants and an indigo shirt draped over muscles that appeared far harder than a gym membership usually accounted for, and though no flames clung to his hands, they were crisscrossed with scars that looked like former battle wounds. His high cheekbones were accented by stubble somewhere between five o'clock shadow and a beard, yet instead of coming across as unkempt, it was rugged and enticing. I hadn't seen a man pull off that look so well since Aragorn in *Lord of the Rings*, and his eyes . . .

Opened, a rich copper shade encircled by rings of evergreen. I would have thought they were beautiful, but at the moment, they looked as though they were staring right into mine.

It unnerved me, but I reminded myself it was

only coincidence. No one ever knew it when I used my abilities to establish a link. I could be the world's biggest voyeur if I wanted, but my most fervent wish was to know less about people, not more—

"Who are you?"

I jumped. If I hadn't seen his finely shaped lips move, I would've thought I'd imagined the words. *Coincidence*, I reminded myself again. Any second someone would come into my line of vision and I'd see who he was really talking to—

"I'll ask a second time," his deep, slightly accented voice said. "*Who* are you, and how the hell are you inside my head?"

That scared me into dropping the link at once. The ornate bed with its encircling drapes disappeared, replaced by ass-ugly wallpaper and a bed that would probably result in my getting bug bites. I let go of the silver knife as though it burned me, still reeling over what just happened.

"Well?" Jackal asked. "Did you find him?"

"Oh yeah." My voice was nearly a croak from shock.

"*And?*" he prodded.

No way was I going to tell him the fire starter had somehow realized he was being been spied on. If Jackal knew that, he'd kill me on the spot so the fire starter couldn't follow the link back through me to find him. It was possible. If he could feel me in his head, the fire starter could probably hear me, too . . .

With a flash of inspiration that was more reckless than smart, I knew what I had to do.

Chapter 4

Twitchy, Pervert, and Psycho had already left the room, but Jackal stayed by the tiny desk. From the belligerent expression on his face, he had no intention of moving.

I let out a sigh. "You think I'm going to escape out the window if you leave me alone? Come on, the others would hear it and stop me. Can't call 911 and say, 'Help, a bunch of vampires kidnapped me!' either. Even if they didn't think it was a crank call, you'd just mesmerize any cops into leaving. Or eat them. Either way, I'm not going anywhere and I know it."

"You're up to something," Jackal stated.

It took all my willpower not to flinch, but I schooled myself to stay absolutely still. *Don't panic, don't panic . . .*

"I don't know what," he went on, "but I can smell that you're plotting something."

I cleared my throat. "What you smell is someone who's been breaking out in cold sweats ever since she was kidnapped by *vampires*. If you want more information on your fire guy aside from how nice his drapes are, then leave. How am I supposed to concentrate when I'm being stared at by a pack of creatures that keep looking at my neck and licking their lips?"

He was suddenly in front of me, his hand gripping my chin. "What are you really trying to do?" he asked, forcing me to look into his now-glowing eyes.

Their effect was immediate. I felt drowsy, unconcerned, and talkative even as a part of me screeched in alarm.

"Can't link to him with all of you watching," I mumbled. "Can't get deep enough in his mind for it to work."

His eyes brightened until it almost hurt to look into them. "That's all?"

The words *He sees me, too* hovered on my lips, about to fall and seal my fate. But though I felt like I'd just smoked a pound of weed, I found the strength to say something else.

"Too scared . . . with you here."

That was the truth, but the reasons why remained unspoken. Jackal released me, his gaze still lit up. "You won't call anyone or try to leave this room."

His words resonated through my mind. I nodded without thinking. He shoved me and I fell back onto the bed, but to my relief, Jackal then headed to the door.

"You have an hour, Frankie. Find him again, and more importantly, find where he'll be in the future."

He opened the door, and then paused. Before my next blink, Jackal had ripped the phone cord in two.

"That's for insurance," he muttered, and finally left.

I waited a few seconds and then let out the breath I'd been holding. Holy shit, that was close! I had no idea how I'd managed not to spill everything when Jackal turned his lite-brights on me, but I'd count my blessings later.

They say the devil you know is better than the one you don't. Maybe that was true, but considering what Jackal and the others had planned for me, I was going with Option B. It gave me better odds than trying to fight off four vampires with one puny knife—which Jackal had taken with him, I noticed. Must not want to risk me attempting suicide, although what I was about to do might turn out to be the equivalent.

There wasn't time for me to second-guess my decision, so I picked up the charred piece of fabric, and Raziel's death washed over me again. As usual, the impressions were fainter, the first touch always producing the most intense experience.

I pushed past Raziel's tortuous last moments to latch on to the fire starter's essence. What had been a thread before now felt like a rope because of my previous connection, so I grabbed it and pulled with all my might. My dingy surroundings fell away, replaced by a huge room with soaring ceilings, elegant furniture, and tapestries on every wall. It wasn't empty; two men stood in front of a fireplace that was big enough to fit both of them. I saw with relief that one of them was the fire starter, and the other a bald, brawny African American who was shaking his head.

"Of course I don't think you're joking, but it still doesn't seem possible—"

"Shhh!" the fire starter hissed. Very slowly, his head turned. When those burnished copper eyes seemed to land on me, I fought my instinct to drop the link and run like hell.

"Oh, it's too late for you to run," he said coldly.

The words slammed into me, shocking me. I'd hoped with a little time—and a lot of luck—I could send him specific messages. It never occurred to me that the fire starter could read my mind as soon as I established a link. *What kind of creature was he?*

"A dangerous one you shouldn't have trifled with," was his response. "Whoever you are, rest assured that I will find you."

Fear paralyzed my mind. He was pissed, and I'd seen what he did to people when he looked to be in a *good* mood.

His friend glanced around. "Who are you—?"

"Quiet," the fire starter said. "Leave."

The brawny man walked out of my sight without another word. The fire starter stayed in front of the enormous hearth, those orange and yellow flames growing as if they longed to reach him through the screen.

"Quit calling me fire starter, it's insulting. You're spying on me, so you know who I am."

"I don't," I said aloud, then cursed myself. If Jackal heard me and came to investigate, I might not be able to resist a second dose of his gaze before I spilled the truth.

Look, you've got me all wrong, I thought rapidly, hoping his antennae into my head hadn't lost its signal. *I have no idea who you are, but four vampires kidnapped me and they're forcing me to locate you for them.*

"Oh?" Amusement replaced the former harshness in his expression. "If that's true, I'll make it easy on you. I'm at my home. Tell the others to drop by anytime."

Flames coated his hands with the words, a warning I didn't need because I was terrified of him already. That fear combined with the death Jackal had planned for me made my reply snappy.

That's great, but I'm not only supposed to find out where you are now. I'm supposed to find out where you'll be in the future, and I'm guessing you won't be as flip about that.

His brows drew together at once, making those coppery green eyes all the more riveting—and frightening.

"You can see the future?" All traces of humor left his expression.

I heaved a mental sigh. How to explain an ability I didn't fully understand?

If I touch someone—or an object with a strong emotional essence on it—I catch glimpses of things. If the glimpses are in black and white, they're from the past. If they're in color but hazy, they're from the future. And if I concentrate, I can trace someone's essence from an object to find that person in the present, which looks clear and normal to me. That's how I found you. Jackal gave me pieces of things from people you killed.

He continued to stare at me until I squirmed. Aside from it being unbelievable that he could hear me, he seemed able to *see* me, too! How? I wasn't there, after all.

"I don't see you like you're thinking," he answered, a tight smile playing about his lips. "You're a voice in my head, but when I concentrate, it's though you're here yet you're invisible." That sounded creepy. I didn't have time to ponder it, because he went on.

"Someone named Jackal is after me? I don't recognize the name, but it's likely an alias. He kidnapped you, you say?"

He and three of his buddies snatched me right off my trampoline this morning, I answered, grimacing at the memory.

"Do you know where they're holding you?"

I knew exactly where I was. Even if I couldn't tell by touching items in the room, the phone had the hotel's full address printed on it. Still, I wasn't about to tell Mr. Inferno where that was until we agreed on some terms.

He grunted in amusement. "Terms? You want a reward for turning them in to me?"

I want to live, I thought at him grimly. *I saw what you did to Neddy and Raziel, so I want your word that if I tell you where Jackal and the others are, you'll kill them, not me.*

"Depends," he said, voice crisp as though this were a business transaction. "If you truly were forced into this as you claim, then I vow you'll come to no harm. But if you're lying in an attempt to lead me into a trap . . ."

He flashed one of those charming smiles that had been the last thing Neddy and Raziel had seen. I shuddered.

I'm not lying, I sent to him. *The only people I'm trying to trap are Jackal, Pervert, Psycho, and Twitchy.*

"Then you have nothing to fear from me," he said, not commenting on the other names. He clasped those deadly hands in front of him. "And it's time we were properly introduced. I'm Vlad, and you are?"

I hesitated, but replied with my real name because I didn't want to risk even a white lie with this creature.

Leila. My name is Leila.

"Leila." He said my name as though he could taste the syllables. That charming smile widened. "Now, tell me where you are."

Chapter 5

 Jackal tossed the partially melted belt at me. "Try again. Knowing he's at his house is worthless. We need to know where he'll be when he's *away* from that fortress, not safe inside it."

I glanced at the clock on the dresser. Almost two a.m., more than eight hours since I'd spoken to Vlad—who was taking his vampire status *way* too seriously with that name. What was keeping him? Had he decided these men weren't worth the effort to kill? I'd love to touch the melted belt and find out, but I didn't know if I could get all of them to vamoose again. Jackal had promised me an hour alone before, but he'd barged into the room only thirty minutes later.

"I'm exhausted," I said, rubbing my forehead for effect. "Reliving all these deaths, repeatedly trying to connect to someone in the present . . . it takes a toll." And I also had a nasty headache, but I didn't think they'd care about that.

"You want me to wake you up with these?" Psycho snarled, baring his fangs at me.

Jackal laid a hand on him. "That's not necessary," he said in a soothing tone. "Poor Frankie's tired. We should let her get some sleep. I know— let's go grab dinner. I saw a tasty-looking family in Room 302. Plenty for all of us."

My stomach heaved, because the cold glint in his eyes said he wasn't bluffing. Pervert, Twitchy, and Psycho smirked, silently daring me to make their night. I got off the bed.

"Let me pee and splash some water on my face, then I'll try to find him again," I said, silently cursing them. I walked the short distance to the bathroom and shut the door. At least none of them tried to insist on coming in with me.

That stalling tactic only bought me a few minutes. Soon I was back on the bed, shivering under the air-conditioning and reaching for the silver knife.

"Why not the belt?" Jackal asked at once, stopping me.

I glared at him, too mad over his dinner threat and worried that Vlad had changed his mind to feign politeness. "It's easier to develop a connection through something I've already used."

He grunted. "Fine. Get to it, and we're not leaving unless you want us to find that family."

More rage flared, but I pursed my lips and said nothing, picking up the cold blade. Neddy's death washed over me again, and I pushed through those memories until I found the link to the fire starter. To my surprise, it barely took any time. A vast expanse of indigo replaced the hotel room around me. Vlad was in the middle of that dark expanse, stretched out full-length, his eyes glowing emerald as he looked at something I couldn't see.

For a moment, I was confused. He almost seemed as though he was swimming in his inky surroundings, except he had on a long gray coat that wasn't wet. What . . . ?

"I'm not swimming, Leila. I'm flying."

Vlad's voice flowed over my mind, sounding amused. I realized that the endless expanse around him wasn't water, but the night sky. He had to be high up, too. I didn't see any lights below.

If I lived through this, I was kicking Marty's ass for not telling me some vampires could fly! What if Marty could fly, too? What if *all* vampires flew? My escape chances would be blown to hell if that were the case—

"Who is Marty? You didn't mention him before." Vlad's cool voice interrupted my train of thought.

Marty's a vampire, too, I thought, still trying to absorb this new information. *But he's not involved in any of this except for probably being worried sick about me.*

"You belong to another vampire?"

A note of suspicion was back in his voice, and the way he said "belong" implied sexual or edible benefits. Or both. I scowled, forgetting Vlad couldn't see it.

No! We work together and we're friends, but that's it.

Ew, I couldn't help but add. Marty was like a second father to me. The idea of him poking his fangs—or anything else—into me was repellent.

What's taking you so long? I thought, getting back to the most important topic. *It's been hours. Did you change your mind?*

It sounded like he snorted, but with the whooshing wind all around him, I couldn't be sure.

"I didn't change my mind. I was very far from Florida."

So he was still coming. Relief competed with anxiety. *They made me find you again*, I told him. *I tried to stall, but they threatened to eat a family. Said telling them you were at your house wasn't good enough and they'd need to know where you were when you were away from that place.*

A grin stretched his mouth. I didn't find anything funny in my statements, but we must have a different sense of humor.

"Are they with you now?"

I couldn't see them at the moment, but I knew Jackal, Twitchy, Pervert, and Psycho were still clustered around me.

Yeah. They wouldn't leave me alone this time.

"Good."

If I didn't know the others could hear me, I would've let out an audible scoff. Vlad could at least *pretend* to care that my neck was in danger of becoming a Capri Sun.

He chuckled, flipping up his coat sleeve to glance at something. Whatever it was seemed to please him, because his teeth flashed in another grin.

"I want you to start narrating, Leila. Tell the others exactly what you see me doing."

Why? I almost blurted aloud, catching myself just in time.

That emerald gaze seemed to laser on me. "Because I told you to," he said, his tone implying that he didn't appreciate having his directives questioned.

I hope this doesn't get me killed, I sent to him irritably. My hand tightened around the silver knife. It might be my only hope if this stunt backfired and Jackal realized that my tie to Vlad went both ways.

"I can see him," I said out loud. If I believed in God, I would've started praying.

In the midst of the wind whistling around Vlad, I heard Jackal's voice. Felt his hand shaking my shoulder.

"In the present? Or future?"

"Present," I said, again hoping I wasn't signing my death warrant. "He's not in his house anymore. He's flying."

The shaking grew rougher. "What's he flying over, Frankie?"

"How should I know?" I replied truthfully. "It's dark. I can't see much . . . wait."

Vlad had angled his body downward. The noise from the wind increased. In the distance, I saw tiny dots appear.

"He's over somewhere populated now. I can see lights. Lots of them."

A slap burned the side of my face. "Where? I need something more specific than 'populated' and 'lights,' you stupid bitch!"

I wanted to cradle my cheek, but didn't because I needed all my attention on my link with Vlad. *I hope you go medieval on his ass when you get here!* I mentally spat.

Vlad's grin widened, showing those sharp-looking upper fangs. "I'll remind you that you said that."

Then he angled his body in a steeper slant. The

glow of lights beneath him became brighter, objects forming distinguishable shapes instead of blank nothingness. I squinted to try and see better, hoping he wasn't hours away.

"It looks like . . . he might have just flown over an amusement park," I continued. He was going so fast, it was hard to be sure. "I think I just saw a roller coaster."

He didn't slap me again, but if Jackal shook me any harder, he'd dislocate my shoulder. "*What* park?"

"Stop that!" I snapped, anger getting the better of me. "You want me to lose the link? Then keep breaking my focus by roughing me up."

The shaking stopped, but Jackal's hand felt like a concrete boulder on my upper arm. "What park?" he repeated.

"Too late to tell, he's past it now. I see lots of roofs and buildings coming up . . ."

And water. Excitement threaded through me. Florida had theme parks set near water and large cities. If Vlad had just flown over Disney World, he might only be about an hour away.

Is that where you are? I sent to him. *Florida?*

Another grin was the only reply I got, but the blur of scenery below him began to take clearer shape. It took me a second to realize why.

"He's slowing down. Dropping lower . . ."

My heart began to beat faster. I wasn't adept at recognizing landmarks from a bird's-eye view, but I thought the cluster of buildings Vlad just flew over looked familiar.

"Well?" Jackal's grip tightened again. "What do you see?"

That thumping in my chest continued to increase when I saw a harbor that I was now positive I recognized.

"He's over a marina. I can't see any street names yet, but he's . . . he seems to be slowing down even more."

"A marina?" All of a sudden, Jackal sounded uneasy. His hand loosened on my arm.

I clutched the silver knife like it was a lifeline. "Yes. Now he's heading toward a city. I see lots of buildings . . . he's dropping down even lower . . . I see a sign on one of them—"

"What does the sign say?" Jackal interrupted, his voice tight with urgency. "What's it say, Frankie?"

I dropped the link to Vlad, not needing it anymore. The hotel room seemed to rush around me in a series of colors, swallowing up the inky darkness that had surrounded Vlad. My heart pounded like it was trying to free itself from my chest and sweat slicked the knife in my hand.

"It says," I rasped, nerves and determination making my voice rougher, "Red Roof Inn, Tampa."

I only had a moment to savor the shock in their expressions before the hotel window imploded from a large form hurtling through it.

Time seemed to switch into fast-forward. One second I was being pelted by flying glass, the next I was shoved into a corner, staring at the back of a dark-haired man in a trench coat. Before my next blink, flames coated the walls in orange and red waves, covering every inch of the room except the section where I was.

"I heard you were looking for me," a now-familiar voice said mockingly.

The instant heat and smoke had me looking for a way out, but before I could attempt to crawl away, a blur of violence erupted in front of me. It was so fast I was reminded of the cartoons I'd watched as a kid, only this whirling mass of limbs was frighteningly real. With their incredible speed and the smoke making everything hazy, I couldn't tell who was winning, or if more than two people were involved in it.

If I got caught up in that deadly maelstrom, I'd be finished, but this was my chance. I took in a deep breath for courage, coughed at the smoke, and crawled to the nearest light socket. Then I placed my right hand over it, feeling the instant surge as the currents in me connected to the voltage in the socket.

Energy flooded me like an adrenaline shot to my heart, followed by a searing ache along my nerves. The lights blinked out, but even with the sudden darkness and my eyes watering with pain and smoke, I could still see the window Vlad had decimated. Flames and some jagged pieces of glass clung to the frame, making it look like the mouth to hell. A few feet away, several vampires were locked in a death match that defied tracking with the naked eye. None of that made me hesitate. I took in another coughing breath and then hurtled toward the window, jumping at the last second as if the floor were a springboard.

Chapter 6

 "Leila, don't!" a harsh voice shouted.

Too late, not that I would've obeyed anyway. My jump was high enough to clear the three-foot ledge, and I tucked into a ball immediately, rolling as soon as I hit the ground. My arms protected my head for another few bruising, scrape-inducing tumbles until something hard stopped my momentum. Air burst from my lungs at the impact, pain radiating through my body.

I wanted to stay hunched in a protective ball, but there was no time. I rose, assessing my options. I'd slammed into the front of a car with my wild dive, but beyond that was the welcoming darkness of the parking lot. I shook my head to clear the ringing that probably indicated a mild concussion and sprinted toward it as fast as my aching muscles could take me.

"Stop her!" a voice commanded behind me.

I glanced back while adding some extra oomph to my stride. Smoke and flames still poured from the ruined window, but no one chased me. With luck, they'd be occupied long enough for the fire department to distract them from coming after me. *Bye bye, biters!* I thought, smiling despite pain radiating through me. Too bad I hadn't been wearing my running shoes when I was kidnapped.

Out of nowhere, something snatched me from behind with what felt like bands of steel around my midsection. I doubled over, almost vomiting from the abrupt resistance that made me instantly come to a stop. For a dazed second, I didn't know what happened, but then I saw dark arms looped around my waist and felt something large and solid behind me.

"I've got her," a male voice called out. Then a cool mouth pressed to my ear. "Don't bother with the stun gun again. It won't be enough against me."

Wait until my new assailant realized my entire body was a stun gun. He must be another vampire or he'd be on the ground from touching me after the extra voltage I'd absorbed from the light socket—and that was just what my body gave off. My right hand was now a formidable weapon, but I needed more leverage to use it to its best advantage.

"All right," I said, trying to sound meek. "You're hurting me," I added to see if that made him loosen his grip.

It did. So my captor wasn't cruel like Jackal or the others. Without that unyielding grip cementing me in place, I was able to step away enough to glance behind me.

The vampire who'd grabbed me was the brawny African American I'd spied Vlad talking to earlier today. Guess the fire starter had arrived with backup, but holding me hostage hadn't been part of our deal. The man looked me up and down, grimacing when his gaze followed the scar that zigzagged from my temple all the way to my right hand.

I was so used to that pitying reaction; it didn't even elicit a twinge of self-consciousness. Right now, I was grateful for every sympathy-inducing advantage I had.

"I think I sprained my ankle," I said, holding one foot off the ground for effect. Hey, I was getting better at this lying thing! "Could you look at it?" The vampire let me go, starting to kneel just as I'd hoped. His attention was on my ankle as I extended it, leaning forward like I was having trouble balancing. One touch of my right hand on his head should incapacitate him long enough for me to run away. I reached out—

"Touch him, and I revoke my promise not to harm you."

Vlad's voice cut through the night air, freezing my hand an inch away from its goal. The other vampire stood at once, back on full alert. *Shit!* I silently screamed. How had Vlad known what I was going to do?

"The same way I knew you were spying on me before," he replied with sardonic amusement. "You have your unusual abilities. I have mine, and mind reading is one of them."

Mind reading. No wonder he'd been able to hear me when I established a link with him! Slowly, I turned toward his voice. Flames still shot from the hotel window, illuminating Vlad in an orange glow. He strode toward us while dragging someone who was so covered in soot and scabs, I couldn't tell which of my former captors he was.

"Where are the others?" I asked, striving to sound calm.

His features were still hazy from smoke and shadows, but I caught a glimpse of white teeth as he smiled.

"Ashes."

His captive tried to pull away, but Vlad's grip tightened until his fingers disappeared into the blackened flesh beneath them. I looked away, my stomach twisting. Sirens cut through the mutterings of people who came out of their hotel rooms to gawk at the blaze. Vlad was unperturbed, as if torching a hotel room and then restraining a charred vampire was what he normally did on a Thursday night.

"You have what you wanted," I said, still managing to sound composed. "Now hold up your end of our agreement and let me go."

That emerald gaze seemed to pierce me to the quick. "I agreed not to harm you and I haven't. As for letting you go, I will . . . after we have a more detailed conversation."

Despair crashed over me. Vlad's idea of a detailed conversation probably meant torture followed by execution. I should have known someone who'd callously burned several people to death wouldn't honor his word to let me go. But then, unbelievably, I heard Marty's voice over the blare of sirens.

"Run, Frankie, run!"

Vlad swiveled toward the sound just in time to see Marty barreling toward him as though he'd been fired from a cannon. I'd wondered why he hadn't done anything when I was kidnapped, but he must have followed me and stayed hidden until he thought he had the best chance to rescue me. Problem was, this wasn't it.

Everything seemed to happen in slow motion instead of fast-forward this time. Vlad's companion pulled out a silver knife and shoved me to the ground. Vlad made no attempt to avoid Marty's assault, but kept his grip on the charred vampire and widened his stance as if daring Marty to take him down. It was dark, but I thought I saw Marty's determined expression the instant before his body crashed into Vlad's. As if trapped in a nightmare, I watched Vlad absorb the blow while remaining on his feet, his deadly free hand erupting in flames as he reached for my friend.

"No!" I screamed.

Instead of running like Marty commanded, I flung myself at Vlad. My right hand landed on his leg, desperation making those hated inner currents rocket from me and into him with far more power than normal.

With my panic and the voltage I'd channeled from the light socket, Vlad should have been blown clear across the parking lot. Instead, he remained where he was, the only effect a shudder wracking him and the smell of ozone briefly overcoming the scent of smoke. That flaming hand snatched Marty up before I registered that he'd moved, and then Vlad's dark head swung in my direction, bright emerald eyes meeting my shocked gaze.

"That," he bit out, "was rude."

The sight of him restraining two struggling vampires was the last thing I saw before my vision went gray. The parking lot and burning hotel vanished, replaced by towering trees and a twisting, ice-filled river.

I knelt by its rocky bank, my clothes soaked, but I paid no attention to the cold. I couldn't feel anything beyond the pain that roared like an inferno through my veins, building until I threw my head back and howled at the overwhelming anguish.

The woman in my arms didn't react. No breath stirred her lips, and her eyes continued to stare sightlessly ahead. I clutched her closer, more agony ripping through me as if it were my body that had been broken beyond repair instead of hers. For all my new power, I had never been more helpless. Death had stolen her away, and she would eternally remain beyond my reach.

That knowledge made a new howl erupt from my throat, despair mixing with the grief that threatened to rend me apart. This was my doing. The river might have washed away all traces of her blood, but I would forever carry its stain on my hands.

"Hold them," a curt voice directed.

The woman, river, and forest vanished, replaced by billowing smoke and the Red Roof Inn parking lot. Marty was still alive, to my vast relief, though he looked like he'd gotten a good scorching. Vlad handed him and the other, far more charred vampire over to his friend. I was on the ground, kneeling, tears streaming down my cheeks from reliving Vlad's darkest memory. To be honest, I'd expected a far more gruesome image after touching the fire starter, but what scarred his soul appeared to be loss, not murder.

Once Marty and the other vampire were secured,

Vlad knelt next to me. His hands were no longer engulfed with flames, but that might be because the fire truck had pulled up and that would draw too much attention. The wailing siren seemed to pierce my skull with its screech, but though vampires had better hearing, Vlad didn't seem bothered by it.

"Stop crying," he said shortly. "I'm not going to kill you, if that's what you're so hysterical about."

He thought I'd fallen sobbing to my knees because I was afraid to die? The lingering echoes from his anguish made my ironic snort come out more like a sniffle.

"Those tears were yours, not mine. Whoever she was, you were *really* broken up over her death."

His brows drew together. He was close enough for me to notice that despite igniting several things—and people—he didn't have so much as a charred speck on him.

"What nonsense is this?"

"Don't tell him anything, Frankie," Marty hissed.

I looked up at my friend, but Vlad's cold voice snapped my attention back to him.

"Take them away, Shrapnel. I'll catch up with you later."

I stopped myself before touching Vlad in instinctive appeal. Electrocuting him again wouldn't help my cause.

"Don't kill him, he was only trying to protect me. That's Marty, and he didn't know that I, ah, called you. He probably thought you were with the crew that kidnapped me."

Poor Marty. He'd followed Jackal and the others, biding his time until he thought the odds were better. How could he have known that Vlad was tougher than four other vampires combined? Of course, if Vlad had already made up his mind to kill Marty, my plea not to harm him would fall on deaf ears. He was capable of murder, but the memory I'd pulled after touching him made me hope there was more to Vlad than his tendency to torch people.

His features hardened. "What memory?"

Right, he had mind reading abilities. That made Marty's urging not to tell Vlad what I'd seen pretty much moot.

"You and the dead woman by the river," I replied. "I told you I pull images from people or things I touch. I saw her when I touched you, and I was crying because I felt everything you felt that day."

He stared at me with such unblinking intensity that it hurt to hold his bright gaze. I didn't look away, though. He might be able to read my mind, but I'd ripped open the wound he held closest to his soul. The least I could do was not take the coward's way out by staring at the ground.

"Keep them both alive, Shrapnel," Vlad said at last. "I'll rejoin you later."

Out of the corner of my eye, I saw the other vampire nod. Then he just . . . vanished. Either teleporting was another vampire ability Marty had neglected to mention, or Shrapnel moved faster than greased lightning.

Vlad stood, his eyes changing from glowing emerald back to burnished copper.

"You're coming with me," he stated, holding out his hand.

I looked at it but didn't move to take it. "So you *are* reneging on our deal."

"I don't like being called a liar, which is something you'd do well to remember," he replied in a tone that made shivers of trepidation run through me. Then a small smile touched his mouth. "We need to talk, and there are too many people here for that. You know I can overpower you despite your unusual talent, so the smart move would be to take my hand."

Yeah, I was aware that he could overpower me. I'd given him the biggest dose of voltage I'd ever harnessed and it hadn't so much as made him lose his balance. Right now, it wasn't just the smart move to take his hand. It was my only move.

I reached for him with my left hand. He ignored that, mouth twisting as he clasped my right one instead. A current slid into him, but he didn't pull away.

"Sorry," I muttered.

He let out a short grunt. "I can handle the effects from your touch if you can."

I was about to tell him that I only pulled impressions of sins from people through a *first* touch, but the feel of him when he drew me close distracted me. It wasn't just his hands that were unusually warm. His entire body gave off heat, searing through my flimsy leotard as he enveloped me in his arms. Normally vampires were room temperature, but Vlad felt like a furnace. Before I could ask what was up with that, or why the impromptu hug, he vaulted us into the air, the wind snatching away my yelp of surprise.

Chapter 7

After a pulse-pounding half hour of flying, Vlad set us down in a large patch of dry vegetation. Once my eyes adjusted to the dark, I saw the small plane ahead in the clearing. So he had more than one way to fly, but that didn't mean I was game.

"You can't expect me to go anywhere in that," I stated.

His brow arched. "You'd rather stay and be a feast for mosquitoes? I can think of better uses for your blood."

If he meant to intimidate me with that comment, he'd succeeded, but it didn't change anything. "I didn't get a chance to grab my rubber glove when I was kidnapped, so you put me in that and my hand will fry every circuit it touches—"

"Then we won't let it touch any circuits," he interrupted, clasping it firmly as he led me forward.

I tugged away, but that had no effect on slowing his stride. "Even if I agreed to get on that plane, which I haven't, you can't hold my hand the whole time we're in the air. You should've figured out that I don't just zap someone once. The longer you touch me, the more voltage you'll absorb, and eventually, it'll cook you from the inside out."

And then I'll cause the plane to crash and get killed, too, I mentally added, which was what concerned me the most. Even Marty had to limit his contact with me to no more than an hour when we trained, or risk his entire body breaking out in what looked like radiation blisters.

The grin Vlad flashed me was amused and a touch feral—a combination I wasn't sure I liked. "And *you* should have figured out that I'm fireproof. You can't harm me, Leila, no matter how much voltage you channel into me."

That stopped me in my tracks. Yes, I'd seen him wield fire without the slightest burn to show for it. Even his clothes seemed immune to the flames, but I was so used to my touch being dangerous that my mind immediately rejected Vlad's statement that I couldn't harm him.

He didn't attempt to pull me forward this time, but waited as I digested this information. It seemed inconceivable, but I supposed if there was someone in this world I wasn't able to harm, it would be a vampire who could call forth fire from his flesh. The danger from electrocution was stopping someone's heart—not an issue for any vampire—and the inevitable, ever-increasing burns. If burns didn't affect Vlad due to his pyrokinesis, he really was immune to me.

No wonder I hadn't taken him down when I'd shot him full of voltage earlier. All that must have done was annoy him.

I looked at the plane with a sense of exhilaration this time. I'd never thought to fly in one again.

Sure, I could keep protesting, but why? Vlad didn't need to go elsewhere to torture or kill me; this deserted area would make a great spot, if that's what he intended. The most logical assumption was he did want to talk, and if he wanted to do that while on a plane . . . well. Hopefully he wouldn't talk the whole time. If I closed my eyes, I could pretend it was before the accident, when there was nothing special about me except my aptitude for gymnastics . . .

"Okay," I said, trying to suppress my grin.

His snort told me I hadn't been successful. "Then come."

He jumped into the plane, pulling me along as if I was weightless. Once inside, I admired the plush cream interior with its sleek tables and leather reclining chairs. I'd only flown coach before, which was night and day compared to this luxurious aircraft. Vlad said something to the two pilots in a language I didn't recognize, and then they closed a small curtain, giving us the illusion of privacy.

"Where's Marty?" I asked, seeing no other passengers.

"Taking a different route," he replied, shrugging off his coat. "Here."

The air-conditioning felt like it was on full blast. Since I was no longer in his toasty embrace, I *was* chilly. Had he read that from my mind? A glance down made me stifle a groan. Nope. With nothing more than thin spandex covering my chest, even the blind would notice that my nipples were so hard, they could cut glass. I took his coat with a mutter of thanks, not looking at him as I settled it around me. It felt like an electric blanket from his body heat, cocooning me in warmth. The inner lining had heavier objects in it, but I didn't explore. Probably silver knives, though Vlad's most formidable weapon was his hands.

Guess we had that in common.

He sat in one of those the comfy-looking leather chairs and I followed suit, choosing the one to his left since he'd need to keep my right hand in his throughout the flight. The plane immediately started to taxi, no safety instructions or admonitions to buckle up, and I was surprised to feel it lift off moments later. Must not need much of a runway.

Vlad's hand was still warm, but it didn't give off the same scalding heat it had before. It felt strange for anyone to touch my right hand, let alone for this long. If he wasn't a dangerous vampire whose intentions toward me were still suspect, I'd have reveled in a smolderingly attractive man holding my hand. For the past decade, that had only happened in my dreams.

With a flash of discomfiture, I remembered Vlad could hear my musings. A current slid into him, powered by my embarrassment. Instead of pretending that he hadn't caught my thoughts, his mouth curled into a sly smile.

"That one tickled. If electrocution is your way of flirting, I commend you on your originality."

"Yeah, well, I remember you weren't impressed by the word *please*," I responded tartly, my brief embarrassment gone.

"Were you born with these abilities?" he asked, changing the subject.

"I was electrocuted by a downed power line

twelve years ago. It kept me in a coma for months. When I woke up, I had extensive nerve damage and this scar." My finger swept from my temple to my wrist for emphasis. "The nerve damage eventually healed, but that came with unexpected side effects."

I couldn't stop the memories that followed my summary of the accident and its aftermath. *Me going back to school, trying not to notice how the other kids stared at my awkward gait or extended scar.* Then my horror when I glimpsed people's darkest secrets through my right hand, let alone the realization that I shocked everyone I came into contact with. The whispers I was meant to over-hear in the halls and classrooms. *She's a monster now . . . All scarred and weird, like some sort of Frankenstein monster . . .*

"I've met monsters. You're not one of them."

Vlad had been unrepentantly listening again. I tried to clear my mind, but it's not like it had an off switch.

"You told me your name was Leila, but your friend and those other vampires called you Frankie," he continued. "You took the Franken-stein insult and shortened it into a nickname?"

I lifted my chin. "Yes." I'd needed to change my identity, and after I got over my hurt feelings, I used my classmates' pettiness for inspiration. If they'd thought their favorite taunt would make me crumble, they'd thought wrong.

"What made you choose the name Vlad?" I asked, unable to resist adding, "It's not the most *original* vampire name you could have picked, after all."

Instead of being offended, that little smirk was

back. "I'm the only authentic Vlad. Everyone else is merely an envious imitation."

I snorted, giving him a deliberate once-over. With his long dark hair, striking features, frightening charisma, and seductively muscled body, he looked like he could pass for the infamous Prince of Darkness, but how naive did he think I was?

"You've got the obligatory dangerous-yet-sexy thing going on, but I'll believe you're the real Dracula when you believe I'm the real Frankenstein."

"Dracula is a caricature born from a writer's imaginings," he snapped, that tiny smile gone. His hand flared hotter, too. "It bears no resemblance to me any more than Mary Shelley's story is an accounting of you."

Wow, he took his little fantasy seriously. *And he just heard you say that,* I reminded myself as his look grew pointed.

"What did you want to talk about?" I asked, shaking my head as though it could rattle any incriminating thoughts loose.

"Your survival chances."

His tone was casual, expression back to that pleasant one I found more frightening than a menacing scowl. I'd seen the faces of countless murderers, but none of them had mastered the look of detached friendliness like Vlad did when he killed.

"Is this the part where you tell me how I'm going to die?" I asked, steeling myself for whatever came next.

He squeezed my hand in a companionable way. "You should have seen that I don't waste my time with monologues before I kill. In fact, it's in my best interest to protect you."

I didn't reply, just raised my brows at this dubious statement.

"I doubt I'll get any useful information from your remaining kidnapper no matter how much I torture him," he went on. "He strikes me as a pawn, so he probably has no idea who sent him after you."

I continued with my doubtful stare. He rolled his eyes. "I forgot your generation is only familiar with mobile phone games like Angry Birds. In chess, pawns are the lowest level of—"

"I know how to play chess," I interrupted. "When you can't touch a cell phone or play electronic games without frying them, you learn to make do with the classics."

He grinned, revealing those lovely white teeth. I reminded myself that if I mentally recited that famous line from Little Red Riding Hood, he'd hear it.

"Good. If you checked your e-mail every five minutes, or keep texting and Tweeting in the middle of our conversation, I might snap your neck out of sheer principle."

"You'd feel right at home in some retirement communities with a technophobic attitude like that. You probably love to tell kids to get off your lawn, too."

Cell phone addiction annoyed me, too, but I'd never fantasized about murdering anyone over it, unless you counted people who talked on their phones during a movie . . .

His smile didn't slip. "You're still half expecting me to harm you, yet you don't hesitate to needle me. Aren't you afraid to make me angry?"

He could read my mind, so I didn't bother answering with anything except the truth.

"You're scarier when you're nice, and you've already decided if you're going to kill me. No amount of bantering *or* begging on my part will change your mind, so I'll keep on being myself. You're not the only one who doesn't care for pretense."

This time, his smile widened into a full-fledged, wicked grin that made him almost devilishly handsome. I looked away, not wanting my thoughts to inflate his ego. To distract myself, I concentrated on the scarred hand holding mine. His grip was light, as if I could pull away at any moment, but we both knew better.

"You're right on all counts," he said in that smooth, accented voice. "But you'll be relieved to know that you're not about to die. I said it was in my best interest to protect you, and I meant that. If I'm right—and I always am—your remaining kidnapper will be a dead end. That leaves you as my best chance to discover who sent those vampires after me."

"Me?" I repeated, my gaze flying back to his.

"Your ability to divine information through touch as well as locate people in the present *and* future is priceless. Vampires all over the world would kill to use you as an instrument against their enemies. I'm astounded that you've remained anonymous as long as you have, considering your friendship with another vampire."

"Marty would never use me like that," I flared. It was bad enough to feel like a pariah because of my condition, but being reduced to "instrument" status was worse.

"Perhaps, which is why I'm letting him live," Vlad replied. "That's a kindness I don't usually bestow on anyone who attacks me, but because of his affection for you, he'll also be invested in finding out who was really behind your kidnapping."

What if neither one of us wants to help you? I couldn't help but wonder. Marty and I had nothing to do with whatever feud Vlad had going on with another vampire.

Those coppery eyes sparked emerald for a second. "If I let you go, how long do you think it would be until that same vampire sent another crew to snatch you up? You need me to find this person far more than I do. I'm hard to ambush." He gave me a callous rake of his gaze. "You're not, and since you seem to be an intelligent girl, you already know that."

His hand didn't so much as twitch, but I imagined I could feel it tightening over mine until it formed an unbreakable snare. My pride wanted to refute what he'd just said, but my abilities meant I'd relived too many instances of the unwary falling victim to the unmerciful. I might have a chance against one vampire, maybe two thanks to my electrocution capability, but against a horde of them? Even if Marty fought with me, I'd be setting us both up to fail, and damned if I'd be that stupid.

"Wise decision," he said, still watching me with that unblinking gaze. "You keep thinking like that and you'll live long enough to dance on your enemies' graves."

"I thought vampires didn't do graveyards," I said with a sigh. I hadn't asked for this fight, but Vlad was right. I was in it now regardless.

He chuckled. "We don't. Graveyards are full of dead people. Vampires want to be where living, drinkable blood is."

I closed my eyes, weariness hitting me all at once. It had been a long, stress-filled day, and according to Vlad, it was only going to be the first of many.

"Where are we going? You never told me."

"My home in Romania."

Wow, this guy wasn't kidding with his Dracula fixation.

I heard a snort but didn't bother to open my eyes. Rustling noises sounded like he was getting more comfortable. I did the same. If we were headed to Romania, we were in for a long flight.

Chapter 8

Eleven hours and one stop to refuel later, we landed at a tiny airport that only had one runway and two hangars, one of which our plane taxied into. I glanced down at my bare feet with a mental sigh. Here's hoping we didn't have a long walk to a car. The ground was covered in snow. Vlad had loaned me his coat, but I doubted he'd give up his shoes, too.

My frostbite worries were put to rest when I followed him out of the plane and saw a shiny black limousine waiting inside the hangar. Either Vlad had lots of his own money or he had friends in high places. Of course, he might also have had a vampire associate mesmerize a limo driver into picking us up. That mind-manipulation thing had come in handy when a customs officer asked for our passports during our refueling stop.

A blond man with a Viking-like build opened the limo door when Vlad approached, executing a bow. My brows rose, but Vlad nodded as though having people bow to him was an everyday occurrence. I tiptoed after him, again grateful that I didn't have far to walk. The ground was concrete, but it felt like ice.

The blond man barely glanced at me, which I didn't mind because most people just stared at my scar first anyway. I ducked inside the limo, careful not to touch anything with my right hand. The driver shut the door, saving all the precious interior warmth from escaping. As soon as I sat down, I shoved my bare feet toward one of the lower heat vents.

"On the way to your house, we need to pick up some things," I said. "My leotard will be able to walk around by itself soon, and shoes are a necessity in this weather."

Vlad reached out, pulling my right hand into his. "It's already been taken care of."

I might have spent the past dozen-plus hours like this, but I still couldn't get over having someone touch that hand without jerking back in pain. True to his assertion, he seemed to have suffered no ill effects though I must have dosed him with enough electricity to kill a regular vampire three times over.

"Was ordering me clothes part of what you were doing when you were on the phone?" I asked, slanting a look at him. He might have disparaged cell-aholics, but he'd been on his cell for most of the hour before we landed. Even one-handed, he could text like the wind.

"Among other things," he replied. His fingers grazed my knuckles in a light stroke. "While you're a guest in my home, I'll provide for all your needs, but be careful that you don't abuse my hospitality."

I stifled a snort. What did he think I was going to do, demand only designer outfits? I'd be happy with any clothes as long as they were warm. It looked like we'd landed in an arctic wonderland from the scenery we drove past.

"That's not what I meant."

Damn him for always listening to my thoughts. I couldn't wait until I had my mental privacy back.

His gaze became cold even as he continued to draw little patterns on my hand. "You should be grateful I can hear your thoughts. It's kept me from employing more invasive methods to determine if you were telling the truth about your kidnapping."

I flashed back to the memories I'd relived from the vampires Vlad had burned to death, and a shudder went through me. Yeah, I'd much rather have him read my mind than experience his fiery abilities personally. Even the thought made me want to snatch my hand away from his potentially deadly grip.

"You're still afraid of me," he stated. "Good."

"You get off on people being afraid of you?" Was he some sort of *insecure* undead killer? Great, then I could look forward to him scaring the shit out of me on a regular basis just to make himself feel better.

In reply, Vlad pressed a button and the dark glass window separating us from the limo driver came down.

"Maximus, do you fear me?" Vlad asked.

"Yes," the blond driver replied without hesitation.

Vlad pressed the button again, and soon that privacy glass was back in place. Once more, I resisted the urge to pull my hand free because the atmosphere between us had changed. Gone was the sense of truce I'd felt for the past several hours, and in its place was tension thick enough to choke on. Invisible currents seemed to circulate around Vlad, making the hair on the back of my neck stand at attention in warning.

"I want you afraid of me for the same reason I want my people to fear me," he said, his voice as much of a caress as his fingers on my hand. "Then you won't attempt to cross me. In the future, someone may try to persuade you to betray me. If that happens, remember this: I find and kill my enemies no matter how long it takes."

I swallowed to relieve my suddenly dry mouth. "I have no intention of switching sides. You're not the one who sent child murderers to snatch me up, and they were going to kill me once they were done with me; I saw it when I touched Jackal. I don't see my death when I touch you, so I'm Team Vlad all the way."

Some of that coldness left his gaze. "Good, because I wouldn't enjoy killing you. Thus far you're not boring or irritating; a rarity. I also reward those loyal to me, so keep your fear of me, Leila, but know this—you need not fear anyone else as long as you're under my protection."

He said those last words with a quiet intensity that sent shivers up my spine. I might not have bought his vow of protection despite the convincing pitch, but the memory I'd relived through him made me a believer. He knew what loss felt like. For loss to be the wound that scarred his soul more than any other made me think he didn't take vows of protection lightly. Slowly, I nodded.

"Once again, we have a deal."

A brief smile curved his lips. "You dislike that

I can read your mind, but that pales next to your abilities. I don't need to tell you never to reveal to anyone what you saw, do I?"

You just did, I thought pointedly.

"So I did." Another quicksilver smile. "You'll learn far more once you're in my home. Many of my furnishings are centuries old and must hold numerous memories. I trust you'll treat any new information you glean with the same discretion."

"Yes, but believe me, I'll try to touch as little as possible." *Antiques*. Oh, how I hated those essence-heavy things!

He continued to study me, his expression a mixture of pitiless calculation and curiosity. "You said you've had this ability for a dozen years, which must be half your life judging from how young you look. I was already old when I developed the power to read humans' thoughts, yet the depravities I uncovered still managed to disturb me. Your gift reaches much deeper than that. I'm amazed you haven't snapped under the strain of it."

I shrugged as if I hadn't been driven to a suicide attempt over the countless atrocities I'd relived. "Sometimes it's helped. I know who to avoid. People can perfect whatever façade they want, but everyone holds their sins close to their skin."

His laugh held a hint of grimness. "How true that is."

The limo bounced over a rut, jostling me. I looked out the window. Trees laden with snow and ice were most of what I saw, but if I craned, I could see the terrain was starting to get steep. After a minute, my ears began to pop. I forced a yawn to relieve the pressure, missing Florida's sea-level altitude.

"Is it very far to your house?"

I hadn't eaten in almost two days since I'd skipped breakfast the morning I was kidnapped. Then again, this was a vampire house. I remembered what Marty used to stock in the refrigerator, and it hadn't been anything I wanted to sample. I regarded the wooded landscape bleakly. Probably wasn't a grocery store or restaurant within fifty miles of here, either.

An amused grunt directed my attention back to Vlad. "I have ample food, Leila, and this is Romania. Not the northern wilds of Siberia. We'll be at my house shortly, and on the way, we'll pass through a town that has both grocers *and* restaurants."

I flushed at his mocking tone, once again reminding myself to watch my thoughts—if I could figure out a way to do that.

"You eat regular food? Marty was never into that. Said it all tasted like clay to him."

"It does, and I don't, but I have an abundance of food for the humans who live with me. If they were undernourished, then they wouldn't be able to feed me or my staff."

His tone was completely casual, but I was starting to realize that Vlad never said anything by accident. I met his gaze, noting the hint of challenge. He was almost daring me to be offended by his flesh version of a pantry.

"Marty always drank from tightfisted tourists," I said, arching a brow in answering challenge. "Said it served them right for not tipping after our performance. He never tried to drink from me, of course, because he said that business and food should be kept separate."

Vlad's lips curled. "Subtle you're not. If you're wondering whether I'm intending to drink from you, don't play games. Ask."

"Are you?" I responded at once, adding, "I don't want you to. I know it won't kill me or turn me into a vampire, but I'm already an 'instrument.' I don't want to be dinner, too."

"No, I'm not," he replied calmly. "Nor will any other vampire while you're under my protection. Your friend Marty and I agree about keeping food and business alliances separate."

That was a relief. Maybe staying with Vlad wouldn't be too different than living with Marty, though hopefully it would be much shorter than the four years Marty and I toured together.

"What did the two of you do?" Vlad asked, lacing his free hand behind his head.

"Traveling circus performers," I answered, braced for the scorn most people showed upon hearing that.

Nothing changed in his expression. "Clever, with your condition. If anyone noticed your tendency to electrocute people, they would assume it to be a circus trick, and you wouldn't remain long enough in one place for more serious questions to arise."

"That's exactly it," I said with surprise. If only my dad and my sister could grasp that logic so easily. My job was an embarrassment to them. The last I heard, they told people I was a stage actress.

Vlad shrugged. "Vampires have experience hiding what we are. Ah, here is the town. Beyond it is my home."

I glanced out the window to see us whizzing by

a small town that did indeed look like it had shops and restaurants. With all the snow and the quaint, picturesque architecture, it also could've doubled as a snapshot of the mythical Santa's Village.

"Pretty," I said, "but I hope your driver doesn't get pulled over. I doubt the speed limit here is eighty."

It sounded like Vlad stifled a laugh. "No need to worry."

I kept looking out the window, seeing large rocks peek up amidst the trees. A shift in balance leaned me farther back into my seat, confirming that the road was getting steeper. Still, the driver didn't slow down, whipping around the bends and turns with what seemed to be total disregard for life and limb. I glanced at Vlad, but he appeared unconcerned. Of course. *He* could survive the car careening off a cliff or hitting a tree.

"No need to worry," Vlad said again with more amusement.

"Oh, I'm glorious," I replied through gritted teeth. Closing my eyes was probably the best way to get through this.

It might have only been ten minutes before the car came to a stop. To me, it felt like a solid hour. I'd probably sent enough nervous currents into Vlad to power a small locomotive, but he hadn't let go of my hand. Now, however, he entangled himself from my grasp.

"We've arrived."

I opened my eyes. His body briefly blocked my line of vision, but once he was out of the vehicle, I saw the house we'd stopped at. And stared, my mouth falling open.

Chapter 9

The word *house* didn't begin to do justice to the white and gray structure in front of me. I actually had to tilt my head back to see all the way up to the roof. It was at least four towering stories high, with additional floors on the triangular turrets that rose dramatically on each corner. A myriad of carvings decorated the exterior, from intricate balconies in front of soaring windows to stone gargoyles that glared down from their perches. They weren't the only sentinels of this gothic-looking palace; at least a dozen people were stationed in various spots around the house, some standing so still that at first glance, I'd thought they were statues, too.

The only thing more startling than the mansion's height was its length. I couldn't tell where the right side ended because a line of lofty evergreens blocked my view, but everything to the left of me went on for the length of a football field. A high stone wall with manned lookout towers encircled the property. Beyond that and the surrounding forest, dark gray mountains acted as a natural barrier, adding to the imposing feel of the place. *No wonder Jackal didn't want to try anything until Vlad was away from here*, I thought, awed. This wasn't a house; it truly *was* a fortress.

"Leila."

Vlad's voice jerked my attention back to him. He didn't bother to hide his grin as he glanced down at my feet.

"Don't you want to come inside before you catch a chill?"

I followed his gaze as if I needed proof that I was standing barefoot on the icy ground. I'd forgotten about the cold, being so caught up in the splendor around me, but now sharp needles of pain pricked my feet.

"Coming," I said at once.

Two huge double doors opened and Vlad entered through them, nodding at the men who bowed to him as he passed. This time, the obsequious gesture didn't seem out of place. Anyone who lived in a palace like this would expect to be bowed to. Hell, it was bigger than some royal castles I'd seen on TV.

I followed after him, unable to keep from looking around like a kid. We were inside an enormous hall with ceilings that were decorated with artful beams, frescos, and shields. Off to the right, the ceiling lowered and became domed glass. Below it, an indoor garden with plants and flowers arranged around chairs, couches, and a marble fountain.

Vlad strode by the garden and I followed, catching glimpses of more magnificent rooms as we continued down the main hall. Finally he stopped in front of a staircase that was wider than the trailer Marty and I had lived in.

"Maximus will show you to your room," Vlad stated.

I hadn't noticed the blond driver behind me, but he appeared before my next blink, so he couldn't have been far.

"Wait. Is Marty here? I want to see him." Vlad had promised not to kill him, but what if something happened with the other vampire on their way?

"I'll send him up after you've showered and eaten," Vlad said without hesitation.

Relief filled me. He must've confirmed that Marty had arrived in one piece for him to sound so sure.

Vlad turned and began to walk away, but my second "Wait!" stopped him.

"I, um, can't shower until I release all my excess electricity," I said with a shrug. "Don't suppose you have any lightning rods?"

"I'll get some," he replied, coming closer. "Until then, use me."

"I can find something else," I hedged.

A brow arched. "I insist."

He grasped my hand with those words. His coppery eyes stared into mine, silencing my next protest before I voiced it. He was so close that I imagined I could feel his unusual heat in the scant space between us. The warmth from his hand was certainly real. It seemed to slip inside my skin, teasing me with memories of what it felt like to be enveloped in his embrace, that hot, hard body pressed along every inch of me.

I cleared my throat to distract myself from the unexpected tightening of certain parts down below. It didn't help that he stroked my skin as he waited for my response, even that small touch sending more pleasant tingles through me.

"Are you sure?" I had to drain myself in order for this to be effective, and though he was fireproof, it might still hurt.

He leaned down, his long hair brushing my face. Those dark strands shouldn't have felt like teasing caresses, but they did, and again, I cursed my strange reaction to him.

"I never do anything unless I'm sure."

His voice was lower, and his fingers tightened on my hand. A bolt slid into him that I hadn't meant to send, but he didn't appear to mind. A slow smile spread across his lips.

"More."

The soft word was filled with challenge, as if he were daring me to hold anything back. Still bewildered over how he affected me, I took in a breath and then released the hold I kept over myself. Those inner currents unleashed in a burst of power that would've made the ground shudder from its intensity, but Vlad absorbed it without flinching, emerald sparks in his gaze the only visible indication that he felt anything. I was the one who swayed, feeling slightly dizzy at the expulsion of so much energy, so fast.

"I—I think that's enough," I said, the words uneven from the sudden weakening in my knees. I didn't usually feel like this after releasing my excess voltage. Maybe it was just because I hadn't eaten in almost two days.

Vlad stared down at me, not moving. "Are you able to manage the steps, or do you need assistance?"

My knees still felt wobbly, and though the idea of being in his hot embrace was dangerously appealing, I was *not* going to be carried to my room like some sort of war spoils. "I'm fine."

He let go of my hand and stepped back, nodding to Maximus. "Prepare her food immediately after you show her to her room." Then to me he said, "I'll see you at dinner."

I used the banister for balance as I followed Maximus up the curving staircase. Thirty hard-fought steps later we came to a landing. I was relieved that Maximus exited there instead of continuing up the staircase. Maybe I was suffering from jet lag combined with an emotional crash from all the stress of the past couple days.

Off the landing was a wood-paneled sitting room with views of the forest and mountains from windows that took up most of one wall. A long hallway was at the end of the lovely space, and I fought the urge to touch the walls to see if the material covering them really was velvet.

Maximus opened the third door in the hallway, standing aside to let me enter. I tried to act nonchalant when I saw that it was just as opulent as the rest of the house. I'd originally hoped it wouldn't take long to help Vlad find the person who directed Jackal and the others to kidnap me—if he was right and there *was* a mastermind behind the plot. But now, the idea of the hunt stretching out a few weeks didn't bother me. I couldn't get used to this kind of luxury because I was going back to my borderline-poverty life as soon as this was over, but in the meantime . . . life was too short not to enjoy a windfall.

"This is amazing," I told Maximus, who seemed to be waiting to see if the room met with my approval.

"I'm glad you're pleased," he replied. His formal manner seemed at odds with his formidable appearance and direct gaze. Maximus was a foot taller than my five-six height, and his thick muscles and rugged features made me think "scary bodyguard" more than "mild-mannered butler," but who was I to judge?

"You will find a change of clothes in the wardrobe," he went on. "Also, the electricity in this room was rewired to be voice activated. Lights on," he commanded, and sure enough, the bedside lamps and wall sconces flared to life.

I was stunned. "How did you—?" Then I stopped. *Vlad.*

He'd not only made good on his promise to provide me with clothes, he'd also managed to have his guest room rewired since without my glove, I couldn't touch a light switch without frying it.

Maximus waited to see if I would complete my sentence. When I didn't, he continued on as if I hadn't spoken. "You can also say 'dim' or 'lights off' when you want to retire. Dinner is served at nine in the main dining room on the first floor. Will you need me to show you where it is?"

"No, I think I remember seeing it," I said, still taken aback by this unexpected kindness from Vlad.

"Then I will leave you. Your lunch will be delivered shortly, but if you have need of anything in the meantime, pull this cord."

He illustrated the statement by pulling on a long

tassel that hung near the door. I didn't hear anything, but I took him at his word that it worked.

"Thank you," I said, feeling like I should tip him. Not that I could. My wallet was back in Florida.

He inclined his head. "My pleasure."

I waited until he closed the door behind him before going into the bathroom to check it out. It had a glass shower big enough for two and a sunken garden tub I could almost swim in, plus various other amenities.

I'd longed for a shower, but the thought of soaking my aches away in that tub changed my mind. "Lights on," I said, and then used my left hand to turn on the water.

Chapter 10

 Several covered dishes were on a tray in the sitting area when I came out of the bathroom. Good thing I'd closed the door or I'd have given whoever brought it a free show. I flipped the lids off to find a four-course meal spread before me. I glanced around, almost expecting people to pop out of woodwork and join me. *I have ample food*, Vlad had said. No shit. If his blood donors ate like this at every meal, they must weigh three hundred pounds each.

My stomach yowled, a warning to stop staring and start eating. I sat down and dug in without bothering to get dressed.

By the time I was finished, I was so full that all I wanted to do was nap, but Vlad had said he'd send Marty up after I'd showered and eaten. The antique wardrobe turned out to be filled with clothes that were new or rarely worn from the pristine look of them. They were all my size, too, as were the shoes at the bottom of the solid wood piece. I began opening drawers in the nearby dresser and found more of the same. Even the cup size on the bras was correct. Either Vlad had been staring *real* hard at me while I slept, or he had a lot of experience guessing women's sizes—and a lot of chick's clothes stockpiled at his house.

The latter was no doubt true, but the thought of him checking out my breasts made things stir in me that I normally kept locked down. Then I reminded myself that Vlad might as well have a "Hazardous to Your Health!" label stamped on him and chose a sweater, slacks, and thick socks. The fireplace was lit, making this room cozily warm, but the rest of the mansion might not be as comfortable. As soon as I was dressed, I tugged on the tassel. Less than a minute later, a knock sounded at the door. I opened it to reveal Maximus in the hallway. I wondered if his speed meant he was a vampire, or just extremely attentive.

"Do you know where my friend Marty is?"

"Yes. Shall I bring him up?"

Relief filled me. Vlad was now four for four on his promises. "I can go to him," I told Maximus. I still felt a little drained, but I wasn't nearly as woozy as I'd been before.

"I will bring him to you," he stated. "Wait here."

Then he was gone in a blur of motion. All right, that answered whether or not Maximus was a vampire. I waited, sitting on the bed after ten minutes standing in front of the empty doorway. Ten minutes into waiting in there, I was starting to get nervous. What was taking so long? Maximus had produced a gourmet meal faster than this!

After thirty minutes, I raced down the staircase to the first floor, trying to remember which direction Vlad had headed off in. The huge hall with its multiple adjoining rooms that had so impressed me before seemed like a maze designed to confound me now. I didn't see a single soul, either. What had happened to all the bowing guys? Where the hell *was* everyone?

"Maximus!" I shouted, a hard knot forming in my stomach. Something was wrong. I just knew it. "Where's Marty? I know you're a vampire, so don't pretend you can't hear me!"

"I'm here, Frankie."

The words came from directly behind me. I whirled and almost smacked into Maximus, but what filled me with relief was seeing my friend. Marty stood next to the blond vampire, a small, tired smile on his face.

"Glad you're okay, kid—"

He didn't finish the rest of his sentence because I grabbed him, crouching down so I could hug him. A shudder wracked him as my previous fear sent a current into him, but he tightened his arms and didn't let me pull away. I might be almost twice Marty's size, but he had ten times my strength.

"You really okay, Frankie?" Marty whispered against my ear.

"Fine," I whispered back, surprised at the strain in his voice. "Didn't you hear? I arrived at least two hours ago."

He let me go, glancing up at Maximus. "I was busy."

The edginess in his tone made me take a good at him. Marty wasn't in the same charred clothes he'd worn the last time I saw him, but his new outfit didn't look much better. Both his shirt and pants were splotched with suspicious dark stains, not to mention his shirt had a big, ragged hole in the middle of it . . .

I darted behind him before Marty could guess what I intended. By the time he spun around, I'd already seen the matching hole on the back of his shirt. It didn't take much imagination to figure out what had caused the bloody entry and exit hole.

"What. The. Hell!" I spat.

Marty grabbed my arms. "Calm down. I'm fine."

"You're not fine," I shot back, waving at him as much as his grip would allow. "You've been stuck through the torso with a huge frigging pole! Where is Vlad? Did he know about this?"

Marty glanced at Maximus again, and fresh fury shot through me as the other vampire's countenance became stony.

"He ordered it, didn't he? Son of a bitch, he had you impaled! Why? To act out one of his crazy Dracula fantasies?"

"Shhh, he'll hear you!" Marty gasped. His face paled, too, something I'd never seen before.

I was too pissed to worry about Vlad's feelings. "I don't care. It's one thing to pretend with the name and the big Romanian castle, but this is *insane*—"

"For the love of God, shut up!" Marty interrupted.

"Good advice," Maximus muttered.

I couldn't believe Marty was more upset about me calling out Vlad for his sick role-playing than being speared like a fish. Maybe Vlad reacted violently to anyone questioning his fantasy. If so, he wasn't just a little deluded, he was a madman—

"I can't listen to this anymore," an annoyed voice stated.

Marty's face managed to drain of more color. Even if I hadn't recognized Vlad's voice, that alone would've told me who had come up behind me.

"Don't hurt her, she didn't mean anything by it," Marty said at once, moving to stand between me and Vlad.

I wasn't about to let him take more abuse, especially on my behalf, so I tried to angle myself in front of Marty. He kept sidestepping me with that damn vampiric speed until it looked like we were engaged in some sort of strange dance.

"Fine, I'll talk to you like this," I snapped to Vlad, Marty still in between us. "You promised you wouldn't hurt him, but you had him *impaled*. Tell me why I shouldn't break our deal right now, and threatening me with death isn't good enough. Been there, done *that* a thousand times, remember?" My lip curled. "Besides, you need me and we both know it."

Vlad smiled with luxuriant coldness, coming closer. "Calling me a name I detest and accusing me of madness and lying. I've killed people for less, but you're right. I do need you. So let's settle the first two issues."

Marty was suddenly gone. Vlad had thrown him aside before I'd even seen him move. A thud by the stone staircase told me where he'd ended up, but when I started to go to him, Vlad grasped my arm, his coppery green gaze boring into mine. My heart skipped a beat, but I didn't flinch. I wouldn't give him the satisfaction.

"What now?" I asked with open challenge.

His brow arched. "This," he replied, and shoved a small, hard object into my right hand.

Chapter II

Images exploded across my mind, but unlike most impressions, they weren't through the perspective of just one person. They came from multiple people.

First, I relived the memory of an older man being cornered by soldiers. They held him down, jeering, as one of them cut away all the skin on the man's face before slitting his throat. The next memory was even more brutal—a burning hot coal used to put out a young man's eyes before he was buried alive. The third was of an even younger man who bore a striking resemblance to Vlad being ambushed and then stabbed to death inside a church. The last was that young man's murderer, pleading to no avail, as a dirty and blood-streaked Vlad shoved a long wooden pole through his midsection, then hoisted him aloft and sat watching the entire two days it took the man to die.

When reality at last replaced those grisly images, I found myself backed into a wall, Vlad's grip on my arms the only thing holding me upright. His gaze was hooded, lean face utterly expressionless as he looked at me. Phantom pains still lingered in various parts of my body, but they faded until only a dull ache from clutching whatever Vlad had given me remained.

I opened my hand, glancing down to see a thick gold ring with a dragon emblazoned across the wide, flat stone—the same ring each of those men had been wearing when they were killed. It was so filled with the essences from its former owners' murders that I half expected it to start dripping blood.

The deaths I'd been forced to relive had conveyed more than the horror of knowing what it felt like to have my face cut off, which had been a new one even for me. I'd also gotten a glimpse into the murdered men themselves. From that, I knew all but the last of them had been members of Vlad's family, and now I also knew exactly who held me against the smooth stone wall.

Shock made my voice come out hoarse. "You're Vladislav Basarab Dracul, former *voivode* of Wallachia, but over five hundred years ago, they used to call you Tepesh. The Impaler."

Vlad didn't blink. "They still do," he replied in a caressingly lethal voice, and then released me.

I was glad my legs managed to hold me so I didn't slump to the ground. Falling before Vlad's feet would be cliché in the extreme, even if he was the *real* Vlad.

I glanced at Marty. He was still by the staircase, but he seemed okay. Maximus was there, too. From the other vampire's grip on his shoulder, he'd been keeping Marty from interfering.

"Could you hear what I experienced from touching that ring?" I asked, unable to contain a shiver at the memory.

"Yes and no." His lips twisted into a humorless smile. "When you utilize your power, your mind is locked behind an impenetrable wall. But when you're finished, you think about what you saw, and I hear that."

I tried to chase away any remaining thoughts of those murders, which was easier to do when I focused on Marty.

"Okay, now I know you're not suffering under a delusion from too much role-playing." The last of that trembling left my limbs and I took a step toward him, my voice sharpening. "It doesn't excuse you from breaking your word not to harm Marty."

Vlad folded his arms across his chest, drawing my attention to the dark stains on his shirt that smelled like one of Marty's foul-tasting shakes.

"No, I promised not to harm *you*," he countered. "I only promised to keep him alive, which I have. But though it never occurred to you that Marty might have been in collusion with the vampires who kidnapped you, the thought did occur to me."

My mouth dropped. "No. Marty wouldn't do such a thing."

"Thanks, kid," he muttered from across the room.

"I believe that now," Vlad said, glancing at Marty without the slightest hint of remorse, "but I wasn't about to take a stranger at his word."

His expression hardened even more. "I come from a line of princes who all have one thing in

common: They were murdered. I've been surrounded by death, betrayal, and power coups for
hundreds of years, yet I've survived and kept my
people safe by being smarter and more ruthless
than my enemies. What I did may disgust you, but
only the naive or the foolish would have trusted
Marty on his word alone, and I am neither."

He came toward me, and once again, I fought
the urge to back away. Vlad might have kept his
promise in the strictest sense of the word, but torturing Marty on the mere chance that he might
have been involved with my kidnapping also proved
that Vlad was one of coldest people I'd ever met.

Then again, after the glimpses I'd seen of his
past, not to mention what I'd seen of him since we
met, *I* was the naive fool for expecting anything
different.

He stopped when he was only inches away, still
nailing me with that hard, copper-colored stare.
Then he held out his hand.

"My ring."

I put it in his palm, forgetting to switch it to my
left hand before touching him. A current sizzled
into him with the contact, which I expected, but I
didn't expect what came next.

*The gothic hall vanished, replaced by the hazy
cocoon of midnight-green drapes encircling the
bed I was on. I wound my hand into the thick
fabric while a moan left my lips, sharpening into
a cry at the incredible pleasure shooting through
me. My grip on the drapes tightened as I writhed
under the erotic combination of wet, deep strokes
and lightly chafing stubble against my most sensitive flesh.*

"Please," I gasped.

Vlad lifted his head, his hair like dark silk against my thighs and his gaze lit up with emerald.

"No," he said throatily. "More." And he lowered his mouth again.

Vlad's face crystallized in front of me, but instead of green drapes all around us, we were back in the hall and he was staring down at me, frowning.

"I know you caught a glimpse of something when you touched me. Your mind went silent. Tell me what it was."

My cheeks flamed with heat. At the same time, disbelief washed over me, covering the remains of pleasure more intense than I'd ever experienced while masturbating. That hadn't been a vision of him with another woman, yet still, denial screeched across my mind.

No. Not me and Vlad like . . . like that!

His frown cleared, replaced by a brow going up. *Damn* his mind reading. *Think of something else! I* mentally screamed, avoiding his stare. *ANYthing else!*

I no longer looked at Vlad, but I could almost feel his gaze roving over me, noting my newly tight nipples, accelerated heartbeat, and probably picking up on that damn lingering throb between my legs, too.

"Not surprising," he said at last, his voice thicker with things I didn't want to name. "I predicted the same thing myself."

My cheeks continued to heat until I expected them to burst into flames like his hands. I brushed past Vlad and headed for the staircase, not daring to look at Marty, either. How could I? I'd just gotten a glimpse into a future where I was in bed with the man who'd tortured him.

"Nothing's set in stone. I've changed my premonitions before," I muttered, both to Vlad and myself. Still, I took the stairs two at a time.

Chapter 12

An hour later, Marty opened my bedroom door without knocking. He'd changed out of the torn, bloody clothes and had taken a shower, from the damp look to his hair. I was sitting cross-legged in bed, trying without success to pretend I'd misunderstood the image I'd glimpsed. Yeah, right. Because Vlad had been between my legs looking for a set of keys he'd lost.

"Frankie?" Marty said gruffly. "I don't wanna bother you, but I don't have long to talk."

"Why? What's going on?" I asked at once, leaping up.

Marty shut the door behind him, scratching one of his long, bushy black sideburns. "I'm leaving for a scouting mission."

I didn't ask, *Scouting for what?* "Vlad might not even be right," I muttered. "Maybe no one told Jackal and the others to snatch me up. Maybe they thought of it all by themselves."

"They didn't," Marty replied, grimness clear in each syllable. "That vampire from the hotel, Shrapnel, spent the whole plane ride grilling the redhead who took you—and he was creative. But that was nothing compared to what Vlad did once we got here. Next to that, I got off easy. They didn't act alone. They were sent after you, but they didn't know by whom. All they had was a phone number and a big deposit in their bank account with promises of more if you gave them the goods on Vlad."

I sighed. I hadn't really thought this would be over so quickly, but I'd hoped. "I'm so sorry, Marty." I gestured at his chest, wanting to cry at what he'd been through. "He shouldn't have hurt you."

Marty snorted. "I'm happy to be alive. You probably guessed that I tailed you from Gibsonton, waiting until there were fewer vampires guarding you. When I realized it was Vlad I attacked, I thought I was done for. The only reason I'm not toes-up is because you made him promise not to kill me. I'd heard that he holds to his word. Never thought to find out personally."

I managed a limp smile. "Since I'll be spending time with him looking for this mysterious puppet master, is there anything else I should know about Vlad?"

"Yeah." Marty's expression became hard. "What you saw in that last vision . . . don't let it happen."

I closed my eyes, feeling my cheeks warm again. So Marty had figured out what I'd glimpsed, too. Not a shock; he was a vampire, and I'd been anything but suave in my reaction.

"Marty," I began.

"I wouldn't care if it was someone else," he cut me off. "This isn't about your inexperience with men."

"Announce that to everyone, why don't you!" I hissed, my eyes flying open. With how well vampires could hear, he may as well have tattooed a big V onto my forehead.

He waved a hand impatiently. "You're missing the point. Vlad isn't your typical vampire. We're all ruthless at one time or another, but he's in a class by himself. You let yourself get involved with him, he'll rip your heart out *and* destroy your life, and if I didn't love you like the daughter I used to have, I wouldn't say this when I know damn well that he's listening."

The raw pain in his voice took away my embarrassment.

"Don't worry." I forced myself to sound nonchalant. "I know how dangerous he is and I *don't* want to get involved with him. I must've had a case of temporary insanity because he's immune to the electricity in my touch." A shrug. "I'll get over it."

Marty chucked me on the hip. "That's my girl. I don't know how long I'll be gone, but you watch your back."

"I will," I promised Marty. "When do you leave?"

Marty sighed. "Now. Give me a hug, kid. Love you."

I knelt down and wrapped my arms around him, careful not to touch him with my right hand.

"Love you," I whispered. "You watch your back, too, Marty. Don't you dare let yourself get killed."

He laughed a trifle grimly. "I'll try not to."

At nine o'clock on the dot, I came down the staircase. I'd considered refusing to join Vlad for dinner after what he did to Marty—among other reasons why I didn't want to see him—but avoiding him would be pointless. We had to work together to find out who'd ordered my kidnapping. I wasn't about to let that person get off the hook.

Besides, I'd gotten over my embarrassment for my naughty vision about Vlad—and for Marty trumpeting the news of my inexperience for every vampire to hear. Was I supposed to be ashamed for valuing other people's lives over my own needs? I wasn't that coldhearted and ruthless.

I couldn't say the same about the vampire who rose when I entered the dining room, his expression showing a flicker of surprise as he took in my appearance. To show that I wasn't suffering from damaged modesty, I'd changed into a strapless black dress, the tight fit clinging to curves honed by countless hours of gymnastics. My normally straight black hair now had waves of curls in it, and the red lipstick and smoky eye makeup looked good against my lightly tanned face.

That's right, Voivode, I thought as his gaze swept over me a second time. *I might be scarred, but I'm still tasty-looking, aren't I? Too bad you're not getting any of this no matter what that vision showed.*

His lips twitched, but he held out my chair without comment. It wasn't until after I sat down that he responded to my mental gauntlet.

"If your goal is to dissuade me from seducing you, taunting me with promises of failure won't work." He settled himself into his chair with an easy, arrogant elegance. "I enjoy challenges, but I don't think it will be long until you're in my bed."

I'd been in the process of unfolding my napkin,

but at that, I froze. He did *not* just talk about me with the same casualness as a dessert he'd eventually get around to eating.

Out loud, I said, "Ooh, someone's got an ego."

He picked up his wineglass, taking a sip before replying. "It's not ego, I'm used to women chasing me. With your age and inexperience, you normally wouldn't stand a chance. But your abilities cut a swath of darkness through all that youth and innocence, making you quite intriguing."

"Lucky me," I gritted out, still steaming at his presumption.

Vlad smiled, as threatening and enticing as a whip curled around a champagne bottle. "Yes. People frequently bore me, sometimes amuse me, most often irritate me, but rarely intrigue me. You do, which is why I'll enjoy having you as a lover."

I couldn't decide which was more insulting—him lumping me together with women who had "chased" him, or his continued conviction that I'd fall into bed with him. I glanced at the room with its cathedral-like ceiling, barbarically gorgeous chandelier, and seating for two dozen.

"No wonder you need such a huge house. Your overconfidence wouldn't fit in anything smaller."

He shrugged. "Confident I might be, but it's not without cause. You think I'm dangerous and you're angry at me over Marty, but even before your vision, I could tell you wanted me."

"You're hot, big deal," I shot back, refusing to let his knowledge of my most intimate thoughts daunt me. "I'm attracted to a lot of hot guys. If Chris Hemsworth were here, I'd light him up like a firecracker with how fast I'd jump on him."

"And that would kill him," Vlad noted.

"Him and everyone else with a heartbeat, which is why I couldn't date after the accident. I could've branched out to vampires, but Marty told me to avoid them because he was worried they'd try to use me for my power." *And he was right*, I thought emphatically before going on. "Now I'm thrown together with an attractive man I can't kill, and you feel special because I responded like any normal, healthy woman would?"

I leaned back with a huff. "Give me a break. Another reasonably good-looking dead guy would rev my engine, too, so don't break your arm patting yourself on the back."

"You're deluding yourself, but as I told you, I don't run away from challenges," Vlad said, stroking the tight stubble along his jaw. I refused to follow the movement; staring at his mouth would only lead to more thoughts of that vision.

"Let's put it to the test," he went on. "Maximus!"

He hadn't raised his voice, but the blond vampire appeared almost instantly.

"Yes?"

"He's just one of many men available for you to choose from," Vlad stated with an arch smile. "All muscular, virile, single, and good for at least an hour before you'd electrocute them into oblivion."

I had a sense of where this was going, and I squirmed in my chair. *Drop it*, I thought warningly.

He ignored that, gesturing to me with his wineglass. "Now look at our guest, Maximus. Full lips, ice blue eyes, long black hair, and strong, shapely body. Beautiful, isn't she? So beautiful I'm confident you and several others in this house would like to fuck her, yes?"

I gasped at his bluntness. Maximus blinked, his gaze flicking to me and then to Vlad. "Is this a trick question?"

"Not at all," Vlad said, eyeing him with cool appraisal. "For the length of Leila's stay, all of my people are free to pursue her, if she's agreeable. Or, if she wants to skip the preliminaries and fuck one of you right now, that is allowable as well."

I could feel the heat rise to my face, but I wasn't sure if it was embarrassment or fury. Maximus seemed at turns uneasy and interested, like he didn't know whether to leave in case I was about to electrocute everyone in my rage, or stay and see if I demanded that he whip out his cock and get started.

"I have a question," I said, my tone bright although I was still seething inside. "Who do I have to screw to get any dinner around here? You have all these shiny plates but no food. It's like you're a terrible tease."

A little smile played about Vlad's lips. "Sorry, Maximus. Seems our guest has chosen other cravings."

"Or maybe I'm not into him or anyone else being ordered to service me as if they're sex slaves," I countered.

"He's not ordering me; he's telling me the normal rules concerning guests don't apply to you, if I'm interested."

Maximus stared at me as he spoke, and he'd

dropped the formal vernacular he'd used in our prior conversations. Guess with this topic, formalities were redundant.

Then he looked at Vlad. "You want her. Why are you offering us this chance?"

"Because she's wrong about me," Vlad said with that infuriating sureness, "and she needs to realize that. Besides, in the unlikely event that she's right, then she's not worth my time."

I threw my napkin on the table and stood. "I'm done listening to this."

Maximus touched my arm. "Please, wait. I *am* interested. Before anyone else jumps into the equation, I want a chance." A hint of green flickered in his dark gray eyes. "Not to be too blunt, but working with Vlad doesn't leave much time for meeting women. Besides, you're beautiful, ballsy, and your abilities fascinate me. So if you're interested, too, I'd say yes, and it would have nothing to do with being *ordered*."

My gaze flew to Vlad, who continued to stroke his jaw in relaxed contemplation. *You smug bastard*, I thought, and then turned my attention to Maximus, torn between my anger over Vlad's ruthless manipulation and awkwardness because Maximus did seem genuine in his offer.

"It doesn't have to be sex tonight or nothing," Maximus went on. "Say you'll let me show you around the house tomorrow."

Again I looked at Vlad, but his brow rose as if daring me to decline. I cursed. This was what I'd wanted—an attractive, nondangerous man I couldn't easily kill asking me out. Vlad might be convinced that I held a special attraction for him, but I'd prove him wrong and have fun doing it.

"A tour sounds great," I told Maximus, sitting down again. "How about one p.m. tomorrow, or is that too early for you?"

"One is fine. I'll look forward to it," he said, smiling. He had dimples and they made his rugged features look younger, making me guess he was my age when he was changed over. Then he turned to Vlad, bowed, and left.

Silence fell on the dining room, broken only by the crackling sounds from the triple fireplace that took up the wall behind Vlad. I stared at him, silently assuring him that he'd made a huge mistake.

Finally, Vlad spoke, but it wasn't to me.

"You may serve dinner now."

The room was suddenly filled with half a dozen attendants, each bearing a large domed platter that had delicious scents emitting from it. But although the food they uncovered and placed on the table looked even better than it smelled, oddly enough, I was no longer hungry.

Chapter 13

I'd figured Maximus would be prompt, and I was right. As soon as the clock struck one, a knock sounded on the door.

I opened it, forcing a smile even though that was the last thing I felt like doing. Despite the bed being the softest, most comfortable one I'd ever lain on, I'd hardly slept and my whole body felt sore. All the various scrapes, bumps, and bruises over the past few days must've caught up with me. Add that to disturbing dreams I had the few times I did fall asleep, and I was in a miserable mood.

Some of that must have shown on my face, because Maximus's smile faded as he looked closely at me.

"Are you feeling all right?"

"I'm fine," I lied. "Just a little groggy. Guess I had too many things on my mind to get a good night's sleep."

"It might be the altitude," he offered, though the faint furrow in his forehead told me he wasn't sold on my excuse. "It can make humans feel very tired until they're acclimated to it."

His "humans" comment didn't faze me. After living for years with Marty, I was used to it.

"Must be it," I said, putting more effort into my smile.

The slight flaring of his nostrils told me it worked. "You look lovely," he said, voice deepening as his gaze moved over me with more than concern this time.

"Thank you." I ran a hand through my hair, letting a swath fall over the scar by reflex. "You look good, too. Very *GQ*."

I wasn't lying. He wore a crew-neck navy sweater that looked like it was woven from silk, and his black pants were dressy yet casual. Add that to his great height, attractively hewn features, and thick, muscular build, and he'd make most feminine hearts flutter.

Most, but not mine. I appreciated him taking care with his appearance, but I didn't feel any spark when I looked at him. If my hormones could've been hooked up to a machine, only a flat line would have registered. *You're tired*, I reassured myself. Maybe Maximus was right about the altitude messing with me.

The altitude didn't stop you from lusting over Vlad yesterday, a dark little voice taunted.

I ignored it. I was tired, that was all. Soon, I'd be thinking half a dozen sleazy thoughts about Maximus. Hell, I might even act on some of those thoughts.

"Shall we?" he asked, drawing my attention back to him.

I'd show that egotistical Romanian prince he was nothing special. "Absolutely."

"Where would you like your tour to begin?" he asked.

I shrugged. "Wherever you want."

"Let's start at the beginning," Maximus said as led me down the ornate hallway. "This was originally a monastery built back in the fifteenth century."

"This house is a former *church*?" I asked in disbelief.

"Monasteries were more than that back then," he replied, gesturing to the huge windows we came to. "They were also strategic strongholds. At that time, the Ottoman Empire was trying to invade Western Europe, and Romania was one of the countries in its way."

"So that explains the high walls and lookout towers," I said musingly before adding, "And they're still used today."

"Vlad has enemies," Maximus replied, slanting a look at me.

I snorted. "Yeah, I noticed after I was kidnapped by them."

"This wasn't where he lived when he was prince," Maximus went on, leading me past the parlor to the staircase. "He didn't move in here until the seventeenth century. The walls and monastery were practically in ruins, but he restored them. Built the third and fourth levels of the house on top of them, as well as added new amenities to the first and second floors."

"Like the indoor garden?" I asked jokingly.

Maximus grinned. "Shrapnel insisted on that. He's a horticulturist at heart, but he'd never admit it."

The huge vampire Marty had described as "creative" in his torture techniques secretly liked to play with plants?

"What other surprises do you have in store?" I asked, adding dryly, "Let me guess: You're the real Roman commander that Russell Crowe portrayed in *Gladiator*."

He chuckled, running his hand along my arm and not drawing away at the currents that flowed into him.

"No, but with the right incentive, you could get me to wear that short leather skirt and pretend to be."

His tone was light, yet underneath was a tinge of sensuality. I might not be thinking any naughty thoughts on this date yet—dammit!—but Maximus was letting me know he was.

"Tell me more about the restoration process," I said, wondering why I didn't feel so much as a twitch at the thought of kinky role playing with Maximus. "Were you around back then?"

If he was disappointed at how I'd changed the subject back to the house, he didn't show it.

"Oh yes. I was in charge of the rebuilding, in fact. By then I'd been with Vlad for centuries and he trusted me to make sure everything was completed while he was off in Slovenia . . ."

Three hours later, my head was whirling. Maximus took me through the first three floors, which were staggeringly huge. Vlad's house was also littered with enough priceless artifacts to make any museum curator weep with envy. Forget the tapestries, portraits, furnishings, and various jewel-studded objects—the Weapons Room was like walking back in time. It had armor, chain mail, swords, shields, and various other items of war, many with the Dracul family standard or the Order of the Dragon emblazoned on them.

I kept my right hand plastered to my side when Maximus showed me that room. I knew these had been used in battle; the dents and scratches were mute testimony to that. It almost seemed like the room gave off a pulse from all the essence-heavy items in it.

Despite my interest, I felt steadily worse as the day wore on. By the time Maximus brought me back to my room, I was so tired and achy that all I wanted to do was sleep. Maybe my brain was over-whelmed from everything I'd learned, and the lack of a decent sleep was catching up with me.

"Thanks for a wonderful afternoon, Maximus," I told him. "See you at lunch tomorrow?"

He leaned against the wall in a casual way. "No, Oscar or Gabriel will bring you your food."

"Sick of me already?" I teased.

His smile remained but his gaze became serious. "It's harder to seduce someone when you're also clearing her plates. That's why I assigned others to take care of you while you're here."

Inwardly I sighed. Despite telling the truth about having a wonderful time, I still hadn't felt any telltale twinges around Maximus—and I'd *tried*. I stared at his ass when he walked ahead of me, envisioned my nails digging into that broad back . . . hell, I'd even stolen some looks at his package. Aside from admiring the shape he was in, nothing. I could just imagine Vlad chortling to himself.

I wasn't about to give up, however. Maybe what I needed was some tactile interaction. Thanks to my electrocution issues, I hadn't been kissed since Johnny Staples in the eighth grade. A kiss was bound to kick-start my libido. I smiled, moistened my lips, and hoped Maximus wasn't the shy type.

He wasn't. He bent down, his hand curling around my neck, and lowered his mouth onto mine. His lips were cool, full but firm, and he used far more finesse slipping his tongue into my mouth than Johnny Staples had. I kissed him back, glad it was like riding a bike and I hadn't forgotten how. Our tongues twined together and I had a further flash of gratitude that he didn't taste like blood. I liked being able to put my arms around someone and be held close, though I was careful not to touch Maximus with my right hand. His little moan when he gripped me to him was nice, too. Glad my years without practice hadn't made me the world's worst kisser, and—

Aw, hell, this wasn't working! His large, hard body was pressed to mine and his tongue was doing very enjoyable things in my mouth, but I still didn't feel a rush of heat. Figures. For years, I'd been frustrated over my forced singlehood, but now that I had means and opportunity in the form of a very willing, very attractive blond vampire, I wasn't into him. Maybe I should get myself sized for a promise ring. Did they give those to nonbelievers? Or was it a members-only thing?

"Maximus, I'm sorry," I said, pulling away from him.

"Too fast?" he asked thickly. "Don't worry, I don't mind waiting. It'll take Vlad weeks to gather personal items from all his enemies for you to touch, so we have time."

Attractive, understanding, and not falling to the floor with a heart attack from the electricity in my touch. I drew in a frustrated breath. Wasn't he what I'd longed for all those lonely nights? So why wasn't my pulse speeding up? Why was my reaction to him so damn *flat* compared to what I'd felt when I was with Vlad?

I was so screwed.

"Maximus," I began.

He put a finger to my lips. "Don't. I know that tone, but . . . wait. If you still want to say it after a week, fine, but give me that long before letting another man make a move." Wry smile. "What else do you have to do?"

What else, indeed? Certainly not think about a dangerous vampire who was so sure of himself that he'd set me up with another guy and also practically dared me to sleep with any member of his staff.

"Okay," I said, and forced a smile.

He kissed me again, and I hoped that I'd feel more this time, but while it was enjoyable, that telltale spark was still missing.

"Good," he said when he let me go. "Then I'll see you tomorrow."

Chapter 14

 I trudged down the staircase at nine o'clock with all the enthusiasm of a condemned prisoner going to the electric chair. This time, I wasn't wearing a slinky black dress. I was in gray slacks and an olive turtleneck sweater, my black hair twisted into a ponytail, not a speck of makeup, and lips thinned into annoyed slits. Everything about me should've screamed "Do not engage" to the vampire already waiting in the dining room.

Vlad rose when he saw me, which for some reason angered me. Why did he keep pretending to be mannerly? Someone with manners didn't torture innocent people or offer to pimp out their staff in order to prove a point!

Then I gave myself a mental shake. Just because I still felt like crap and was unable to prove him wrong didn't mean I had the right to spew venom all over him. *Sorry*, I thought, assuming he was tuned into my thoughts as usual.

The sardonic smile that curled his lips when he held out my chair confirmed my suspicions.

"Your date wasn't everything you'd hoped?"

I sat down with a small sigh. I hated lying and he could read my mind, so what was the point trying to deny it?

"No, but Maximus wants to give it a week, and I agreed."

Once I was settled at the table, Vlad returned to his chair, again making the simple act of sitting appear commanding. Give him a throne and he'd look right at home. Then again, he probably had one stashed away somewhere. Maximus hadn't shown me the fourth floor because he said it was "private." I translated that as "Vlad's personal territory" and wondered why he needed the equivalent of an apartment building for his quarters.

Or maybe that was where he did all his torturing. I could understand Maximus not wanting to show me *that* room.

"No, I do my torturing in the dungeon like any other respectable castle owner," he said, amusement clear in his voice. "And the fourth floor isn't merely mine. My most trusted staff members have their rooms there, too."

"You really have a dungeon?" Talk about old school.

"Of course." Spoken as he gestured with two fingers. An attendant appeared, pouring dark red wine into my glass.

At least, I hoped it was wine.

"It is." With more amusement. "Aside from its obvious purpose, the wine should assist you in getting a better night's sleep tonight. It will also help to soothe some of your aches."

Your ability is so *intrusive*, I thought, glaring at him.

He only smiled and raised his glass in silent salute.

I took a small sip of mine, letting the liquid roll around my tongue before swallowing. Hints of violets, black cherry, and . . . smoke. *Very nice*, I decided, and took a larger sip. Some of the tightness started to leave my shoulders.

Vlad watched me, whatever he was thinking hidden behind that enigmatic half smile. I'd dressed down for dinner, but he hadn't. The rich material of his aubergine shirt made it far more elegant than your average button-down. Lights from the chandelier gleamed off jeweled cuff links, and his charcoal-colored pants fit him so perfectly, it was hard not to stare. His hair was brushed into smooth, dark waves and that eight o'clock shadow hugged his chiseled jawline, making me forget myself long enough drink in his appearance along with my wine.

I'd expected him to smirk over my obvious admiration, but his expression didn't change as he stared back at me. His long, tapered fingers stroked the stem of his wineglass, and I flashed to how it felt when he'd caressed my hand as I unleashed all my electricity into him. Warmth spread through me that I told myself was the effects from the wine, but I knew better. Three hours and two kisses with Maximus hadn't made me feel as much as a glimmer of heat, but less than five minutes sitting across from Vlad and I was mentally fanning myself.

Now his expression did change—into a slow, knowing smile.

"You see? You *don't* react this way with every man," he said with satisfaction.

Nothing would make me happier than to tell him he was wrong, but I did feel something for Vlad that I hadn't felt for anyone else. Maybe he was right and it was that damn darkness in me recognizing a kindred spirit. That didn't make him any less hazardous to my physical or emotional well-being, however.

"Stop," I said quietly. "Find someone else to toy with. We both know I lack experience, so I don't know how to play the game without getting hurt. Besides, I hate games. I prefer knowing straight up what's real and what's bullcrap."

He sat back, something lurking in his gaze that tempted me despite knowing better. I gulped my wine for a distraction.

"It's your directness and refusal to lie to yourself that I find most appealing. And I'm not toying with you. I'm very serious about making you mine."

I held the wine in my mouth for a long moment before swallowing. Not to test the flavors this time, but in an effort to gain control. Two Leilas seemed to be battling it out inside of me. The first was outraged that he still considered it a fait accompli that I'd give in to him, and the second . . . that slutty bitch was wondering what Vlad looked like naked.

His teeth flashed in a wicked grin. "Many women wonder, but few find out. I'm very selective in my lovers."

"Because you're so special?" I couldn't help but ask with open sarcasm.

That grin faded and his expression became serious. "Because at points in my life, I've lost everything. This house, my other homes, the cars, planes . . . they're my possessions, but anyone could own them. My body is the only thing that's truly mine, so I don't give it away as though it's worthless."

I'd lost everything before, too. It was worse than death in some ways, so I wasn't surprised that it had had a lasting effect on Vlad. Loss seemed to haunt him, from the source of his darkest sin all the way to this.

"Again I say my mind reading doesn't come close to your abilities," Vlad said softly. "You saw right into my soul with one touch. How does overhearing a few thoughts compare to that?"

I glanced away, clearing my throat. "I don't know. Some of those thoughts I'd *really* rather you not have heard."

He chuckled, low and decadent. "Ah, but those were the ones I most enjoyed hearing."

"Any luck rounding up items for me to touch?" I asked, desperately trying to change the subject.

Vlad still had a devilish glint in his eye, but he let the previous topic drop.

"I have enemies, but they're not open in their stance against me. Probably because I tend to kill my adversaries rather quickly, so first I have to determine who's paying me lip service, and who's wishing me dead."

"I could help with that." I leaned forward, anxious to find the person who'd dragged me into this. "Get me items from the top ten people you think might be double-talking you. I'll touch them and tell you who is and who isn't."

His sly grin was back. "Oh, Leila. Now you're just making yourself irresistible to me, aren't you?"

I drained the rest of my wine, wishing he'd stick to being either terrifying or charming. Being both wreaked havoc on my equilibrium. "Serving dinner yet? I'm starving."

I woke up with a groan at the sunlight streaming in. My sleep had been interrupted by dreams that had me waking with my heart pounding and my nightgown damp with sweat. They weren't nightmares where I relived Jackal kidnapping me, but they did feature a vampire. One who hadn't been doing anything against my will, but had left me gasping and pleading for more—and my dream lover hadn't been Maximus.

I swung my legs over the side of the bed. I was no stranger to wanting something I couldn't have, and there were two remedies I knew that could help. One I couldn't indulge in because the mind-reading vampire who haunted my sleep would *know* what I was doing, and worse—he'd know I was thinking about him while I was doing it. That left the other remedy.

Even though I still felt like a piece of meat someone had hammered for maximum tenderness, I got up and went over to the dresser, pulling out a pair of pants and a runner's bra. Maximus told me this house had an exercise room. I was going to find that room and burn off all my misdirected, useless lust until I was too tired to fantasize about anything except a nap.

Once I was dressed, I went downstairs. The great hall looked empty, but I knew better.

"Hello? I need to know where the gym is," I stated.

Before I could mentally count to three, a figure slipped out from behind one of the tall stone pillars.

"It is below this floor," the vampire said, an Irish brogue adding a pleasant cadence to his speech. "I will escort you."

I'd started to smile in thanks when a familiar, far more subtly accented voice made me freeze.

"No need, Lachlan. I'll show her where it is."

I mentally groaned. It was bad enough trying to exorcise Vlad from my thoughts when I only saw him at dinner. If I ran into him during the day as well, I didn't stand a chance.

And thanks to his damn mind reading, now he knew that.

Lachlan bowed to Vlad and vanished again. I waited, not turning my head. A scarred hand slid along my arm, leaving gooseflesh in its wake more from my reaction to his touch than the result of his heated flesh compared to the hall's chillier temperature.

"Are you always this warm?" I asked, not looking at him.

Something tall and dark filled my peripheral vision. "If I'm utilizing my power, I'm even warmer, but you know that. If I'm asleep, my temperature drops to that of a normal vampire."

So every part of him would be at least this heated. Didn't *that* invite musings I was better off not having?

"Gym," I managed to say. "Where is it?"

His fingers closed over my arm. "Come with me."

He knew I'd follow him, so his hand on my arm wasn't necessary. He'd chosen my right side, too, so if I wasn't careful, my hand would brush him and I might glimpse that erotic vision again. *I never do anything unless I'm sure*, he'd said. Was he daring me to see if that vision remained unchanged?

Vlad had to hear what was churning inside my head, yet he made no comment. He also didn't drop my arm or move even an inch away. Instead, he led me down a staircase located behind the winter garden that ended in an enclosed stone hallway.

"What else is down here?" I asked to break the silent standoff between us.

"Aside from the gymnasium, there are the lower kitchens, laundry rooms, servants' entrance, storage facilities, swimming pool, root cellars, and humans' living quarters."

I did look at him then. In shock. "You keep your live-in blood donors in the *basement*?"

"It's a very nice basement. Much better than the dungeons. Those tend to be quite cold in winter."

I couldn't tell if he was serious. He might indeed think nothing of housing his blood donors next to his root cellars, or he might find it hilarious to let me believe that.

"I'd love to meet them one day," was what I said.

His lips twitched. "Would you, or are you trying to discover if they're shivering in a dark room even now?"

"I never said *that*," I muttered.

He stopped walking, but his hand remained on my arm. "I don't shirk my responsibilities, and everyone here is a member of my line directly or indirectly. Their living quarters contain normal bedrooms, and you are welcome to see that for yourself."

"Thanks," I said, adding, "I didn't really think you kept them housed in tiny underground cellars."

His mouth quirked. "You gave it fifty-fifty odds."

"Well, you *do* have an active dungeon," I pointed out.

He laughed, the sound rolling over me more than once with the echoes in the enclosed hallway. His laughter was so unique—part amused growl, part purr, and all self-assured male. Its effect on me was tangible, turning up my own lips and making me step closer to him before I realized what I was doing.

Emerald flared in his gaze and his fingers tightened on my arm. A throb started inside me, low but unmistakable, making my mouth go dry and my pulse begin to speed up. One more step would have our bodies touching, we were standing that close. But that single step would probably seal my vision into reality. *Don't let it happen*, Marty had urged me. *He'll break your heart* and *ruin your life* . . .

I took not one but two steps backward, slipping my arm out from Vlad's grasp. He let me go without trying to stop me, and I expelled the breath I hadn't realized I'd been holding. Anxious to defuse the unspoken tension, I pointed at a door with stone ivies carved around the frame.

"What's in there?"

"The entrance to the chapel," he replied.

I let out a nervous laugh. "Maximus told me this place used to be a monastery, but you actually kept the chapel?"

"No, it was destroyed," he said, not commenting on my edginess or the reason behind it. "I had this one rebuilt on the ruins of the old citadel tower. Would you like to see it?"

"No thanks," I said at once.

"How emphatic. Not the religious type?"

"No, why? Don't tell me *you* believe in God?"

"Many vampires do. The story of our origin states that the mark of Cain was God turning him into the first vampire by forcing him to drink blood as penance for murdering his brother."

Then he leaned forward and his voice dropped to almost a whisper. "Surprised? Is it impossible to believe that I think a day will come where I'll be held accountable for each life I've taken, every drop of blood I've spilled . . . and yet I continue to do whatever is necessary to keep my people safe?"

I swallowed, as unnerved by that thought as I was by his nearness. Vlad was such a study in extremes that I couldn't figure out if he was being rhetorical or serious, but maybe that was for the best. It was easier to walk away when I wasn't being pulled further into his intriguing complexities.

He still stood very close. Without thinking, I rubbed the place on my arm where his hand had been. The spot felt oddly barren now. *Ridiculous*, I told myself. *You came down here to unload tension. Quit stockpiling more of it with your idiocy.*

His lips curled as he glanced at my arm. He'd heard that, of course. How I wished I could shut him out of my mind.

"Is the gym far?"

He inclined his head toward a door on the opposite wall.

"Right there."

We'd been standing only a dozen feet away and he hadn't said a word? I would've demanded to know what sort of game he was playing, except I didn't think he was playing one. Instead, as his brow rose in silent challenge, I wondered if he was doing something worse—intensifying his pursuit of me.

If so, then the next move was mine, and with my attraction to him growing, I didn't know if I'd choose wisely.

Chapter 15

 The gym turned out to be filled with state-of-the-art equipment. Good for whoever lived here, but useless for me. However, it had a large exercise mat, some free weights, and a knotted rope suspended from the high ceiling. I made the most out of those three things, forcing my aching body through a series of routines I'd used when I was training for competition.

I had the room to myself for the first two hours, then I heard voices right before the door banged open. A group of twenty-somethings entered, chatting in what I now recognized as Romanian. They stopped short when they noticed me dangling from the rope upside down, my black hair fanning out underneath me.

"Hi," I said, feeling self-conscious as I realized that I probably looked strange. "Any of you speak English?"

"Most of us," a husky, curly-haired guy replied, to other murmurs of assent. He started to grin. "What are you doing?"

"Sit-ups," I said, demonstrating by hoisting

myself up until my face touched my thigh. "Works more muscles this way."

"I bet it does," he said, still staring at me.

I uncoiled the rope from around my leg and climbed down. My abs had been killing me anyway. Once I was back on the ground, I smiled at the group.

"I'm Leila," I said, using my real name because everyone else here called me that.

I knew the moment they saw the scar. A collective wince seemed to ripple over the group, though it took longer for some of the guys since they checked out my body before getting to my face. I kept my smile in place, used to this reaction.

"It's from an accident when I was a kid," I said by way of explanation. If I didn't offer any information, people would just ask. That I was also used to.

"Oh, how awful," a pretty, petite, strawberry-blond girl said in heavily accented English.

"Glad you, uh, healed up," the curly-haired guy replied awkwardly. "Nice to meet you. I'm Ben, and as you can tell from my accent, I'm American, too. This is Joe, Damon, Tom, Angie, Sandra, and Kate, but her English isn't good so she'll probably just grunt at you."

"Well, her English is better than my Romanian, so she's got me beat," I replied, waving at everyone.

"Are you . . . new to residing here?" the strawberry blonde introduced as Sandra asked.

I assumed that was a nice way to inquire if I was going to be a live-in donor, and I stumbled over my reply.

"Ah, not really. I'm just helping out Vlad with, uh, a project, but I'm leaving once it's done."

"Vlad?" Ben looked surprised. His gaze swept over me again. "You're human, right?"

"Yep." The rest of them still seemed taken aback, so I had to ask. "Why? Is it unusual for Vlad to work with a human?"

Ben's brows rose. "We wouldn't know. None of us see him unless he's hungry. Then it's bend, get bitten, and beat it."

Now my brows went up, too. "*Bend?*" Did he mean—?

My expression must have given away my thought, because he hastened to add, "I mean bend as in this." Ben tilted his head to the side, exposing his neck. "Most of the others chat with us a little first. Vlad doesn't."

"Oh." I felt like I should apologize even though I wasn't the one with the wham-bam-bite-'em-ma'am record.

He shrugged. "Not a big deal. Can't beat the benefits." Then he smiled, looking me over again. "Hey, we're going to a club tonight. If you're not too busy, wanna join us?"

"There he goes again," the tall, rangy brunet named Damon muttered.

That was my cue to leave. "Thanks, but I can't."

"What, too good for us breathers now?" Ben teased.

Sandra elbowed him. "Rude," she hissed.

I gave the group a measured stare as I reconsidered leaving. They all looked normal, which meant I would usually hide the reason behind why I couldn't go to anything as contact-heavy as a club and then avoid them at all costs. But they weren't normal. They were the willing blood donors to a house of vampires, and either I told them about me, or I stayed away from them the whole time I was here.

I decided to take a chance. "It's not that." I held up my right hand. "My accident changed me. I can't touch anyone or I'll electrocute them, for starters."

I had their full attention now.

"What do you mean, for starters?" From the goateed guy with the black hair named Joe. "What else can you do?"

I drew in a breath. "I see things when I touch people. Bad things, mostly, but sometimes I catch glimpses of the future."

"No," Sandra breathed.

"Yes," I said a trifle grimly. Maybe I shouldn't have told them. This might be too weird even for vampire blood donors.

Ben started to grin. "That is so *cool*. How bad do you electrocute people? If you touch me, can you tell me my future?"

"Ooh, I want to know mine, too!" Angie said, blue eyes bright with anticipation.

The rest of them seemed equally excited. Okay, this I wasn't prepared for. I'd hoped they wouldn't be repelled by me. I didn't think I'd suddenly be popular.

"I don't always see the future," I hedged, starting to back away. "Most of the time, I just see people's sins."

"Really?" Ben looked fascinated. "If you're not going to zap me into next week, I don't have any sins, so touch away!"

I didn't want to, but it had been a long time since

anyone looked at me like this: with acceptance and enthusiasm. A lonely part inside me reared up and roared, *Don't screw this up, Leila! Do it!*

I sighed. "Let me offload some energy first."

So saying, I went over to the bench press. It was made of metal and bolted into the concrete for safety, so it would do. When everyone was on the rubber and foam mat, I laid my right hand on the weight bench and released my strict inner hold.

An audible *zzt!* followed by a flash of white later, and I felt slightly dizzy. Now I didn't need to dump energy into the lightning rods before showering. Vlad had been quick to get those set up for me.

"Come here," I said to Ben, waving him over.

He approached, still smiling. He was a nice-looking boy in his early twenties, and I envied his blondish-brown curls. My hair couldn't be straighter if I ironed it every morning.

"Hold out your hand," I said. The farther my touch was from his heart, the better, even if I had drained myself.

He held out his hand and I gently laid my right one on it. A far softer bolt left me, causing him to yelp, but he didn't fall over or start peeing himself, thankfully. Then, as usual, a slew of colorless images crowded my mind. True to his word, they weren't violent, but I saw no full-color, hazy images afterward.

"Sorry, I didn't see anything about your future," I said.

His smile was expectant. "What'd you see from my past?"

The others looked interested, too. I glanced away. "You don't want me to say, trust me."

"Come on, how else will I know it worked?" Ben pressed.

"Yes, tell us," Joe added.

"Tell us" came in a chorus from the group. I shook my head, muttering, "It'll embarrass you," but I was swamped with more demands for proof.

I threw up my hands. "Fine, but I warned you. When you were twelve, you stole your little sister's favorite Minnie Mouse DVD and beat off to it every night until your dad caught you and made you buy her a new one out of your allowance money."

Stunned silence followed. Ben's face went red.

"I don't believe it," he muttered, but that was soon drowned out by laughter and good-natured ribbings. I let it go on for another few moments and then cleared my throat.

"I bet the rest of you have some embarrassing sins, too, so give him a break or I'll start copping feels."

The teasing subsided to lingering grins and the occasional giggle. Ben shot me a grateful look. Hey, compared to the sins I'd seen from other people, his was steeped in innocence.

"When I was a little girl, I wanted to be Miss Piggy so I could marry Kermit the Frog," I told Ben, winking. "*Kermit*. Talk about shameful."

"Ouch. You shoulda kept that to yourself," he said, giving my arm a friendly knock.

The brief contact meant only a tiny bit of electricity sizzled into him, but he winced. Then he grinned.

"My sister used to rub her socks on the floor and then chase me. Reminds me of that."

"She owed you for the stolen DVD," I quipped.

"Like you said, I bought her a new one," he replied, still grinning. "Hey, what's wrong with your ear?"

"What?"

I reached up and felt something wet. *Ew, I'm still sweating like a pig*, I thought, but when I looked at my hand, it was red.

Sandra gasped. That was the last thing I heard before everything went hazy and the exercise bench reared up to hit me in the face.

Chapter 16

"Leila, can you hear me?"

I opened my eyes, blinking. Vlad's face materialized in front of me, blurry at first, and then clear enough for me to notice that he looked concerned.

"Hey," I said, surprised at how weak my voice sounded.

"Will she be all right?" I heard Ben ask.

"All of you, leave," Vlad responded curtly.

"That's not nice," I mumbled. "You should talk to them before you bite them, too. Common courtesy."

His brow went up, but he said nothing to that. I heard shuffling feet and then moments later, a door closed.

"Did I faint?" I asked, trying to remember what happened. I'd been attempting to make Ben feel better about his former Minnie Mouse fetish, and then I saw something red . . .

"Yes. You were also bleeding from your ears, but it's stopped now."

Vlad's words were blunt, but they lacked the

brusque tone he'd used with Ben. I tried to sit up, but his features started to get blurry again.

"Slowly," Vlad said. He grasped my shoulders, easing me into a sitting position. Then he slid behind me so that my back rested against his chest.

"Don't. I'm all sweaty and bloody," I protested.

"Heavens, not sweat *and* blood," he replied mockingly.

I managed to smile. Smartass vampire.

"Are you anemic?" Vlad asked, surprising me.

I frowned. "I don't think so, but I haven't been to a doctor in a long time, for obvious reasons."

He grasped my hand. Before I realized what he intended, he had my red-smeared fingers in his mouth.

"Stop!" I gasped.

His other arm went around my torso, holding me in place against his chest. Between that and his grip on my hand, no way was I breaking free even if I had all my strength back, which I didn't. I could do nothing but wait as he slowly sucked on my fingers, his warm tongue snaking in between them to get every last drop of blood.

"You're not anemic," he said when he finally let go and I yanked my hand away from his mouth.

I still felt rattled by what he'd done, and it wasn't because I'd found it repellent. "You can tell from *that*?"

"You'd be surprised by the things I can tell from tasting someone's blood," he replied in a lower, darker voice.

I shivered, acutely aware that my neck was only an inch from his mouth. As if to accentuate that point, his jaw grazed my cheek. *His stubble doesn't feel as rough as it looks*, raced across my mind. Then again, it hadn't felt rough in that vision, either . . .

"I think I can get up now," I said, trying to scoot away.

His arm stopped me before I got more than a few inches, drawing me back against that hard, heated chest.

"Stop fidgeting, I'm not going to bite you."

"Going to lick the blood off my head instead?" I asked before cursing myself. *Give him the idea, why don't you?*

I couldn't see his face, but I could almost feel him smile. "No, not that, either. Has this ever happened to you before?"

Being held against my will by a vampire? Sure, lots of times, I thought sardonically.

"Leila . . ." His voice held a note of impatience.

I thought back, ruling out the times I'd felt dizzy after falling during practice and banging my head.

"Years ago, right around the time I met Marty. Once I fainted when he and I were performing. Then Marty started making me these awful-tasting health shakes, and I got better. Maybe I hadn't been getting enough vitamins before or something—"

I stopped, because Vlad had tensed. If I thought his chest felt hard before, now it was like leaning against steel.

"How often did he make you those shakes?"

I didn't like the sound of his voice. Too controlled and pleasant—the same voice he used when he killed.

"About once a week. Why?"

He didn't answer, but pulled out a cell phone, dialing one-handed. With our close proximity, I heard the person answer.

"Yes?" Marty's voice, tight with tension.

"Why are you—?" I began, but Vlad's hand sliced the air in the universal command for silence.

"Martin," he said genially, "did you forget to tell me something very important about Leila?"

Silence, and then Marty's guarded "I don't know what it could have been—"

"Because she's right here, blood staining her hair after it leaked from her ears when she fainted," Vlad cut him off, his tone sharpening. "Does *that* stir your memory?"

I didn't understand where Vlad was going with this. He clearly thought Marty had something to do with my fainting, but why? How?

My uneasiness wasn't abated when I heard Marty's heavy sigh.

"I hoped she'd built up enough of a resistance that she'd be okay until I got back, but . . . well, fuck."

"Well *what*?" I demanded, struggling to rise to my feet.

Vlad's arm tightened, keeping me pinned to his chest. "He's been feeding you his blood in those shakes," he said flatly. "That's why they tasted terrible to you. I should have picked up on that the other day when the scent from my bloody shirt reminded you of them, but I was preoccupied."

I was stunned, my mind immediately rejecting the idea. I'd seen what Marty put into those shakes! Carrots, celery, tomato juice, protein powder, some vitamin drops . . .

Red vitamin drops in an unmarked bottle that

he claimed he got from a friend who sold them on the side. I never questioned Marty about it. Why would I? I trusted him.

"Kid." Marty's voice flowed through the silence. "I'm sorry I didn't tell you."

My teeth ground together until my jaw ached. "Hold the phone near my ear," I directed Vlad. "Why?" I asked as soon as it was close.

Marty sighed again. "You were dying when we met. You didn't know it, but I could smell it. You're only human; you don't heal fast enough to undo the harm inflicted on your body from all that power inside you. I thought if I gave you a little bit of my blood every week, it might reverse the damage and even build up your resistance to the repercussions from your power. I was right about the first, but not the second, obviously."

In that moment, I was glad Vlad hadn't let me get up because I felt like all the strength left my body. I'd been *dying*? Could I believe him about that after he admitted he'd been lying to me the entire four years we'd known each other?

"Why didn't you tell me this before?" My voice sounded strong, at least. Anger helped with that.

"I wanted to, but I was afraid you'd say no." It sounded like Marty sniffed even though he didn't need to breathe. "You know what happened with Vera. When we met, you reminded me so much of her that I couldn't . . . I *wouldn't* let you die, too."

I shook my head, still furious but with tears in my eyes now. I wanted to beat Marty for his deception until my arms grew tired, and then I wanted to hug him and tell him Vera's death was *not* his fault and to quit punishing himself.

"I gotta go," I said, sniffing myself now.

"I don't blame you if you hate me," Marty said gruffly.

"I don't hate you, you dumb shit," I snapped. "But I *am* taking it out on your ass when I see you again. Count on it."

He let out a choked laugh. "I'll look forward to it, kid."

Vlad took the phone and at last released his hold. "Martin, I am not pleased," he said coolly. "The next time you withhold information from me, rest assured that I'll burn you to death."

Marty started to say something, but Vlad hung up. I slid away from him, my emotions still torn.

"I'd want to kill him for withholding that, too, if not for how messed up he still is about his daughter," I muttered. "Dwarfs can have regular-sized children, but you must know that. Vera was thin, long dark hair, blue eyes . . . she looked a little like me, and she was twenty when Marty killed her. I saw it the first time I touched him because it was his worst sin."

Vlad said nothing, but his brow arched in silent invitation to go on.

"In the early nineteen hundreds, Marty and Vera had an act together like he and I do now. After a show, some vampire attacked him, but he didn't stop there. He turned him and just *left* him. Marty rose as a vampire to find Vera crying over what she thought was his dead body. You know what happened next. No new vampire can control their hunger."

"No," Vlad said evenly, "no new vampire can. You're right that her death wasn't his fault, but I meant what I said. If he withholds information from me again, I'll kill him."

I stared at him. His burnished copper gaze was utterly dispassionate, the words spoken as if they had no meaning. Or maybe he just didn't care about how much that would hurt me.

"Sometimes I think you're the coldest person I've ever met," I said, rising to my feet.

"You could have died."

When he started to speak, Vlad was still seated on the exercise mat, specks of my blood staining his gray shirt and ruining his otherwise elegant yet casual three-piece ensemble. But before I drew my next breath, he was right in front of me.

"When someone threatens me or endangers a person under my protection, I make an example of him. This is the second time I've let Marty live out of consideration for you, but he won't get a third pardon. I can't afford to let others think they can get away with similar behavior."

"Because then you'll lose your scary reputation?" I asked with a bitter scoff.

"Yes, and my people will suffer for it," he replied, tilting my chin up so I had to look at him. "I don't kill out of a perverse sense of enjoyment. I do it to protect those who are mine because once life is lost, it's lost forever." His voice thickened. "You saw into me. You know what loss has cost me."

Oh, how I wished he was lying. It would be so much easier if Vlad was a homicidal narcissist who placed no value on anyone except himself, but I did know better. In a twisted way, he valued life more than most people, but in his case, it was specific to his people. No wonder they feared no one but him.

"Later, I want you to call Marty so I can talk to him again," I said steadily. "Give him a chance to come clean on anything else without your death threat hanging over him. After that, he hides something from you at his own peril. Deal?"

His lips curled. "Deal."

I started to walk away, but his voice stopped me before I got more than a few feet.

"We're not finished yet, Leila."

I wished I didn't know what he meant, but Vlad unbuttoning his shirt cuff and rolling up his coat and sleeve only confirmed my suspicion.

"What if I said no?" I asked. "Would you force me?"

He gave me a jaded look. "I don't have to force you. You might not want to do this, but you want to live more."

With his shirt and jacket rolled up, I saw the scars on his hands continued up his forearm, a fine dusting of dark hair covering some of them. I rubbed my own scar reflectively. I didn't remember the pain of my skin splitting open when the electricity from that power line ripped through my flesh. Did he remember what happened when all those scars were made, or had the passing of centuries erased that from his mind?

"I remember."

I jerked my gaze up to meet his unblinking stare. "When I was human, I led my armies from the front, and I kept my scars for the same reason you chose to keep yours—so I'd never forget."

I flinched at his correct guess that Marty had offered to slice my scar off. If he poured his blood over the wound right after, the incredible regenerative qualities it contained would heal my skin back to the same unblemished smoothness I'd had when I was a baby. But I'd wanted to keep the evidence of what happened. Every time someone winced when they saw my scar, I was reminded of how my self-ishness cost my mother her life.

"I told you once before," I said, the words husky from remembrance. "Everyone holds their sins close to their skin."

Fangs gleamed for an instant before Vlad bit into his wrist, pooling up two deep crimson holes.

"Then come," he said, holding it out. "And taste mine."

Chapter 17

I walked over and took his wrist. If I hesitated or thought about it, I might lose my nerve, and he was right. I did want to live more than I was repelled by the thought of drinking vampire blood. Vlad had only met me a few days ago and he knew that. Marty had lived with me for years and hadn't counted on it enough to tell me what he was doing.

When my mouth sealed over his wrist, I closed my eyes. *Pretend it's wine. Really sharp, coppery-tasting wine.* My first swallow made me grimace, but I forced my tongue to slide over his flesh, catching any spare drops. His arm was hard as oak with all those muscles, but his skin was smooth. As heated as my lips, and when I ran my tongue over him a second time, it was because I couldn't help myself from finding out what he tasted like without the harsh flavor of blood tainting his skin.

A low growl preceded his hand fisting in my hair, drawing my head back. Vlad's eyes were bright green as he stared down at me, his expression almost frightening in its intensity. My mouth parted, lips still wet from tasting him, but I didn't speak. I knew I should tell him to stop, to back away, but I didn't want him to.

He closed the scant space between us, pressing our bodies together, reaching out with the same hand I'd licked his blood from. Slowly, deliberately, he traced his thumb across my lower lip, capturing that lingering moisture. Then he brought his thumb to his mouth and tasted it, his eyes never leaving mine.

All the breath seemed to leave me and my heart began to pound. I couldn't resist reaching out and resting my hand on his chest, feeling his taut body beneath that crisp gray shirt. His muscles bunched as a current slid into him, and then his hand closed around mine. He pressed it flat, inch by inch dragging my palm over his chest, up to the smoothness of his neck and past the seductively rasping stubble of his jaw until it finally reached his mouth. My breath came faster, both from touching him this way and the look in his eyes as he placed a kiss onto my palm, his tongue flicking out to tease my flesh.

The gymnasium door banging open made me jump as though burned. Vlad released his grip on my hair, but not my hand, and his gaze slid to the left with visible irritation.

"What?" he asked coldly.

Maximus walked over, one glance taking in our compromising position. I backed away, shame replacing the desire that seized me the moment I licked Vlad that second time. I'd agreed to give Maximus a week to see if we clicked, but only a day later, he'd caught me nearly kissing his boss. *Slut*, I lashed myself.

"You have visitors," Maximus stated. His face was impassive, but I still cringed, trying to discreetly tug my hand out of Vlad's.

He let me go and folded his arms, smiling in that scary, pleasant way at Maximus.

"And they are so important that you had to find me at once and enter without knocking?"

I heard the threat behind those silky words and blanched. He wasn't about to throw down on Maximus over this, was he? *Don't*, I sent to him, not adding *please* only because I knew the word didn't work on him.

"Forgive me, but it's Mencheres and his co-ruler," Maximus stated, not sounding apologetic even though he bowed. "Their wives as well."

I started to slink away, sanity returning now that I wasn't caught up by Vlad's mesmerizing nearness. What had I been *doing*? Nothing smart, that was for sure.

"Leila, stop," Vlad said.

I kept heading for the door. "You have company, so I'll just make myself scarce—"

"*Stop*."

I did at his commanding tone, and then cursed. I wasn't one of his employees—he had no right to order me around.

"No," I said defiantly. "I'm sweaty and bloody and I want to take a shower, so whatever you have to say, it can wait."

Maximus lost his impassive expression and looked at me as if I'd suddenly sprouted a second head. Vlad's brows drew together and he opened his mouth, but before he could speak, laughter rang out from the hallway.

"I simply *must* meet whoever has put you in your place so thoroughly, Tepesh," an unfamiliar British voice stated.

"Did I mention they were on their way down?" Maximus muttered before the gym door swung open and four people entered.

The first was a short-haired brunet whose grin made me assume he was the one who'd greeted Vlad with the taunt. He was also handsome in a too-pretty way that made me think with less muscles, a wig, and some makeup, he'd look great in a dress.

Vlad's scowl vanished into a smile as the brunet's gaze swung in my direction as though he'd somehow heard that.

"Looks as though she's put you in your place as well, Bones," Vlad drawled.

"So it seems," Bones replied, winking at me. "But while I've worn many disguises, I draw the line at a dress."

My mouth dropped. *Another* mind reader?

"You're shit out of luck, because almost all of us in this group are mind readers," announced the redhead by his side. She gave me a sympathetic smile. "Annoying, isn't it?"

"Yes," I said emphatically.

Behind the brunet and the redhead was an Arabian-looking man with black hair as straight and long as mine, and a slender blonde who must be the other aforementioned wife. If most of them were mind readers, then I guessed none of them were human.

Maximus bowed once more and then left the room. Vlad walked over to me and rested his hand on my shoulder.

"Leila, this is my friend and honorary sire, Mencheres, and his wife, Kira," he said, indicating the long-haired Middle Eastern man and the blonde. "Also let me introduce my friend, Cat." The redhead, and for some reason, she looked familiar. "Her husband, Bones"—here Vlad smiled coolly at the short-haired brunet—"is *not* my friend."

"You two," Cat muttered, shaking her head. Then she held out her hand to me. "Great to meet you, Leila."

I looked at it and cleared my throat. "Ah, sorry."

"Leila has unusual abilities," Vlad said, breaking the awkward moment. "She gives off electricity, particularly her right hand. She also divines psychic impressions through touch and can glimpse events from the past, present . . . or future."

Cat whistled through her teeth. Mencheres blinked once before turning his unsettling black gaze onto me.

"Extraordinary."

The way they all looked at me made me feel like the instrument Vlad once casually likened me to. *I also jump through flaming hoops for REAL,* ran through my mind before I could squelch the derisive thought.

"Oh, you're right," Cat said, aghast. "We're giving you the freak stare! How *rude.*"

"I'm used to it," I replied. At least they hadn't gawked at my scar as openly as most. Then I looked at Cat again. *Now* I knew why she'd seemed familiar! She was the really depressed girl I'd glimpsed when I touched the door frame in my room. Whatever she'd been upset over at the time had been strong enough to leave a mark.

"Huh?" Cat said, frowning. "I've never met you before."

I rubbed my head. "No offense, everyone, but it was bad enough when only Vlad was eavesdropping in my mind. I don't think I can handle a group of people doing it."

Mencheres stepped forward and laid his hand on Vlad's arm. "Leila, a pleasure to meet you. Vlad, my friend, walk with me."

He didn't move. "I'll see Leila to her room first. She injured herself only a short time ago."

Bones looked at Vlad and then at me. He sniffed, oddly, and a slow smile spread across his features.

"No need, Tepesh, we'll be glad to escort her. If it's the same room my wife stayed in, she'll remember where it is."

Vlad bristled, and if I didn't know better, I'd swear I smelled smoke.

"What makes you think you can tell me what you will do with *my* guest in *my* house—"

"Vlad," Mencheres said, drawing his name out with a touch of censure. I expected him to round on the other vampire with even more anger, but he let out a frustrated sigh.

"You brought him here. You knew this would happen."

"Let them escort her," Mencheres said in a more cajoling tone. "Besides, you requested that I come here because you have a question to ask, and you won't want to ask it with Cat or Bones nearby."

"Hey, why not me? We're friends," Cat protested.

"Yes, but you tell him everything," Vlad said

with a jerk of his head toward Bones. "Kira can come, though."

Kira grinned mischievously at them before linking her arm with Mencheres. "Good to meet you, Leila."

"Yeah, you too," I said, piqued that I didn't get to hear this question, either. It was probably about how best to use my abilities, so you'd think I should at least be privy to it.

The three of them departed, leaving me with the vampiric versions of Ken and Barbie—which I regretted thinking as soon as Cat let out a snort.

"Thanks, I think."

"Sorry," I said while grinding my teeth. "It *was* a compliment because the two of you are really, uh, pretty."

Perfectly so, and not just their features. Their skin was pale and creamy, not a visible flaw on an inch of it. Just looking at them made me feel as though my scar stretched and widened until it covered half my face and all of my arm.

"Oh, I have scars, too," Cat said, tapping her leg. "Stake puncture, right here. Stab wound in my stomach, another one on my back—"

"Stop, please," I said, holding up my hand.

"Really intrusive when your thoughts aren't your own, isn't it?" Bones stated, giving me a speculative look. "Used to drive my wife barmy before she changed over, but"—here his voice lowered—"there's a way to limit what someone can listen to, if you're interested."

My eyes widened. Was I interested? I'd give all my teeth for some mental privacy right about now!

Bones grinned. "Thought so. See, it takes a rare

form of willpower for a human to block a mind-reading vampire from their thoughts, and most people don't have that. But what you can do whenever you suspect you're being eavesdropped on is sing something wretched to yourself."

"Sing?" I repeated doubtfully.

A nod. "In your mind, of course, but remember—it has to be so annoying and repetitive that it distracts the person from breaking past that mental melody."

Cat looked at Bones with open suspicion. "I think I know why you're doing this, and it's *mean*—"

"Tepesh has it coming," Bones interrupted, his tone hardening. Then he smiled at me. "Go on, try to block me."

I understood that Bones wasn't helping me for altruistic reasons, but if it gave me a shield against Vlad reading my mind whenever he wanted . . . well, then his enemy was my friend. Annoying and repetitive, huh? I thought back to the eighties music my mother had loved listening to. It had certainly made me crazy when she'd play the same songs over and over.

I began to mentally sing the lyrics to "Relax" by Frankie Goes to Hollywood. Bones tapped his chin.

"I like where you're going with this, but dig deeper."

I sighed and began to think of other songs. Madonna's "Like a Virgin" had been played to death, but it was too apropos considering my own state. I decided on Whitesnake's "Here I Go Again" and repeated the chorus a few times in my mind.

Bones nodded. "Better, but still not slit-your-own-throat annoying. Come on, Leila. Do you want this or not?"

I let out a frustrated noise while shooting him a dirty look. Then inspiration struck and I smiled. *Take this!*

After the first few lyrics of the new song, Bones laughed.

"Perfect. Repeat that whenever Tepesh is around you, and he'll run screaming in no time."

Cat shook her head. "You are really twisted, honey."

Bones just smiled. "As I said, he had this coming."

Chapter 18

 Hours later, I dressed for dinner with more enthusiasm than I had the previous nights. Part of it was because that former lethargy combined with all-over body ache was gone. Even the bruises from my kidnapping and window dive had vanished. Vlad's blood was clearly more potent than Marty's, or I'd had more of it than Marty normally slipped into my shakes. Either way, for the first time in days, I felt great.

I was also anxious to try out my new mental defense. It made me look forward to seeing Vlad even though I berated myself for abandoning common sense with him earlier. To make matters worse, a part of me couldn't stop wondering what would have happened if Maximus hadn't come in right when he did.

As if you don't know, an inner voice taunted.

I sighed. Yeah, I knew. But an affair with him might indeed break my heart. I'd felt lust before—I was a virgin, not *dead*—and this was more than that. I also wanted to crack Vlad's shell, discover his secrets, and explore the complexities of his personality to find the man beneath the fearsome protector of his people. The fact that I wanted all this after knowing him less than a week was where the danger lay. A lust-based affair was so simple in comparison.

I'd slipped into a conservative yet flattering navy sweater dress when a rap sounded at the door. I opened it, my quizzical expression freezing when I saw Maximus.

"Uh, hi," I said, not sure if I should've started with an apology. Some dating experience would've helped right about now.

"Vlad regrets to inform you that he will not be dining with you tonight," Maximus said, speaking as formally as he had when we first met.

Disappointment coursed through me that I hoped didn't show on my face. Then I forced a smile.

"Will Cat, Bones, and the others be there?"

"No, they've left. You can still dine in the main room, if you'd like, or I can have your supper brought to you here."

I couldn't keep pretending like nothing had happened. "I'm so sorry, Maximus. You have every right to be mad at me. If I were smart, I wouldn't go anywhere near Vlad. I—I don't know why I can't seem to stop—"

"I do," Maximus interrupted with a grim smile. "For the same reason so many Wallachians fought and died for him over the course of three separate reigns when he was prince—because he draws you in even if you know it will end badly."

I grimaced. That wasn't too subtle of a warning. "Hopefully I won't end up like them."

He shrugged. "Either way, you're his now."

That made my brows shoot up. "Oh really? How odd, because I don't remember agreeing to that."

"He offered you his blood and you drank it. I could smell it on you." Maximus looked at me as though I were slow. "What did you think that meant?"

"That I needed it because apparently, without ingesting vampire blood my abilities would kill me," I replied, a chill going through me despite the room being warm.

"Think, Leila," Maximus said coolly. "This house has dozens of vampires. Vlad could have summoned any one of us to give you blood. He gave you *his* blood instead. That makes you his more than if he'd branded his name onto you."

"Wait." I held up a hand even as I continued to shake my head in denial. "Marty has been secretly giving me his blood for years. If I belong to anyone, it's him!"

"Marty didn't claim you. Vlad has. Earlier today, he rescinded his offer to let me court you, as if I hadn't figured out for myself that you were his now." Maximus gazed at me almost pityingly. "And if you care for your friend, you will never tell Vlad you think you belong to Marty. He'll kill him."

This was too much. I closed my eyes, drawing in a deep breath.

"Where is he? I need to talk to him."

Maximus's face closed off into polite stoniness. "He's detained at present."

My teeth ground. "Please stop the formal talk, and tell Vlad that he needs to *un*detain himself."

He snorted. "That's not how it works. No one gives Vlad orders. When he's available, he'll see you. Having a fit in the interim won't change anything."

"I'm not having a fit." I *would*, that was for sure, but I'd save it for the vampire who'd declared me his without asking my opinion on the subject.

"Then would you like to eat here, or the main room?" Maximus asked, returning to his original query.

I was too mad to have an appetite, but refusing to eat would only be churlish.

"Here."

Vlad continued to be "regrettably detained" the next morning and afternoon, too. I was torn between being madder than hell and worried. I didn't know if he was here and refusing to see me—Maximus wouldn't say, and neither would any other vampire I asked—or if he was out somewhere. It was ridiculous to worry about Vlad considering his age and power, but people *were* out to kill him. That was how I'd been thrust into his life in the first place.

By evening, when someone other than Maximus came to tell me that Vlad was still "regrettably detained," I'd had enough. He might not want to see me, but I wouldn't sit here stewing any longer. I changed clothes and then almost ran out of my room.

I went down to the level where Ben and the others lived. I hadn't gone far past the chapel when I heard voices. I followed the sounds to a kitchen where several people were gathered.

"Leila," Ben said in surprise when he saw me poised by the open door. "Hey, come in."

I gave Ben a big, almost desperate smile. "You know that club you mentioned? Are you guys going tonight?"

He came over, scratching a hand through his curls. "Yeah, but I thought you couldn't go because of, you know. Your condition."

"I can't dance," I said with a short laugh. "But I can drain my excess energy into something safe, keep my right hand holstered, and drink with whoever else is knocking 'em back."

"That'll work," Damon said, his mouth still full of whatever he'd been eating.

"Well, then, sure." Ben smiled. "I'm glad you're feeling better. What was wrong, anyway?"

My abilities are killing me and vampire blood is the only cure.

"Low iron? I'm okay now. No bleeding or fainting, promise."

"All right, we'll be ready in a minute."

Then a depressing realization suddenly filled me. "Wait. I don't have any money, and I'm not about to hit up one of Vlad's staff for some."

"Money?" Ben laughed. So did everyone else there. "You don't need money," Ben went on. "Vlad owns the town and we're his special plasma kabobs. Everything is free for us, and as his guest, same goes with you, too."

My eyes bugged. "He owns the whole *town*?"

"The counties surrounding it, too. Romania has communes, and while most people don't own the ones they oversee . . . Vlad has his own way of doing things, doesn't he?"

He does indeed, I thought, remembering how he hadn't told me the implications behind drinking his blood. Then I forced that thought back and smiled.

"Then I'm ready whenever you are."

Chapter 19

Eight of us piled into a different limousine than the one Vlad and I had arrived in. Due to the freezing temperature, I wore a long, thick coat over my dress. It also acted as a protective barrier for my right hand, which I kept tucked inside it. Once we were all in the vehicle, however, it didn't move though the driver sat at the wheel with the engine running.

"What's the hold up, Hunter?" Ben asked.

"Getting authorization," Hunter replied, and then rolled up the privacy glass.

"Authorization? Since when?" Ben muttered.

Since me, I thought, tensing in anger. If Vlad was available to forbid me from leaving, he'd damn well better be available for me to speak with.

From their glances, everyone began to figure out that I was the reason for the delay, but they chatted as though nothing was amiss. After about ten minutes, the privacy glass came down. Maximus now sat in the passenger seat, glaring at me.

"Did you really think you could sneak away?"

That brought the conversation to a halt. I stared back at him, my temper flaring.

"I'm not sneaking anywhere. I'm going out with the other residents of this house. I notice *they* didn't have to check in with anyone before leaving, so why should I?"

"Because you belong to Vlad," Maximus said at once.

My fists clenched. *Not this again.*

Ben caught my frustrated clenching. "Hey, it's cool. We all belong to Vlad," he said, patting my knee in a comforting way.

Maximus's gaze went from gray to bright green in an instant. "Not like she does, so remove your hand or I will remove it from your body. No one touches her except Vlad."

Ben's hand flew off my knee as if I'd channeled lightning into him. Maximus's meaning could not have been clearer. I was torn between wanting to sink into the seat in embarrassment—or leaping forward and electrocuting him. The latter was more appealing, but then it would ruin my plans for the evening.

"Now that you've marked your master's territory for him, can we leave?" I asked, icicles hanging off every syllable.

He nodded at the driver, and the car took off. Sandra nudged Joe and hissed, "Raise the glass." He pressed the button, and the front seat was once more blocked off.

As soon as it was up—as if *that* would keep Maximus from overhearing us—Sandra grinned at me. "Leila," she said in an admiring voice, "you must tell us everything!"

I was getting drunk. Rip-roaring, stinking, worshipping-at-the-porcelain-altar drunk. Damn

Maximus for his big mouth, and damn Vlad for his incomprehensible arrogance.

"It's not like that," I muttered, looking out the window rather than at the seven sets of eyes fixed on me. "Nothing's happened between us."

Sandra let out a knowing laugh. "But Vlad must intend for something to happen to make it known that you're his."

Not without me agreeing to it, I thought grimly.

Out of the corner of my eye, I saw Ben shake his head. "I should've known something was up when Vlad came himself after you fainted. If any of us gets sick or injured, we get sent a doctor, but we don't see *him*."

Several murmurs of agreement. I still said nothing, but I filed that away for potential mulling later.

"Tell me about this club," I said, changing the subject.

From their description, even on a winter week night it would be busy since it was the only one in a town of about three thousand. We arrived in thirty minutes. I was by the door, so I got out first, looking around.

FANE'S was on the front of the two-story, wood and stone building. A long stone chimney puffed smoke into the clear night. The other buildings on this street looked closed, but across the street, some of them had their lights on. I liked how the streetlights resembled iron lanterns on tall poles. It added to the aged feel of the town.

Maximus got out of the limo but stayed close to me. "What, are you my babysitter tonight?" I grumbled.

He shrugged. "Call it what you like."

Wait until I saw Vlad. This sort of crap might have worked in the fifteenth century, but it would backfire on him now.

"Do me a favor," I said, not bitching at Maximus only because I still felt guilty over yesterday. "Stay far enough away so I don't look like I've got a Viking-sized backpack?"

Maximus smiled slightly and held open the door. "I'll try."

I went in, surprised to see that on the inside, Fane's didn't look very different from the bars back in Gibsonton. A smattering of tables took up the space leading to the long, curving bar, with a fireplace adding to the restaurantlike atmosphere. Sandra first took me to the coatroom, where all of us unloaded our heavy outerwear. Then I followed her to the bar and took the seat she kindly saved for me.

"What will you have to drink?" she asked.

Red wine was normally my drink of choice, but tonight, I wanted something harder.

"Vodka and cranberry juice, if they have it. If not, vodka and whatever they have to mix it in."

She grinned. "Oslow!" she called out. The bartender turned. "*O vodka si un suc de coacaze in contul voivode.*"

The only word I recognized out of that last sentence was *voivode.* Prince. "What did you say?"

"I ordered your drink and told him to put it on the prince's tab."

"Does everyone know who Vlad is?" I asked in surprise.

Sandra ran a hand through her golden-red hair before answering. "In this town, many know, but few speak of it, and never to outsiders. Romanians revere the heroes of their history and they know how to keep secrets."

Then she slanted a glance at me. "As the object of the prince's desire, many would consider you a very lucky woman."

"It's the 'object' part I have the biggest problem with," I muttered, picking up my drink as soon as it was set in front of me. "And I'm going to need a lot more of these before I feel anything close to lucky."

Six vodka cranberries later, I allowed Sandra to talk me into going to the second floor where the dance area was. Sandra, Ben, and the others seemed to get a kick out of forming a protective circle around me. I kept my right hand glued to my hip and danced like I didn't have a care in the world. I might not understand the lyrics, but a good beat needed no translation.

A few more drinks later, I'd decided that tonight was the best night I'd had in years when a crashing noise sounded above the blaring music. The floor shuddered, too, making me look around in confusion. Did Romania get earthquakes? I wasn't the only one peering about, but then I heard Maximus's roar.

"Hunter, get her out of here!"

That was when I smelled the smoke. Another tremendous boom shook the dance floor, and people began to scream.

"Fire!" Sandra shouted, in case the smoke and panic hadn't clued me in.

My circle of friends disintegrated as the crowd

scrambled en masse toward the staircase. I tried to keep my right hand from touching anyone, but the crush became too tight. The person next to me dropped to the floor when she was shoved into me. Grayish images of shoplifting filled my mind, and when I blinked back into reality, I didn't see her anymore. The rough jostling had propelled me away. I tried to find her, afraid she'd get trampled.

I tucked my right hand into my armpit to prevent any more accidental contact and fought my way through the crowd, heading *away* from the staircase. I couldn't risk trying to get out with so many people around me. I might kill someone, if I hadn't already. Maybe Maximus or Hunter could help me with the woman I'd electrocuted. Where *were* they?

I finally made my way to the balcony. Something blurry caught my gaze below, and another crash shook the rapidly emptying dance floor. That blur became a flash of blond and brawn—Maximus, shaking debris off him as he advanced toward three people who weren't moving even though dozens in the crowd surged against them.

When I saw the distinct flash of silver in the strangers' grips, I understood. This wasn't an accident. It was an attack.

Something hard closed around my arm, whirling me around. I had a second to recognize Hunter the limo driver before he threw me over his shoulder and headed not for the staircase, but the window across the room.

"Wait!" I said, pounding on his back. "Grab the woman, too. She's somewhere on the floor, and she's hurt!"

He didn't stop. "You're important. She's not."

"Asshole!" I spat, pounding harder. "Turn around *now*—"

Glass shards tore the back of my legs as another boom sounded, only this one wasn't below us. It was in front of us.

"Ah, there she is," an unfamiliar voice stated.

Hunter stilled, and I craned to see around him, but his grip on me was too tight.

"Vlad will kill you," he hissed at whoever had smashed through the window.

"Not if we kill him first," the other man replied without concern, and then I was dumped on the floor, my head banging painfully against the hard wood.

Even though stars went off in my vision, I had enough sense to scramble back. The smoke was getting thicker, making me cough as I blinked to clear my gaze. The first thing I saw was Hunter and a young man with prematurely silver hair locked in a death match that lasted only long enough for me to grab the balcony rail and pull myself to my feet. Then Hunter fell back, a knife protruding from his chest, his features starting to shrivel before my shocked gaze. The silver-haired vampire looked up from him to smile at me.

"Frankie, isn't it?" he asked pleasantly.

My first instinct was to turn and run, but I didn't. The fact that he hadn't grabbed me yet meant he wanted to toy with me. Great, a murdering sadist, as if I hadn't met enough of those lately. I glanced to my right and then back at him.

"Yeah, I'm Frankie," I breathed. "Nice to meet you." And then I vaulted over the balcony rail.

My gamble paid off because he clearly hadn't been expecting that. I landed on one of the few patrons who hadn't run out of the club yet, rolling as soon as I felt warm flesh. That lessened the impact, but the person still screamed and then limped toward the exit, coughing at the increasing smoke.

I didn't get more than a step in that direction before a thud sounded behind me and rough hands seized me.

"Ooh, you *do* give off quite a charge, don't you?" Silver Hair commented.

With his grip, I couldn't raise my right hand to zap him properly, and time was running out. Flames crawled up the club's walls as if they had their own agenda. Multiple crashing noises indicated that Maximus was still fighting, but the screams had died down. Almost everyone seemed to have made it out of the club. Music continued to blare, making it hard for me to hear what Maximus and the other vampires were saying, but I caught "Frankie" a few times and knew, with a sinking feeling, that I was the reason behind this attack.

Silver Hair glanced behind me and sighed. "Looks like they need help killing him," he said in mock annoyance. "Stay here."

His foot shot out with brutal efficiency. Two kicks later, and I fell to the ground, tears streaming from my eyes. My calves bent at awkward angles, broken so badly that bone protruded from the skin. Silver Hair smiled and then walked toward Maximus, who had his back to him as he fought the three other vampires. Almost leisurely, Silver Hair pulled out his knife.

Hunter had been slaughtered trying to protect

me. Now Maximus was about to die. I dragged myself toward them, crying out at the white-hot pain of my broken legs scraping across the floor, but not stopping.

Silver Hair must have heard my cry, but he didn't turn around. He had no fear of me stopping him, and that made my fury grow. Fear for Maximus, hatred of Silver Hair, and ever-increasing agony made my right hand do something it had never done before: It began to form a visible sliver of electricity, like a tiny lightning bolt. I looked at it, at Silver Hair—who had almost reached Maximus—and then crawled faster. More blinding pain shot through me, but that sliver increased, growing longer and thicker.

Silver Hair's companions saw him behind Maximus and doubled their attack. Maximus fell back, not knowing he put himself closer to Silver Hair. I crawled faster, almost delirious from the pain, but through my tears and the smoke, I saw Silver Hair raise his knife. Now my cry was one of pure despair. I wasn't going to make it. I was still a dozen feet away—

A blast of white shot from my hand, quick as a thunderbolt and long as a whip. It cracked across Silver Hair's back, ripping his shirt and making his whole body glow for a split second. He fell to his knees, the knife fusing to his hand as the electrical currents melded his flesh around it. Maximus didn't glance away at the distraction, but one of his enemies did, and with a savage swipe, Maximus's knife cleaved through the vampire's neck. He dropped over, headless.

Silver Hair turned around and glared at me. I

recognized that look—I'd seen it on many faces right before someone got killed. I tried to summon another whiplike bolt from my hand, but I felt more drained than I ever had before. I started to crawl away only because I didn't want to die without trying, but I wasn't surprised to be hauled up moments later.

"Bitch," Silver Hair snarled, lifting me until our faces were level. "*Now* you'll stay put."

Then he flung me backward so hard that the last thing I felt was a wall breaking behind me.

Chapter 20

 The pain must've caused me to pass out, because when I opened my eyes, it looked like I was under a blanket, but that was impossible. I was still somewhere in the burning club, wasn't I?

I pushed the blanket off me, and smoke immediately had me coughing so hard, my throat felt stripped. Yep, still in the club, and I hadn't been covered by a blanket, but a coat. Several of them were around me, some still on hooks, some fallen from where my impact had knocked them loose. Silver Hair had flung me right through the wall into the coatroom.

I tried to crawl away—and screamed. Pieces of the wall had collapsed on my broken legs, pinning them. The hole I'd made was too far up for me to peer through to see if Maximus was still out there. And the walls around me were getting hot while the smoke continued to make breathing an effort.

Amidst the searing pain and coughing, I had a moment of clarity. I couldn't get out myself, so unless someone came to get me, I was dead. If I was lucky, the smoke would kill me first. If I wasn't, well . . . the pain in my legs would be bliss compared to what burning to death felt like.

"Maximus!" I shouted, hoping he'd managed to defeat Silver Hair and the other vampires. "Maximus, I'm here!"

Nothing but the still-blaring music and ominous breaking sounds that probably indicated the club was starting to fall apart. I coughed more, feeling light-headed. What had the fireman whose near-death experience I'd relived done to save himself? He'd covered up, for starters.

I grabbed every coat I could and piled them on top of me. The heat was unbearable, but they'd provide a barrier against the flames. Then I took one of the thinner coats and wrapped it around my mouth, trying to use it as a filter against the smoke.

"Maximus!" I screamed again. "Maximus, where are you?"

Still no response. Panic rose but I pushed it back. If there was one thing I'd learned, it was that panicking never helped anyone. Okay, either Maximus couldn't hear me above the music and crumbling structure, or he was dead. I'd have to try something else.

I got as low as I could, keeping the blankets over me and trying to think past the dizziness and searing pain that radiated all through me. If only I had something of Vlad's, then I could link to him for help. Even if he wasn't near enough to come himself, he could tell someone where I was. But I didn't, and I hadn't seen him today.

Maybe desperation gave me the crazy idea, maybe it was the growing lack of oxygen to my brain, but I stuck my right hand under the coat and began to rub my lips. *Please, oh, please, let Vlad have felt something when he touched them yesterday!* If that near-kiss hadn't meant anything to him, then I was a dead woman. But if he'd felt a strong enough emotion, I might be able to find a hint of his essence that I could follow back to him—

The cloak room vanished, replaced by Vlad encased in an indigo background that took me a moment to realize was the night sky. Relief made me want to weep, but before I could say anything, his voice cut across my mind.

"Leila, where are you?"

I didn't answer out loud because I was coughing too much.

In the coatroom at the club.

"Get out," he said tightly. "You must know it's on fire."

Do you think that escaped my notice? I asked in disbelief. *My legs are broken and part of the wall is pinning me.*

His eyes closed. When they opened, they were bright green.

"I'm only minutes away. Cover yourself with whatever is near and stay as close to the floor as you can."

A coughing fit kept me from responding because it took all of my concentration to breathe. I wasn't sure if the roaring in my ears was the flames eating through the walls or an indication that I was about to pass out.

Already done, I managed before my mind started to wander even more. Part of me knew that was a very bad sign, but the rest of me didn't care.

"Leila," Vlad said sharply. "Do *not* pass out."

So arrogant, I thought. *As if you can order someone to stay conscious.* Bit by bit, my coughing lessened, as did the agony in my legs. The relief from the pain was overwhelming in more ways than one. If I couldn't feel my legs, maybe I wouldn't feel the fire.

"You won't burn." Even amidst my drifting away, I caught the vehemence in his voice. "I *will* make it in time."

I didn't respond. Vlad said something else, but it was lost in the beautiful roar all around me. If I concentrated on it, I felt like I could fly. I focused on that, and soon everything began to fade away. I was lighter, floating, free . . .

Pain dragged me back into consciousness with pitiless abruptness. I wasn't on the floor anymore, but wrapped inside a hard embrace as Vlad picked me up. Red and orange flames were all around us, their heat blistering, but then the flames extinguished and a path cleared as if by magic. Vlad strode through it and soon the choking smoke vanished, replaced by flashing lights and soot-streaked people. He bit his wrist, and then something warm and wet pressed against my mouth.

"Drink," he ordered.

His dark hair curtained everything else from view as he kept his face close to mine, making sure I swallowed in between fits of coughing. Pain erupted in my legs before fading into a dull ache and then finally an odd itching. My coughing lessened, too, though I still couldn't seem to draw enough air into my lungs. Finally Vlad removed his wrist, and my head fell back against the cradle of his arm.

"You made it," I said weakly.

His smile was brief—and fierce. "I told you I would."

Vlad flew me back to the house, but instead of stopping at the second floor, he strode up to the fourth and deposited me in a stunningly gothic room with a high, triangular ceiling. With its size and grandeur, I would've thought it was his room, but the bed didn't have those distinctive midnight-green drapes.

"What's wrong with the other room?" I asked, still feeling dizzy and worn out even though his blood had healed my injuries.

He pulled my boots off, tossing them to the floor before he whisked back the covers and set me on the bed.

"Someone wanted you badly enough to attack on my territory. It's been a hundred years since anyone dared such a thing, so you'll stay close to me until I find them."

I closed my eyes, guilt and anger swarming me. "Maximus?"

"I saw him, he's alive," Vlad said, to my vast relief.

He settled the blankets over me. I normally hated anyone treating me like I was helpless—I'd had enough of that when I'd *been* helpless right after the accident—but now, I didn't mind. Having the most dangerous vampire in the world look after me somehow made me feel safe, and after nearly burning to death, I wanted to hold on to that feeling a little longer.

"How did you end up trapped in the cloakroom?" Vlad asked almost casually. "Maximus was supposed to protect you."

I grimaced at the memory. "A silver-haired vampire who looked a little like Anderson Cooper threw me into it after I electrocuted him."

Both dark brows went up. "You attacked him?"

"Maximus was fighting the other three vamps and Silver had just killed Hunter. He was about to jump Maximus, so I zapped him. It gave Maximus time to beat one of the vamps and get out of the way. But Silver Hair was pissed and chucked me through the coatroom wall to show it."

"What were you thinking, risking yourself that way?" Vlad muttered.

Did he miss the part where Maximus was about to get killed? "I'm drunk," I said testily. "I'll try anything if I'm drunk."

His teeth flashed in a quick grin. "I'll remember that. We'll speak more about this tomorrow. Now, you need to rest."

His authoritative tone reminded me of why I'd gone to the club in the first place. Despite feeling like I might conk out, I pushed myself up on the pillows.

"Not yet. We have some things to clear up first."

"Such as?" The question was mild, but his eyes glinted.

"Why have you been avoiding me?"

"I haven't. I was out gathering items with Mencheres and the others. I'd only been back an hour when Ben called to report the attack on the club."

His gaze never wavered, but . . . "Then why did Maximus say you ordered him to shadow me there?"

"He called to tell me what you were doing." Vlad's tone hardened. "Though it seems you did a better job protecting him."

Okay, so he hadn't been ducking me. That left the bigger issue.

"Why didn't you tell me there was a catch to drinking your blood? Maximus said that doing it made me, ah . . ."

"Mine," Vlad finished without hesitation.

My temper rose at his complete self-assuredness. "I didn't agree to that, so forget it."

He sat on the edge of the bed and leaned down, setting his arms on either side of my face.

"You think my blood is the only tie between us?"

His voice was low, yet edged with palpable hunger. It seemed to rub me in places I'd only ever touched before, making my anger fade under a flash of desire. Vlad was so close that his hair was a shadowy veil all around me, and when he began to caress my face with light, sure strokes, it was all I could do not to close my eyes in bliss.

"This is our true tie," he whispered, his breath falling hotly onto my lips. "You're meant for me, and I *will* have you."

Then his mouth lowered in a hard, claiming kiss. A groan parted my lips and his tongue snaked between them to stroke mine with sensual dominance. He tasted like sin made into wine: dark, heady, and impossible to resist. The raw demand in his kiss and his hard body pressing me into the bed made my nerve endings flare with blinding sensation. Need overwhelmed me, causing an exquisitely painful clenching in my loins. I pulled him closer, tangling my hand in his hair and gasping when I felt his fangs slide out. My trepidation vanished when he kissed me deeper, drawing my tongue into his mouth and sucking on it until the throbbing between my legs matched the pace of my pulse.

Suddenly, he was across the room, his eyes scalding green and a bulge straining against the front of his pants.

"If I don't stop now, I'll forget about searching for your attackers or you still being weak. Rest. I'll see you soon."

Vlad was gone before I had the chance to reply. I blew out a frustrated sigh. Rest, riiiight. As if anyone could rest after *that*.

Chapter 21

After some pacing drained away the last of my energy, I finally fell asleep. When I awoke, I'd come to two decisions. The first was that I was having sex with Vlad despite the dangers of a relationship with him. The second was that I needed to go back to the club. Right away.

I showered and got dressed, noting that sometime while I'd slept, the dressers and wardrobe had been stocked with clothes from my old room. This room had two doorways, and after determining that one led to an elegant sitting area, I went out the other into a long hallway with only two more doors until it opened into what looked like a set of interior crossroads.

Damn huge house. I should've paid more attention when Vlad carried me here last night, but I'd still been a little woozy.

"Hello?" I called out. Someone else had to be up here. Vlad said his most trusted staff had their rooms on this floor.

I heard a door open, and then Maximus's voice. "I'm coming, Leila."

He appeared moments later, wearing the same ripped and soot-stained clothes from last night. Once he saw me, he shocked me by dropping to one knee.

"No apologies are adequate for my leaving you in danger . . . nor can I ever thank you enough for saving my life."

I glanced around, glad no one else was witnessing this. "Maximus, get up," I urged. "You were fighting several vampires. It's not like you decided to go out for a beer."

He rose, but his head remained bowed. "I thought the silver-haired one took you. He escaped while I fought the others, so after I killed them, I chased after him. I should have searched the bar instead. You almost burned because of me."

I smiled bleakly. "And Hunter's dead because of me. We could spend the day piling on the guilt, or you can help me make it right by taking me to those other vamps' bones."

Now Maximus did look up at me. In confusion. "Their bones?"

"Vampires might shrivel into beef jerky when they die, but they leave their skeletons behind," I said with grim satisfaction. "Nothing's filled with someone's essence more than their bones. Let me touch them, and I can tell you who they were, and if we're lucky, who sent them."

Maximus began to smile with such savage anticipation that it made me glad I wasn't on his shit list.

"I'll have them brought here at once. In the meantime, you must eat."

I waved a hand. "Not hungry, thanks."

He gave me a stern look. "You barely ate yesterday and you were almost killed last night. Soon you will use more of your power. Vlad's blood cannot sustain all of your body's needs."

Crap, he was right. All I'd had to eat since breakfast yesterday was vampire blood. I wasn't about to get in the habit of blood being the main staple of my diet.

"On second thought, I'm starving."

I'd finished a large helping of eggs Benedict when Vlad strode into the dining room. He dropped a burlap sack onto the table and then stood behind my chair, leaning down to brush his lips against my cheek.

"Beautiful and diabolical. You make me impatient indeed to claim you."

I shivered at the graze of his mouth and his seductively growled words. If he used that same tone of voice in bed, he could probably get away with skipping foreplay.

He laughed, his hands settling on my shoulders. "I very much enjoy foreplay. Didn't your vision show you that?"

I closed my eyes against the flash of memory those words elicited, trying to will away the instant clenching in my loins. *Stop. We have killers to catch, remember?*

"Yes, first things first. Maximus, quit lurking and come in, I might need you. Leila, are you finished eating?"

Did he think I'd want dessert before attempting to find who murdered Hunter and tried to kidnap me *again*?

Vlad came out from behind my chair and swept my dishes aside, his lips curling.

"Straight to business—another thing we have in common. The fire caused the building to collapse so this bag contains random remains, but some are bound to be your attackers."

Maximus entered the dining room, his expression stony as Vlad emptied the bag where my breakfast plates had been. Four skulls and various other bones spilled onto the shiny oak surface, Vlad catching one of the craniums before it rolled off.

"May as well start here," he said, holding it out to me.

I mentally braced myself and then took the skull. A black and white stream of images played across my mind, showing a laughing girl named Tanya who looked to be the same age as my sister and whose worst sin was shoplifting.

I set the skull down, blinking past the sudden moisture in my gaze.

"She's not one of them. She was next to me when everyone started panicking, and she brushed my hand . . ."

And that ended up killing her, whether my touch had stopped her heart or knocked her unconscious long enough for the fire to finish her. I *never* should have gone to the club last night. If I'd stayed in, this girl would still be alive.

"No, Leila," Vlad said quietly. "Her blood is on *my* hands because she was killed by *my* enemies. Even if you'd touched her out of sheer carelessness, without that attack, she would have survived. Don't carry sins that aren't yours."

I swiped my eyes and silently resolved to get another huge rubber glove at once—and never go out without it no matter how much unwanted attention it drew. Then I grasped one of the other charred skulls. Vlad was right. First things first.

More colorless images skipped across my mind. This skull belonged to the vampire Maximus had decapitated. His name was Cordon, and seeing his worst sin made bile rise in my throat. I tried to push past that and the images of his death to see what happened before. It felt like watching a movie on rewind because everything moved so fast as to be mostly incomprehensible. That was one of the drawbacks to pulling information from bones. They held a lot more history than a single object.

Vlad and Maximus remained silent, which helped with my concentration. After several minutes, I caught a scene that seemed promising: Cordon and the silver-haired vampire, their expressions serious as a distinguished-looking man in his forties with a frame like a tree trunk barked at them in a very odd-sounding language.

This was the other drawback to pulling information from bones—I wasn't experiencing everything as though it was happening to me. If I had been, then I'd understand what was being said because I'd be in Cordon's mind, but this was similar to linking to someone in the present. I was merely an invisible observer in the memory I'd stumbled across.

"I think I've got something," I said aloud. "I see two of the vampires from the attack and it looks like they're getting orders, but I don't understand the language."

"I'm fluent in dozens of languages, repeat whatever you hear," Vlad directed.

The other man had spoken rapidly and the language wasn't easy to replicate, but I gave it my best shot. After I parroted some sentences that may or may not have been accurate, Vlad's whistle yanked my attention away from the memory.

"I believe you've found our elusive puppet master."

I disengaged the link to center my attention back on him. "You understood him? What language was it?"

"Old Novgorod." A tight smile twisted his lips. "I haven't heard that since I was a boy. Either he is at least as old as I am, or he's very clever by communicating through a dialect few knew even before it became extinct."

"What was he saying?"

His smile remained, but his expression hardened. "You were missing a few words, but I heard enough to determine that surveillance equipment in the town alerted them to your presence. Once you were spotted, his men were told that if they couldn't succeed in returning with you, they were to kill you."

Considering the silver-haired vampire had broken my legs and left me trapped in a burning building, the "capture or kill" order didn't come as a surprise. Still, it didn't give me the warm fuzzies. Before, I'd wanted to help Vlad catch the mastermind because then I would be safe. Now, I wanted to catch the bastard so he could pay for everything he'd put me through.

"Tell me more and you'll get your vengeance,"

Vlad promised. "Do you know his name or where he is?"

"No," I said, and explained why. Even their surroundings were of no use. The three men had been in small room with wall-to-wall concrete and not much else. Vlad stroked his jaw when I was finished, his expression thoughtful.

"Maximus," he said at last. "Find out who the world's best sketch artist is, and have him or her here by dawn."

Chapter 22

The other bones didn't reveal anything significant. Just more images of their owners' sins and more flashbacks of the distinguished-looking gentleman who spoke Old Novgorod. Vlad left to find the surveillance equipment and to, I assumed, burn the ass off anyone involved with its setup. I kept trying to sort through the deluge of memories to discover more about the people behind the bones, but after several frustrating hours, I called it a day. The truth was that I might be giving myself a headache for nothing. Now that I had a face behind last night's attack, if the sketch artist panned out and Vlad recognized him . . . checkmate would come tomorrow.

That left tonight to settle the other issues between us.

I ate dinner alone in the wood-paneled sitting room that adjoined my new bedroom. Then I stayed there after the plates were cleared away. The modern leather furniture and large flat-screen TV looked out of place next to the antique bookcase containing editions so old, I could barely read the letters on the bindings. Those contrasts in extremes, plus the ancient shield above the fireplace bearing the same dragon design as Vlad's ring, made me guess where the other door in this room led to. Therefore, when I heard it open, I didn't turn my head, but stayed on the couch and continued to stare into the crackling orange flames.

A tall form blinked out of the corner of my eye before I felt warm, strong hands slide down my arms and then the rasp of stubble against my cheek. Despite my resolve to settle a few things first, I couldn't help but think that the heat seemed to travel from his hands down to a specific place in my body.

"Wait," I said, but the word came out wispy.

Dark laughter made my neck tingle where it landed.

"How unconvincing. Try again."

I couldn't stop my eyes from closing when his mouth settled in the same spot where his breath had been. A slow graze of his lips had me exhaling in pleasure, then the sudden firm suction made desire stab me right in the center even as I gasped.

"Vlad!"

Another chuckle before I felt the dangerously sensual pressure of fangs. Vlad continued to draw on my neck, those sharp teeth grazing my skin without breaking it. My pulse jumped against his mouth as if begging to be bitten, but then I slid off the couch, pivoting to face him.

He stalked over, his eyes glowing with emerald highlights. Now that I got my first look at him, I saw that his cuffs were undone and the top buttons of his black shirt open, that V of hard flesh entrapping my gaze even as I backed away. The most I'd seen of his skin before was when he rolled up his sleeve to give me his blood. I found myself wondering if his chest had the same crisp dusting of hair as his arms, or if the hint of darkness I glimpsed was from the firelight's shifting shadows.

His teeth bared in something too predatory to be called a smile. "You'll soon find out."

I stretched out my hands as if to ward him off. "Not yet. I want to know what your end game is first."

Another flash of teeth, this time showing his fangs. "To have you screaming my name within the hour."

Those words made my pulse pound so strongly that my neck felt like it vibrated. His gaze flicked there and then he reached me in the next stride, catching my hands and using them to pull me closer. Excitement shot through me as he pressed our bodies together, his arms a sensual cage around me. When I felt something hard pulsing against my belly, lust burst forth with enough strength to shove my other concerns aside. I wanted to touch him there. Taste him. Feel him so deep inside me that I screamed out his name just like he promised—

"Not until you tell me the catch to sleeping with you," I managed before those cravings washed away all rational thought.

He'd already slipped his hands under my sweater and unhooked my bra, but at that, he paused.

"The catch?"

My rapid breathing made the words come out jumbled. "Yes, the catch, cost, downside, or thing that will make me say, 'Oh, shit' tomorrow when it's too late. Tell me now."

He pulled back to stare at me in the strangest way, like he was amused but also debating whether to ignore me and finish taking off my bra.

"Ah, that catch," he said at last. "To start, if you betray me with another man, I'll burn him to death in front of you."

I'd expected something like that, but I wasn't about to agree without conditions. "Only if you hold yourself to the same standard, and *don't* pull any of that 'You're mine' garbage if things don't work out between us."

His hands left my back to weave in my hair. Then he leaned down until his face was very close to mine.

"I never set a standard that I won't keep myself, and if you ever want out, you need only say the word. But mean it, Leila, because once I leave, I'm gone forever."

Vlad's eyes bled back to deep copper as he spoke, and though they were no longer glowing in that inhuman way, somehow, they were more compelling.

"Right back at you," I said, matching his unyielding stare. "Is that all?"

His lips twisted. "No. I can give you honesty, monogamy, and more passion than you can stand, but not love. That emotion died in me long ago, as I suspect you already know."

I took a deep breath, fighting a twinge that made no sense because he was right. I *had* guessed that about him.

"Good," I replied in a steady voice. "I was worried that you'd turn into one of those obsessed, emo movie vampires, and that would be embarrassing for both of us."

His laughter rang out before changing into something rougher and infinitely more sensual. Emerald overtook his gaze once again.

"Enough talk," he muttered, and lowered his head.

The firm warmth of his lips combined with the dominating flicks of his tongue made me groan deep in my throat. Desire unfurled as he held me closer, his hand slowly tightening in my hair while I gave myself up to the aphrodisiac of his kiss. His other hand left a trail of heat down my back as he explored my curves with possessive hunger. My loins clenched in response, that inner throb almost painfully insistent. I clutched him, digging my fingers into his back and sending a sharp bolt into him before I moved my right hand away.

He clasped it immediately, pressing it back to his body. "Don't take your hands off me even once tonight."

His voice was harsh with lust, the order more growled than spoken. Then he bent, sweeping me up and covering my mouth with another searing kiss as he strode toward the door.

The one that didn't lead to my room.

It took several of his long, swift strides before he set me on something soft. I'd closed my eyes while kissing him, but when he pulled away, allowing me much needed gulps of air, I opened them—and saw darkness all around. It took a second to see that the darkness was drapes surrounding the bed. They looked black, but I knew they were darkest green instead. Vlad was a shadow looming over me, the brightness in his gaze providing the only illumination in the room.

It wasn't enough. "I want to see you," I said, not caring that my voice sounded shaky from passion.

Light blazed in dozens of places as candles I hadn't seen all ignited at once. They showed a staggeringly large room with a high, triangular ceiling and countless rows of shelves, but I only looked behind him for a second. Then my attention was all for Vlad as he drew his shirt off and discarded his pants in one seemingly simultaneous movement.

I sucked in a breath. Candlelight adorned his bare skin as though trying to caress it, showing broad shoulders, corded arms, thickly muscled legs, and a hard chest that was faintly dusted with hair. That hair followed a tempting dark line down his flat stomach before thickening once it met his groin. When my gaze reached that part of him, I stared. Age-old instinct made moisture flare between my legs, yet I also felt a sliver of apprehension. Everyone said the first time hurt, but at least I was no stranger to pain.

I led my armies from the front, Vlad had said. The proof was all over his body, from the scars that adorned his skin in random white patterns to the muscles that flexed and bunched with his slightest movement. If he'd looked like one of those effeminate magazine models, I wouldn't have felt such a powerful swell of lust, but there was nothing boyish or plastic about Vlad. He was devastatingly masculine, and all of that untamed sensuality was now mine to savor. The knowledge caused another rush of heat between my legs.

"If I didn't want you so much," he said in a deadly purr, "I'd let you keep fucking me with your gaze, but you make me impatient."

He grasped my ankles as he spoke, stripping off my shoes. I pulled my sweater and unhooked bra over my head, breathless but also a little self-conscious as his hot stare moved over my breasts. His body was so magnificent that I wished I had more for him to look at, but my chest maxed out at a B-cup.

"Never disparage yourself to me." The words were low, but they vibrated with force. "You're mercilessly beautiful, and it's taking all of my control to go slowly with you."

A stronger wave of desire filled me, causing me to tremble from its intensity. I'd never wanted anything more than this, so I didn't see any reason to wait.

"I wish you wouldn't go slowly."

Chapter 23

 Vlad's gaze blazed a brighter shade of emerald. Then my skirt and panties were yanked off with a distinct ripping sound. My breath caught when he settled his body over mine, his skin so warm that he felt fevered. Then more aching ripples of desire surged through me when he caressed my breasts and pinched my nipples to throbbing tips.

His skillful hands and that taut, muscled body covering mine sent my need into near desperation. I pulled his head down and slanted my lips over his, thrusting my tongue into his mouth with blatant demand. An appreciative rumble sounded before he sucked on it and then ravaged my mouth with kisses hard enough to bruise. I didn't care. Anything less wouldn't be enough.

I made a noise of protest when he pulled away, but he gripped my hair to keep me from seeking out his mouth again.

"Open your legs, Leila."

My heart hammered at the explicit command, yet I didn't hesitate. Vlad's gaze felt like a brand as he stared at me while I spread my thighs. He lowered himself between them, that thick, pulsing shaft so hot against my inner thigh. Then he reached down and I closed my eyes, wanting him so much but also bracing for the inevitable discomfort.

Instead of the thrust I'd expected, his finger delved inside me, stroking and seeking with erotic ruthlessness. Pleasure flashed through me, arching my back and forcing a cry past my lips. Vlad lowered his head and his mouth closed over my nipple, sucking so powerfully that another cry tore from me. Then his finger began to slide in and out, building a rhythm that interspersed my cries with increasingly rapid gasps. All the while, he sucked on my nipple until it throbbed with the same ceaseless insistency as my loins.

I moved without thought, lifting my hips in time to his hand and clutching his head to my breast. Wetness slicked the finger that he circled around my clitoris with firm, undulating strokes. Starbursts of sensation went off inside me, making my nails rake down his back. I didn't care about electrocuting him anymore, couldn't think past the tension growing with every intimate rub and greedy pull from his mouth. My blood thundered through my veins until it felt like my entire body pulsed with passion. Over my gasps and moans, I heard Vlad's roughly seductive voice, but he wasn't speaking in English so I had no idea what he said.

Then his hand was gone and something far thicker pressed at my center. I shuddered at the first feel of him—so hot, hard, and unbelievably tantalizing that the pleasure made me groan. Vlad's hand brushed my face, smoothing my hair away before sliding down to grasp my hip. Then he thrust forward, the blade of his flesh penetrating deep. Pain sizzled inside me, tearing a sound of another kind from my throat. Instinct made me thrash to get away from the searing ache, but he held me tight. Very slowly, he began to withdraw.

I let out a ragged breath, trying to force myself to relax. The pain wasn't excruciating, but it had cooled my passion. *It'll only hurt tonight*, I reminded myself.

When Vlad pulled all of the way out, guilt assailed me. Had my thoughts killed the mood for him?

"You don't have to stop," I whispered.

He kissed my neck, his mouth hot against my flesh. "Sweet Leila, I'm not about to stop."

Then he slid down my body before I registered what he was doing. His mouth descended between my legs, tongue a wet, sinuous brand that knocked the breath out of me. At the same time, he caressed my breasts, those strong fingers squeezing my nipples with exactly the right amount of pressure.

Pain began to fade under the double assault of pleasure. My back arched and his name hoarsely left my lips as his tongue swirled before probing with deep, spine-searing flicks. He used the same addicting strokes when he kissed me, but these were firmer, faster, making cascades of ecstasy wash over me. His fangs grazed my clitoris, applying pressure in shockingly effective ways. Spirals of bliss twisted in my loins, chasing away the remains of pain and replacing it with aching need instead.

My hips rose, seeking more. His fingers tightened on my nipples, worrying them into hypersensitive tips while his tongue moved even faster within my depths. My fingers dug into his arms, currents flowing into him with the seething buildup of pleasure. I couldn't stop writhing underneath his mouth, all control gone, my gasps turned into something very close to sobs. Inner muscles clenched with every new stroke, sending shattering sensations through me. *Yes, yes, just a little more!*

Then his mouth was gone, and a choked noise of frustration left me. Vlad's smile was almost cruel as he rose up, his hips sliding between my legs.

"No. I want to be inside you when you come."

Then he thrust forward, that hot, thick flesh causing a clench of passion along with a whisper of pain. He moved deeper, eliciting more rapture and wounding fullness. I whimpered, and his mouth slanted over mine, swallowing my cry as he sheathed himself to the hilt.

Pleasure gripped me as intensely as the sudden slice of pain. Having him fully inside me was too much and so incredible at the same time. I returned his kiss, panting into his mouth as he began to move with slow yet relentless strokes. His taste was sharper but still intoxicating, drawing me in as completely as those achingly sensual thrusts. Pleasure began to build, edged with slivers of pain that made every sensation more intense. Soon I moved under Vlad's body the way I had under his mouth, gripping his hips with a hunger I hadn't known I was capable of. My gasps became cries, but I couldn't stop those any more than I could stop writhing beneath the excruciating ecstasy of his increasingly harder strokes. *Yes. Please, Vlad, yes!*

His grasp tightened on my hips before he began to thrust so fast, for a second I was afraid I'd feel only pain. Then that fear extinguished under a flood of blistering rapture that culminated in a climax unlike any I'd ever experienced. My loins convulsed over and over, sending shards of bliss throughout my body until every part of me tingled and vibrated.

Vlad's grip turned to steel, his back arching while a harsh groan left his lips. Then he thrust so forcefully that I cried out, but that cry turned into a moan at the new spasms. He ground against me while his orgasm pulsed inside me like hot honey, those final thrusts making my mind spin away into a million glittering pieces.

After a kiss that stole the rest of my breath from me, Vlad rolled to his side, his tight grip curling me against him. The change in our positions made me suddenly aware of the room's chilly temperature. My front almost burned from its contact with his flesh, but a shiver went up my spine at the brush of cold air on my bare back and legs.

Vlad brushed a kiss onto my shoulder before he pulled the bedspread over us. Then with a snap, the fireplace blazed to life, painting the room in brighter shades of orange and cream. *Thanks*, I thought, still too out of breath to say it aloud.

His grin was slow and wicked. "My pleasure, I assure you."

I hadn't been thanking him for *that*. I poked him with my right hand, but only the barest current flickered into him. His smile widened, and then Vlad caught my hand and kissed it.

"Now we know what truly drains your power. This will make traveling with you much easier. No need to pack lightning rods."

"You really are the most arrogant man I've ever

met," I breathed, but my sated tone didn't match the words.

He kissed my hand again, his mouth lingering this time. "Yes, I am."

The way he looked at me—possessive, passionate, and unrepentant—made gooseflesh ripple over me. This complex and infamously lethal man was now my lover; a relationship I'd chosen of my own free will. Part of me wondered what the hell I'd gotten myself into while the rest didn't care. I'd relived enough terrible events happening to cautious people to know that prudence wasn't a guarantee for happiness.

I traced my fingers across his jaw to his neck, brushing some of those dark strands aside. Then I ran it over his shoulders, silently marveling that my touch contained no more energy now than static electricity. It emboldened me to keep exploring with my right hand. I dragged it lower, circling my thumb around his nipple and watching it instantly harden.

Was that pain or pleasure? My gaze flew to his. Vlad's eyes were glowing, his lips parted, expression pure sensual expectation.

"No need to wonder," he said in a voice that flowed over me like darkest silk. "If I don't enjoy something, I'll tell you, as I expect you to do the same."

"Okay," I said softly. Strange that all of a sudden, I was very aware of my nakedness, as if Vlad hadn't touched and kissed every part of me.

"Not yet," he murmured, sliding closer, "but I will."

The bedspread slipped off his hips with the movement. My hand had been on its way down there, so that's where my gaze was, too, but when his groin came into view, I gasped. Another glance revealed scarlet smudges on my own thighs. Was this from my lost virginity, or did vampires ejaculate blood? That was one topic Marty hadn't touched upon.

"Our fluids are tinged pink, but they're not pure blood."

Then this was mine. No wonder it hurt so much at first.

"Sorry about, um, the sheets," I said, that awkward feeling returning.

His hand curled behind my head before he brushed his lips over mine.

"Don't. This blood you can only shed once, and you gifted it to me. That makes it worth more than these sheets, this bed, and most anything else in my house."

I swallowed at the intensity in his voice, suddenly glad my abilities had prevented me from throwing my virginity away on someone who might not have cared past the immediacy of getting laid. Vlad was still terrifying in many ways, but even if I could change the past to where I never touched that power line, I wouldn't want to share this experience with anyone except him.

The realization reminded me of Marty's warning that Vlad would break my heart if I got involved with him. To deflect that thought—and the growing emotion inside me—I smiled.

"Besides all that, I bet your staff has lots of experience removing bloodstains."

His lips twitched. "Yes, they do."

Speaking of blood . . . Vlad agreed not to bite

me when we first met, but that was when we were keeping things professional between us. We weren't anymore, so in fairness, I shouldn't expect him to keep his fangs holstered. After all, how could I take a vampire for a lover and then ask him to ignore his very nature, especially since I had to drink *his* blood once a week?

Vlad heard the thoughts whirling in my mind, but he said nothing. I met his gaze and, decision made, brushed my hair away from my throat in silent invitation.

A slow smile stretched his lips, making me flash to the satisfied expressions I'd seen on lions' faces before they sank their fangs into a gazelle. He leaned down, mouth grazing my neck, so warm, sensual, and scary despite my resolve. Then his tongue slid out, circling over the throbbing base of my pulse in a leisurely yet deliberate manner. Finally, he gave it a long kiss with the faintest brush of teeth before leaning back.

"Not tonight, but soon. And when I do, you will come to crave my bite as much as my kiss."

You are terminally *arrogant*, I thought, but thus far, he'd also been correct in a lot of his predictions. Case in point: I was in his bed and craving his kisses right now, among other things. But those would wait until I cleaned off first.

I pushed him back and sat up. "You have a shower in this room, right?"

"Of course." His gaze slid over me with heated intent, and when he smiled, fangs gleamed from his teeth. "One that's big enough for both of us."

Chapter 24

 I woke up alone in Vlad's bed. All the windows had the drapes drawn, blocking out the sunlight. The candles had gutted out, too, but the fireplace still smoldered, providing enough light that I wouldn't stumble into any furniture on my way out of his lobby-sized bedroom.

I got out of bed, remembering to feel around for the step. I'd learned last night that his bed was on a raised dais when Vlad's quick grip was the only thing that kept me from falling after my foot came down on air instead of flooring. Then I found the robe he'd stripped off me after our long, very erotic shower and put it on, hurrying out of his room. Vlad's stunning black marble bathroom had a shower that could fit four and a sunken tub you could snorkel in, but no toilet. In hindsight, that made sense. A vampire wouldn't need one.

I crossed the sitting area into my room since I didn't want to chance bumping into anyone in the hallway. Everyone in the house probably knew I'd spent the night with Vlad, but that didn't mean I wanted to be seen leaving his room in nothing but a robe. After I finally relieved my long-denied bladder, I looked at the tub with longing. An extended hot soak would help my lingering soreness in certain areas, but the sketch artist might have arrived during the night, so I'd better go with a quicker shower.

Half an hour later, I came down to the first floor and peeked into the dining room. Empty. I could start searching the other rooms in this huge house, or do things the quicker way.

"Hello," I called out. "Need to ask a question."

Before I could count to three, an impeccably dressed black man appeared, his bald head buttersmooth and thick muscles bulging under his beige suit.

"Shrapnel," I said, recognizing him from that night in Tampa. He bowed, which struck me as odd. Normally Vlad got the bows, not me.

"How can I assist you?"

I resisted the urge to compliment him on how pretty the indoor garden was. "Do you know if Maximus got back with the sketch artist yet?"

"He arrived with her an hour ago."

"And where are they?" I prodded.

His expression closed off into a polite mask. "I'll let Vlad know you're awake."

"He knows," a cultured voice stated from across the room.

I turned, my pique at Shrapnel's evasiveness fading when I saw Vlad walking toward me. His wine-colored shirt was a vivid contrast to his black jacket and pants. Both colors accented his emerald-ringed, coppery eyes, but as usual, only his face, neck, and hands were bare. The rest of him was

covered, the elegant cut of his clothes simultaneously flaunting and concealing that lean, muscled
body.

A body that was now mine to explore and enjoy.
All of a sudden, I wished the sketch artist hadn't
arrived.

The sly smile that curled Vlad's lips said he'd
overheard my thoughts—and liked them. Then
he pulled me close, one hand twining through my
hair while the other stroked my back.

"Good morning," he murmured before his lips
closed over mine.

I'd wondered if he would be reserved with me in
front of his people. Obviously not. By the time he
lifted his head, my pulse had tripled and my body
felt flushed. I'd also slid my arms around his neck
without thinking, my right hand flexing against his
shoulders. A week ago, I'd never *forget* about that
hand coming into contact with someone. Now, it
seemed so right to touch Vlad that it hadn't occurred to me not to.

"Good morning, yourself," I said huskily.

He gave me another, far shorter kiss before releasing me. Then he looked over my shoulder.

"Shrapnel, let it be known that henceforth, no
one needs my permission to tell Leila where I am,
or where anyone else is, either. If she has a question, answer it."

I turned in time to see Shrapnel bow, first to
Vlad, and then to me. Then he walked away, disappearing into one of the many rooms in this
house.

"Tell me sleeping with you didn't automatically

upgrade me to bowing status," I said, uncomfortable.

Vlad's chuckle was confirmation enough of my suspicion.

"Really?" How twisted.

His arms slid around my waist as he leaned down, pinpricks of emerald in the coppery depths of his eyes. "Of course my people will now treat you with the utmost respect. I told you; I don't take many lovers. You're also the only one I've shared my bed with, and the first to sleep in the room adjoining mine."

I didn't know what to say. A tiny part of me thought it was chauvinistic that Vlad had had sex with those other women, yet hadn't deemed them worthy to share his bed or the closest room. That, however, was overshadowed by the fluttering of my heart and the sudden urge I had to pump both fists into the air.

But maybe he had another reason. A practical one. Vlad might not want me to relive images of him with other women if I touched the wrong item in one of his usual tryst rooms.

His lips curled. "How admirably jaded of you to think that, but I could always change out the furnishings in another room if I didn't want you to see such things."

That was true. *Way to wreck a nice moment, Leila!*

"Sorry. You know I'm winging all of this, but even if I'd been a through dozen prior relationships . . . I don't know if any of them would've prepared me for being with you."

"They wouldn't," he said with complete as-suredness.

His arrogance really would take some getting used to.

"Then let me say what I should've said in the first place." I placed my hands on his chest and stood on tiptoe. "I'm glad," I whispered near his ear before kissing it.

His arms tightened around me, one hand slid-ing down to press my hips to his with the same sensual authority he'd shown last night. But we weren't in his bedroom anymore—we were in the large hallway where at least a dozen vampires lurked nearby.

"Stop," I said, glancing around to see if anyone saw that.

When I looked back, Vlad's gaze more than half glinted with emerald. "If that sketch artist wasn't here, I wouldn't stop."

Then he let me go, his eyes changing back to deep copper. "But Hunter's death needs to be avenged, as does your treatment. Come. Her name is Jillian, and she's in the library."

The sketch artist was a petite woman with deep laugh lines and blond hair that had mostly faded to white. Maximus bowed when we came in, but Jillian didn't even seem to notice. She was too busy looking around with the same dazzled expression I'd probably had when I first arrived. The library was two stories tall, a spiral staircase leading to the second level and a massive stone fireplace with crimson Louis XV furniture in the center. Thou-sands of books filled the shelves, some regular-sized, some so enormous that they must weigh thirty pounds each.

"*Madame, les voilà*," Maximus said, his gaze lingering on me before he glanced away.

Vlad's hand rested on my waist. Even through my sweater, I felt his temperature suddenly spike. I glanced over, puzzled, but when he addressed Jillian in the same language, he sounded perfectly relaxed. *Must be nothing*, I decided.

I smiled at her while thinking that I should've studied French instead of Spanish in school. Vlad must have told her not to shake my hand because she didn't make a move toward me, but smiled back while speaking in heavily accented English.

"Happy to make your meeting, Leila."

"You too," I said, getting the gist of what she meant.

Several sentences in French were directed at Maximus while she gestured to the chairs by the fireplace.

"She wants you to be comfortable while you describe who you saw," Maximus translated. Then he smiled sardonically at Vlad. "And she wants to be paid in gold instead of euros."

Vlad flicked his fingers as if he could care less. I sat in the place indicated. Then I glanced over at Vlad.

"I'll describe him better if I'm holding one of the bones."

"Maximus," Vlad said, with a nod at the door.

He left. Jillian pulled a large pad and several charcoal pencils out of her satchel, humming to herself. Maximus returned moments later with what looked like a femur. Her brows rose, but

Vlad said something to her in French that seemed to pacify her.

"I am ready," she said to me.

Vlad stood behind my chair, resting his hand on my shoulder. "Speak normally. I'll translate."

I took the bone and placed it on my lap. Then I ran my right hand over it, closing my eyes until I found the man who'd ordered the attack.

"He has short dark hair with streaks of gray," I began, "and a square jaw, kinda like comic book heroes have . . ."

An hour later, Jillian handed me her pad.

"Is him?" she asked.

Staring back at me was a man with ash-streaked hair, wide forehead, generous mouth, and piercing eyes of indeterminate color. All set off by a handsome face with lines that on men were called "character" and on women were considered cause for a Botox appointment.

"That's pretty close," I said, pivoting to hand the picture to Vlad. "Well? Do you recognize him?"

Chapter 25

Vlad looked at the picture, his brows drawn together. After a long moment, he exchanged a glance with Maximus, who shook his head with an expression I couldn't decipher.

Then Vlad turned to me. "The only person I know that this picture resembles died a long time ago."

"Oh," I said, disappointed. "Well, it's not an exact replica. I'll keep linking through the bones. Maybe there's a detail or two about him that I can describe better."

Vlad handed the picture to Maximus. "Make a copy and show it to Jackal. Find out if he's encountered this man before."

"Jackal's still alive?" I asked in surprise.

"Of course. Where do you think Shrapnel has been?"

"I didn't know he'd been torturing Jackal this whole time!" I blurted, forgetting to watch my words in front of Jillian. Hopefully she hadn't understood that.

No such luck. "Someone is *tor*tured?" Jillian

rose, her hand near her mouth. Then a torrent of nervous-sounding French erupted from her as she began to back away.

"*Assieds-toi, ce ne sont pas tes oignons*," Vlad said, his eyes flashing bright green.

Whatever he told her, that combined with the power in his gaze worked. She sat, her expression changing from horror to placidness. Satisfied, Vlad turned his attention back to me.

"Not just Shrapnel. I spend time with Jackal daily, too."

Some things I would never get used to with Vlad. This was one of them. I picked my words with care.

"But you said Jackal didn't know who'd sent him after me, so why all the, ah, extra *effort*?"

Vlad shrugged. "Due diligence."

Only he could describe a week of brutal interrogations so casually.

"My father would love you," I muttered.

His grin was so at odds with the topic that if I hadn't gotten used to Vlad's quixotic nature, I would've been startled.

"Most fathers don't."

"Well, mine's a retired lieutenant colonel who swears that water boarding is an acceptable interrogation technique."

Another shrug. "Fire works faster. Speaking of your family, I have a secure number you can give them. You should contact them soon so they don't worry and report you missing."

I cleared my throat. This was an uncomfortable topic to discuss in front of Jillian, even though she seemed oblivious to us at the moment.

"Not a problem. My dad and I only speak every couple months, and my sister Gretchen and I talk even less."

An inner hollowness spread with those words. My dad had been deployed for much of my childhood, so our relationship had always been more of a long-distance one, but Gretchen and I used to be close. All that changed the day my mother died. We hadn't spoken since my aunt's funeral a year ago, and that conversation had been bitter.

Vlad's smile was gone, his expression now flickering between regret and cynicism.

"Sometimes families bring no peace. On many occasions, my younger brother tried to kill me. Once, he thought he'd succeeded, but I was past mortal death by then." His mouth twisted. "Despite this, when Radu died, I mourned him. Family is always irreplaceable, even when they're also irreconcilable."

Irreplaceable. Yes, that summed up my mother. My aunt Brenda, too. She'd taken over raising me and Gretchen after my mother's death so we wouldn't have to move all over the world following my father's most recent transfer orders. Aunt Brenda had also been the one to break the news to my dad that something very strange had happened when my damaged nerves regenerated and my whole body began giving off an electrical charge.

I shook my head as if that would clear the memories away. "That man you said that picture reminded you of, the one who's dead. Could he have a relative who looked like him?" *One with a grudge against you?* I mentally added.

"He has no biological family left alive."

"Are you sure?" Men fathered secret babies all the time—

"He'd been a vampire for over a hundred years when he died; it was impossible for him to father children," Vlad stated.

I glanced at Jillian to see if the word *vampire* freaked her, but she still seemed to be insulated in her happy place.

"Well, what if he didn't die? The man who ordered an attack on you just happens to resemble a vampire you used to know. What if he's still alive and—"

"He's not." Vlad's smile was chillingly pleasant. "Mihaly Szilagyi was the first person I ever burned to death."

Jillian retired to one of the guest rooms. Vlad wanted her to stay for the next couple days in case I discovered any other pertinent details on the still-nameless puppet master. But though I'd spent the afternoon sifting through a flood of memories from the charred remains, all I'd gotten so far was a funky-looking ring the puppet master wore. And a headache.

Vlad had left me alone to concentrate—and to help Shrapnel do terrible things to Jackal while asking him if he recognized the man in the drawing, no doubt. I hadn't seen Maximus since this morning so I had no idea what he was up to. I wished I could take some headache pills and lie down, but I went to the basement level of the house instead. With the chaos of the past two days, I'd never gotten a chance to thank Ben for calling Vlad when the club was attacked. Without that,

Vlad might not have arrived in time, and I'd be burned crispy.

When I went into the kitchen, however, no one was there even though it was close to dinnertime. Curious, I followed the sounds of conversation farther down the hall, coming at last to a large, open lounge area.

Ben, Joe, Damon, Kate, and several others were lined up in front of one of the tall windows that, to my surprise, showed trees in the background. Not all of the basement must be underground, but since the house was on a steep hill I supposed that explained it. Sandra sat on the couch, flipping through a magazine, but she smiled when she looked up and noticed me.

"Leila!"

Ben left the window at once. "Hey, girl!"

Soon I was surrounded as the rest of them abandoned their places, too. How happy everyone acted to see me reminded me of the camaraderie the carnies had with each other. I didn't know these people very well, but they'd clearly accepted me as one of their own. I was so touched, if I wouldn't have electrocuted them en masse, I would've tried for a group hug.

"I'm fine, really," I said for the third time. "And Ben, thank you *so* much for calling Vlad and telling him about the attack. He got to me just in time."

Ben looked abashed. "I didn't know you were trapped in there. I called Vlad because I was worried about my own ass."

Sandra elbowed him. "Yet you thought to call. We were too panicked to do that. This is why Vlad rewarded you."

"He did?" He hadn't mentioned that.

"Hell yes, he did. Ben will be getting made in the next year!" Joe crowed, thumping Ben on the back.

Maybe I was losing something in the Romanian-to-English translation. "Made what?"

"Into a vampire," Sandra said proudly.

I was stunned. Ben still looked embarrassed, yet hints of excitement and pride clung to him. Obviously, he'd wanted this.

"Oh," I said, unsure how to respond. "Congrats."

"Think about it—next year, you'll be biting one of us." Damon grinned as if amused by the prospect. "Just don't fuck up with Vlad or you'll be the next one harpooned on a pole."

"Hey, we'll miss it," Joe said, going back to the window.

Everyone else followed except Sandra, who shook her head.

"I don't like to watch such things. I am surprised you came to see it, Leila."

"See what?" I asked, getting a sinking feeling in my gut.

Ben turned around from the window. "See Vlad stick Maximus on a pole for leaving you behind in the club."

Chapter 26

I didn't bother to put on a coat, but marched around to the side of the house that was secluded by a tall line of trees. Now I knew the reason why. Any poor tourist who happened to stumble across Castle Dracula would get alarmed at the sight of several long poles stuck in the earth, some of them with remains still hanging from them.

Vlad must have known that I was coming, either from my thoughts or the crunching noises my boots made with my furious stride. The long piece of timber he'd had in his hand when I first glimpsed him through the window was now on the ground. Maximus stood next to him, shirtless, seemingly oblivious to the cold that made my whole body ache, a grim yet resigned expression on his face.

"Leila," Vlad said, voice as casual as if I'd stumbled upon them sharing a beer. "It's too cold for you to be out dressed like that. Go back inside. I'll join you in a moment."

"What, after you finish shish-kebobbing Maximus for no good reason?" I snapped.

He actually had the nerve to look at me as if *I* were the one overreacting.

"No good reason? I ordered him to protect you. Instead, his actions resulted in you nearly burning to death. Did you think I'd let him off with a tongue-lashing?"

"I didn't think you'd go pole-happy on him," I countered, trying to keep my teeth from chattering because that would take away from my hard tone. "He'd been fighting off *three* vampires at the time, which was pretty damn impressive. No wonder he didn't notice what Silver Hair did to me."

Vlad's hands sparked. Maximus muttered, "Stop helping."

"I am the Master of my line." Vlad enunciated each word as though I suddenly had difficulty understanding English. "No matter how Maximus's fighting skills may have impressed you, how I punish one of my people for failing me doesn't concern you."

My temper snapped. I was supposed to be his girlfriend, not a lackey so he did *not* just pull the Big Bad Vampire card on me!

"Ooh, you told me," I mocked, sketching a bow. "You're right, I should've have *dreamed* of interfering. In fact, however long you sentence Maximus to that pole, I'll be sure to think about how wrong I was while sleeping alone!"

"Don't use abstinence as blackmail," he said curtly. "It won't work, and we agreed not to play games with each other."

I marched over, feeling my hand tingle with angry currents.

"This isn't blackmail. It's me being seriously

pissed over you torturing Maximus for something that wasn't his fault. You do what you have to do, Vlad, I can't stop you. But then I'll do what *I* have to do."

Vlad glanced down, his expression changing from irritated obstinacy to concern.

"Leila, your hand."

I looked and saw a sliver of electricity extending from it like a glittering icicle. I fisted my hand, taking a deep breath as I attempted to stuff my power back inside.

"It's fine," I muttered. "It happened before; I whipped a current across Silver Hair's back when I wasn't close enough to grab him. Maybe drinking your blood amped up my voltage."

Vlad stared at my hand before casting a speculative look at Maximus. Then he returned his attention to me. And smiled.

"What?" I asked warily, recognizing his charming "I'm going to do something awful" expression.

"Congratulations, Maximus. Leila has won you a reprieve from impalement." His smile widened. "And I know just the way you can thank her for it."

Maximus stood across from me in the huge hallway, fully dressed now. His features were stoic, but if I were him, I'd be cursing me up one side and down the other. I hoped this hurt less than a pole through the torso, but since Vlad had thought of it, probably not.

"Sorry," I said for the dozenth time. Then I focused on the knife he held and aimed as much electricity toward it as I could. A pure white cur-

rent shot out of my hand, whipping across his wrist
and leaving an ugly burn. His whole body stiffened, which had been his usual reaction, but this
time, Maximus also took a step backward. Still, he
didn't drop the knife.

"Better," Vlad said in an approving tone. "With
more practice, you'll be able to do this."

Then he snapped the whip he held. It flashed out
too fast for me to follow with my gaze, but the
knife in Maximus's hand was suddenly several feet
away on the floor.

Vlad turned to me. "I could take his hand off if
I wanted to, and this is an ordinary leather whip.
You have the ability to channel one made of pure
electrical energy. Wielded properly, you could cut
someone in half, human or vampire."

I doubted that. Vampires healed too fast for my
abilities to be lethal unless I maintained contact
with my right hand for at least an hour. Case in
point: The burn on Maximus's wrist had already
vanished, and his posture was now as straight as
ever.

Vlad strode over, scowling. "If you don't believe you *can* do it, then you *won't* do it. Do you
think my control over fire appeared the first time I
manifested a flame? No. I honed my abilities until I
turned them into the weapon they are today."

"Do you two need a minute alone?" Maximus
grumbled.

Vlad ignored him, grasping my hand and holding it up as if I'd never seen it before.

"This could be a formidable weapon. You've
only ever practiced suppressing your power, but

where has that gotten you? Stop trying to get rid of it and bend it to your will instead."

"What if I don't *want* my power to get any stronger?" Exhaustion from continually manifesting currents made my voice harsh. "Power might be the ultimate status symbol for vampires, but I never wanted these abilities to begin with. They've shattered my life more than once and without drinking vampire blood, they'd kill me. I want less power, not more."

"You want to survive, don't you?" he countered mercilessly. "As you are, most vampires could overcome you. Right now you hope that whoever ordered your kidnapping hasn't spread word of your psychic abilities, but if he has, you'll be very popular in the undead world. If that happens, you can stay helpless, relying on my protection forever, or learn how to defend yourself. Your choice."

Damn him for knowing the right buttons to push. Growing my abilities might have emotional and physical drawbacks, but they beat being helpless against another kidnapping attempt.

"Fine," I said after a long pause. "I'll hone my power into the best weapon it can be."

Vlad traced the path of my scar from my hand all the way up to my face. His voice lowered. "First you need to let go of your guilt over your mother's death. It's crippling you."

The words hit me like a slap. "You have no right," I gasped, knocking his hand away. "I never told you about that, so you stole it from my mind! Do I bring up that day by the river to you? No, because you didn't share it with me of your own free will, so I leave it alone. Leave *this* alone, Vlad. I mean it."

"I'm gonna go," Maximus muttered, slinking away from us.

I ignored him, focused on the vampire in front of me. Vlad stared back, impenitent and uncompromising.

"You don't need to bring up that day by the river because I dealt with my guilt a long time ago. But you're right. You didn't share this with me of your own free will, so I won't mention it again . . . unless you continue to let it handicap you."

Something boiled over in me at that. I could actually feel the current pulsing under my skin as if begging to be freed.

"I'll show you handicapped," I spat, and snapped my right hand at the nearest statue—a life-sized male warrior. A long, white current rocketed from my skin, lashing the statue's neck. Some part of me must've held back with Maximus before, because this time, the current cut all the way through. The marble head smashed onto the floor, breaking into several pieces.

Maximus ran back down the hall and stared at the remains in horror. "That was fifth-century Grecian!"

My surge of fury vanished as I looked at the wreckage. Surprise at what I'd done competed with shame. My sister Gretchen used to break things when she was upset, and I'd sworn never to be that way. Now I'd broken that vow—and a priceless statue along with it.

"I'm so sorry," I began, looking over at Vlad,

but his expression stopped me from saying anything else.

"You see?" he said with supreme satisfaction. "A formidable weapon, just as I told you. Now that *you* know what you're capable of, we'll keep working to improve on it."

Chapter 27

 When I finished with my shower, I saw that my bedroom door leading to the sitting area was open. It hadn't been when I first went into the bathroom. Murmured voices drifted in from the other room. Curious, I wrapped my robe tighter around me and peered around the frame.

No one but Vlad on the leather couch, jacket off, feet up, watching a vampire movie of all things. I came inside the room.

"Didn't know you were a fan of those."

He waved at the TV. "These never cease to amuse. If we're not being portrayed as bloodthirsty eunuchs, then we're angst-filled imbeciles whining about our lost humanity."

"Then you must love the cinematic retellings of *your* life."

"Most of them don't retell my life," he replied coolly, his eyes flashing green. "They retell Stoker's fabrication, which bears no resemblance to me except for the moniker—and even that's incorrect. Dracula doesn't mean son of the devil. It means son of the dragon, as my father was known in his time."

I shouldn't have brought this up. I blamed it on the fact that I was tired and still upset at Vlad for throwing up my mother's death to me, but two wrongs didn't make a right, as the cliché went.

"Forget it," I murmured.

He rose, walking over with the unhurried grace of a predator who knew his prey couldn't outrun him.

"You have the right to know about the man you've taken for a lover. Much of what history's written is false, but some things are true, even if my motivations are often portrayed incorrectly."

When he reached me, he traced his finger up the sleeve of the mulberry-colored robe. The firelight made deeper hollows out of his striking features, and his coppery eyes seemed to hold their own inner flame.

"Go on," he said with soft challenge. "Ask me something."

I glanced away, both enticed and unnerved by the offer. "Really, Vlad, I only know what the movies say about you, which you confirmed was bull. I wouldn't even know what to ask—"

"Liar," he interrupted, the word more statement than accusation. "You have questions, so ask."

"Is Marty right?" It came out before I could stop myself. "Will you break my heart?"

As soon as I said it, I wished I could take it back. We'd agreed that love wasn't an option between us, and here I was talking about a broken heart like a moonstruck teenager. Maybe this was a sign that I was already in over my head emotionally in this relationship.

He leaned against the door frame, his body so

close that a deep breath from me would have us touching.

"Why would I seek to break your heart?"

"Because you can be a merciless bastard at times," I answered honestly.

A smile flitted across his lips. "True, but I want you with me." His head dipped, mouth grazing my neck to send a scattershot of shivers through me.

Even amidst my enjoyment over his actions, I felt a pinprick of disappointment. I hadn't been looking for a promise of forever, but I had hoped to hear something . . . more. He wanted me with him now, but what happened after we caught his mysterious enemy and I no longer needed to live under his roof? Would we attempt a long distance relationship with me back in the States and him here? Would he ask me to stay? If so, would I?

"Do you feel anything for me aside from lust?" I forced myself to ask. Not until the words were out did I realize how much his answer mattered. Yeah, I was in *way* over my head.

His lips continued to brush my skin with feathery strokes that elicited countless tingles despite my nervousness as I waited for his reply.

"You challenged my authority in full view of the lowest order of my people," he said at last. "And what did I do?"

"You had me electrocute Maximus over and over," I replied, not sure where he was going with this.

"I gave him a lighter punishment while also showing you how to grow your powers," he countered in a seductively smooth voice. "If I felt nothing more for you than lust, Maximus would be on that pole for a week, and you, my lovely interloper, would not be here with me now."

Hardly the words you'd find on a Hallmark card, but they caused a glow of happiness nonetheless. Okay, so this wasn't love, but at least it was something real to him. That was enough for now. Before Vlad asked what I felt for him—a question I wasn't ready to answer with my runaway emotions—I changed the subject.

"How like you to kill two birds with one stone: punishing Maximus and working out my powers at the same time."

I meant to sound glib, but it was tough when each brush of his mouth made my toes curl. Either my distraction worked or he didn't want to know what I felt, because he addressed my statement instead of my mental musings.

"As I told you—due diligence."

His reply reminded me of the only tidbit I'd gleaned from sifting through hours of memories today.

"The puppet master," I began, my breath catching when he nipped my neck with teeth that now had two prominent, sharp fangs. "He had a funky ring. It was kind of like yours, only it had a bird on the front instead of a dragon."

Vlad's mouth stilled. "What kind of bird?"

"Maybe a crow? It was hard to tell since I only saw the ring when he was gesturing as he spoke—"

Vlad disappeared into his room before I finished speaking, my robe fluttering from how fast he'd moved. I blinked in surprise. Moments later he was back, holding a torn page.

"Is this the image you saw?"

I took the yellowed page from him, not understanding the language of the antique writing on it, but recognizing the icon.

"Yeah, that's it. I thought the thing in the bird's beak was a twig, but now I see that it's a little hoop."

Vlad muttered something in Romanian. From his tone, I guessed that it translated into several four-letter words.

"What's wrong?" He'd recognized the symbol, so the ring was a lead. That was a good thing, wasn't it?

He stared at me, and the expression on his face was so fierce, I almost took a step backward.

"That ring bears the Corvinus family coat of arms. The last time I saw one like it was on the hand of Mihaly Szilagyi."

"The man the sketch resembled," I said slowly. "You told me you burned him to death, but the coincidences are piling up."

"Yes, they are." His voice was tight. Then his gaze raked over me. "Dress warmly. We're going out."

Chapter 28

 After more than an hour of flying, I thought I'd figured out the trick to it. Don't look down: The icy wind was hell on my eyes. Keep both arms around Vlad: Not because he'd drop me, but because the warmth emanating from his body kept my hands from feeling like ice packs. Keep my legs around him for same reason. Pretend it was a roller-coaster ride: That helped with the fear when he made an unexpected roll or descent.

I figured out the most important tip when he finally set us on the ground: Don't try to walk right away. My frazzled equilibrium made my legs feel like they were different lengths and I misjudged my steps. Had Vlad not righted me, I would've fallen face-first into the snow.

"Why didn't we take the limo again?" I muttered.

He looped my scarf back around my neck. At some point during our flight, it had ended up halfway down my coat. "Because if someone's watching the house, we don't want them to follow us and see where we're going."

I finally looked around and my breath caught. Strategically placed lights illuminated the remains of an ancient castle, church, courtyard, and tower. Some of the structures looked fully restored, like the brick-based pale tower, but others had crumbled. Railed walkways and signs showed that these ruins were a tourist haunt, but the modern insertions looked out of place amidst the aged brick and stone. I could almost feel the ancient remains throb with the essence of thousands of memories, but I didn't reach out. I stayed still, drinking in the beauty around me, the wind and noises from the nearby highway the only sounds aside from my fog-flumed breaths.

"The Royal Court of Targoviste." Something lurked in Vlad's tone that I couldn't put a name to. "I never thought to return here, but this is where I buried Szilagyi's remains."

I stared at Vlad, thinking how *right* he looked in these surroundings. His lean, rough handsomeness, wind-whipped dark hair, and determined expression held as much barbaric splendor as the former medieval palace. In many ways, Vlad reminded me of these ruins; an untamed slice of the past amidst the veneer of modern civilization.

"This was where you lived when you were prince?"

He gave me a brief, jaded smile. "Not for long. My time as *voivode* was spent trying to keep Wallachia from falling prey to her enemies. It left little room for relaxing at court."

Then he started walking toward the tower, hopping over a half-crumbled wall and holding out his hand to me.

I gave him a look as I ignored his hand and leapt over the wall with the same ease as him. "Former gymnast, remember?"

Another sardonic smile. "I do, but not because you told me. You never speak of your time before the accident."

Walked right into that one, I thought as I picked my way through the dilapidated courtyard. Earlier, he'd offered to answer any question I asked him. Too late, I realized that offer came with hooks. But if I was willing to do the asking, I couldn't chicken out on answering when it was my turn.

"As a child, I was very good at gymnastics." He'd already filched this from my mind, but it seemed he wanted to hear it the regular way. "So good that when I was thirteen, I won the chance to compete for a spot on the Olympic team. Problem was, at the same time, my dad got a change of duty station to Germany. He could go unaccompanied for one year, or take all of us with him for three years. If we went, I'd lose my coach, my training facility . . . basically my best shot at the team."

We were at the perimeter of the tower now. Signs around it advertised in Romanian and English that inside was the "real" story of Vlad Dracul, complete with a picture that looked nothing like the man standing next to me. Vlad went around to the back of the tower, beckoning me to follow.

I did, tucking my hands into my coat. Even through my gloves, the cold was biting. Vlad knelt at the base of the tower, running his fingers along the faded bricks.

"Szilagyi's sword struck here when he attempted to take my head off," he said, indicating a crack that I hadn't noticed until he tapped it. Then he rose, pivoted, and took six long strides in the opposite direction before kneeling again.

"And here is where I buried him." He began clearing away the snow. I was about to ask why he hadn't brought a shovel when he shoved his hands through the frozen earth with enough force to make the ground shudder.

Yeah, a shovel would be a little redundant.

I watched him dig with a sense of relief that ended when he said, "And then what?" in a tone that dared me not to answer.

My snort blew out a plume of white. "You want to dig up the past metaphorically and literally at the same time?"

His eyes glowed green through the veil of his hair as he glanced up at me. "Call me a multitasker."

It wasn't because he'd offered to tell me anything that I answered him. It was because he hadn't shied away from his darkest sin when confronted with it, so how could keep refusing to talk about mine?

"I begged for him to take the one year unaccompanied, or to let me live with my aunt Brenda so I could still compete in the tryouts. Making the team was all I cared about, and I was so *mad* that my dad would let his job ruin everything." Bitter sigh at how stupid I'd been. "My mother refused both options, said that nothing was more important than our family sticking together. That's when I told her what I'd found a week before when I rummaged through my dad's foot locker looking for camping gear."

Vlad had dug more than three feet down, piles

of earth he tossed aside dark smudges against the snow. As soon as I stopped speaking, he paused, that commanding stare leveled on me.

"For a smart man, he was dumb for leaving a crumpled-up letter from a woman he'd slept with at the bottom of his duffel bag," I continued. "I told my mom about dad cheating—not because I thought she had a right to know, but as revenge on him for ruining my Olympics dream, and on her for refusing to let me stay at my aunt's. That's who I was. A pathologically narcissistic bitch."

Vlad hadn't resumed digging, but he still knelt in the snow, staring up at me with the oddest expression. It took me several seconds to realize what. *Sympathy*. No wonder I hadn't recognized it. I'd never seen him show that emotion before.

Choked laugh. "*This* is what you finally feel pity over?"

"You were a spoiled child who did a cruel thing. You deserved to be beaten and confined to your room, but you didn't deserve to lose everything."

I swiped at the sudden wetness near my eyes. "Oh? I wanted to stay with my aunt, and I got my wish. My mom, sister, and I moved in with Aunt Brenda when she told my dad to go to Germany unaccompanied while she figured out what to do. Then a month later, tornados knocked a bunch of trees down in our neighborhood. Afterward, I heard a dog whining in the yard. It was so weird; the dog just sat there, tree limbs all around him. I didn't see the downed power line. I went to clear the debris away . . . and the next thing I knew, I woke up in a hospital." Harsh sigh. "The doctors said I was lucky the shock knocked me across the yard. Otherwise, I'd have burned to a crisp while stuck to that power line. But what no one could explain was why my mother died from the leftover voltage in my body when she tried to help me, yet that same voltage didn't kill me."

"Why?" Vlad's lips curled, his sympathetic expression gone. "Some things just are, Leila. You survived. She didn't. Wondering why is as irrelevant as it is futile."

After everything I'd experienced, I knew that to be true. Yet it didn't make the pain of my mother's death go away, let alone my guilt over how I'd ripped my family apart.

Vlad began digging again. Either he was impatient or the ground wasn't as frozen farther down because his progress was faster.

"Again you're being naive. Your father's infidelity ripped your family apart. You were merely the messenger."

I'd never told anyone this next part, and it took two tries before I could force the words past my newly tight throat.

"He wanted to work things out. He cheated on my mom, but he still loved her, and when she died . . . part of him blamed me so much that he avoided me. He never said that, but I saw it when I touched him." My voice cracked. "It's his worst sin."

Vlad abandoned his digging and rose, but I held out a hand. "Don't. Right now I need you to be cold. If you're not, then I have to remember how much that hurt, and I don't want to."

The words were ragged, but I'd managed to stop the tears, at least. Vlad stared at me for a long moment, his expression unreadable. At last he knelt and began digging again. A few minutes and a taller pile of dirt later, he let out a grunt and then pulled something long and whitish from the hole.

A bone.

"Right where you're supposed to be," Vlad muttered.

It did seem to be undeniable proof that Szilagyi couldn't be the puppet master, but I came closer, holding out my hand.

"Let's make sure."

His brow arched, but he placed the bone in my right hand.

At once, echoes of the man's agonizing last moments washed over me. He'd been burned to death, which I expected, but I didn't see Vlad's face through the flames. I saw the puppet master's, his face haggard and gray-streaked hair much longer, but his features were unmistakable. Another jumble of images replaced those in rapid succession, showing a benign sin, long days spent farming the land, and small children playing by a mud-walled house. A name kept reverberating throughout the memories. *Josef*. This was all wrong.

When I clawed my way back to that fiery death again, I saw what I'd missed the first time in the jumble of pain and panic. The puppet master was wearing the ring I'd seen when he ordered my attack, only here, he was doing his own dirty work. The man buried here was named Josef, and he'd been burned to death by the same vampire who had recently tried to kill me.

Chapter 29

Once again, I found myself surrounded by vampires while trying to find a killer through the essence trail left from the man he'd murdered. But this time, I wasn't being forced. Despite the late hour and being exhausted, I wanted to find this bastard now, not later. I would've started looking next to that grave except Vlad insisted that we return to his castle.

When I found the essence thread leading to Josef's murderer, I followed it. The tapestry room with its large fireplace and exquisite wall coverings fell away, replaced by what looked like the inside of a cement box. With the all-gray colors of the room, for a second, I thought I'd stumbled upon a past memory. Then I saw the brown wooden door with thick black iron hinges. Color images, no haziness. That meant I was in the present. In the corner of the drab room, underneath a blanket-sized fur pelt, was the elusive puppet master, asleep.

Or, if my guess was correct, Josef's murderer and the orchestrator of my kidnapping was Mihaly Szilagyi—the vampire Vlad thought he'd killed centuries ago.

"Got him," I said out loud.

The vampire's eyes snapped open, deep brown and piercing. Now that he was in color, I saw that the streaks in his hair were blond, not gray. The lines in his face also looked less pronounced, but maybe that was because he wasn't scowling like the other times I'd seen him. His complexion was typical vampire pale, but his cheeks held a faint tinge of color. He must have fed recently. Marty had always looked flushed after a good meal.

"How unexpected," the puppet master drawled with the same faint accent that Vlad had.

I glanced at the wooden door, but it was still closed. Prickles of fear danced up my spine. *Vlad would have told me if he was a mind reader*, I tried to reassure myself.

The vampire stretched as though waking up from a nap. "Much can change in three hundred years, my little psychic spy."

Oh, crap! "We have a problem," I said out loud. "He's like you, Vlad. He can hear me in his head."

Vlad muttered a curse, but I seized upon the only defense I had. At once, I began to mentally blast the most annoying eighties song I could think of. The vampire winced.

"Stop that."

I turned up the volume in my head instead. *Thank you, Bones!* "Mihaly Szilagyi," I said aloud, "you've been found out in more ways than one."

I was guessing, but thanks to that song blasting away in my mind, the vampire didn't know that. He threw aside his blanket, revealing that he wore black sweat pants and a thick pullover sweater. Then he got up, a mocking smile on his lips.

"Capturing you has surely backfired on me. At least now I know how Vlad located you so quickly. I worried that I had a traitor in my midst, but your abilities are truly extraordinary."

"So I've been told," I replied, still mentally jamming out.

Another wince. "Must you keep thinking of that wretched song? It was unbearable even when it was new."

"How'd you do it?" I asked, not really expecting an answer. "Survive Vlad? He normally leaves behind nothing more than a pile of ash."

That made Szilagyi smile again. "We share the same sire. If Vlad thinks about it long enough, he'll figure it out."

"Can you tell where he is?" Vlad asked in a hiss.

"No," I replied with a sudden burst of insight. "He must've known I'd come looking for him. That's why he's in the same windowless concrete room that I saw when he ordered my attack. There's nothing in it but a big fur blanket, and even his clothes are so average; you can't tell anything from them."

Szilagyi gave a concurring shrug. "I thought it possible that you could locate me through an object I'd touched. Why do you think I wanted to retrieve you so badly?"

"Or kill me," I reminded him in a curt tone.

Another shrug. "Anyone who isn't on my side is my enemy." Then those deep brown eyes gleamed. "You could still be on my side, Frankie. With that clever defense you have against mind reading, Vlad need not even suspect. Lead him to the place of my choosing, and I will ensure that you never spend another day bouncing on trampolines for pennies."

"Yeah, because I'll be dead," I scoffed. "Jackal was going to kill me as soon as my usefulness ran out. I'm supposed to believe you'll be any different?"

"Why would I kill someone with your priceless abilities if I can use you to my benefit?" he asked silkily.

"Ooh, a lifetime of captivity, sounds *nice*," I mocked. "Thanks, but no."

Szilagyi's expression hardened into the merciless one I recognized from other people's memories. "You believe that Vlad will let you go? Is he pretending to be kind? I've seen that act from him before, but only a fool falls for it."

"I'm not getting anywhere with him," I said to Vlad, ignoring Szilagyi's taunt. "Do you have something you want me to relay before I go?"

"Yes." Vlad's voice was pleasant. "Tell him the next time I see him, I'll rip off his head and make a new toilet out of it."

"He hates you a lot," I summarized to Szilagyi.

"Accept my offer while you still can," the vampire replied.

I dropped the link, the confining gray room morphing into soaring ceilings with tapestries depicting various scenes of ancient life. Vlad's fingers drummed on his armrest, the faint smell of smoke emanating from him. Behind him, Maximus was immobile, but Shrapnel paced in front of the fireplace.

"How is he even still alive?" he muttered.

I didn't think the question was to me, but I answered it. "He was vague about the details. Said something about him and Vlad sharing a sire, and Vlad figuring it out if he thought about it long enough."

Nothing but the crackling of flames for a few loaded moments. Then Vlad laughed, but it sounded far uglier than his usual half purr, half amused growl.

"He has Tenoch's gift of degeneration."

Comprehension dawned on everyone's face except mine. "What's that?"

Vlad's fingers drummed against the armrest hard enough to produce tiny splinters.

"Tenoch, the vampire who turned me, had many powers. One of them was the ability to degenerate into a withered husk, mimicking the appearance of true death for a vampire. Szilagyi was also turned by Tenoch, but while I inherited Tenoch's control over fire, Szilagyi must have inherited his gift of degeneration. That's why I thought I'd burned him to death, but he wasn't dead. The filthy usurper was faking it."

Flying. Pyrokinesis. Degeneration. What other vampire powers would I learn were possible?

"What happened between you and Szilagyi?" I asked to distract myself from the scariness of undead abilities. "Three hundred years later, you're still trying to kill each other."

That scent of smoke coming from Vlad increased. "The first time I was imprisoned, I was a boy and the Ottomans were my captors. The second time, I was a vampire and my jailer was the king of Hungary, who was mesmerized into imprisoning me by his uncle, Mihaly Szilagyi. My human allies were unable to free me and as my vampire sire was dead, Szilagyi could do with me what he wished without repercussions from the vampire world. He intended to break me and rule Wallachia through me as he ruled Hungary through his nephew, but"—cold smile—"I would not break. Szilagyi would've killed me if not for Mencheres. He was Tenoch's most powerful progeny and declared me to be under his protection despite my protests that I'd rather die than be subject to a filthy Turk, as I considered Mencheres at the time. But since Szilagyi was afraid of Mencheres, he kept me alive. Years later, as a condition of my freedom, I married the king of Hungary's pregnant cousin and claimed the child as mine. Szilagyi pretended to want my help in overthrowing the Ottomans, so he had the king of Hungary assist me in reclaiming Wallachia's throne, but he'd secretly allied with the sultan."

Vlad paused, a savage smile flitting across his face. "When it came time to war, the Church paid Hungary to join me in fighting the Turks. My armies went. Szilagyi convinced Hungary's army to stay behind, but he never returned the money. Instead, he fabricated tales of my viciousness and spread them far and wide. My people suffered because of his lies and greed, and my reputation had been tarnished so badly that many allies abandoned me. When my brother ambushed me, I allowed my country to believe I'd been killed so that my son could rule. Then he was murdered shortly after he'd begun his reign. Two centuries later, I discovered Szilagyi had sent the assassin, and I trapped him at the Royal Court of Targoviste, where until today, I thought I'd burned him to death."

I winced. There was bad blood, and then there were centuries old virulent hatred.

"Why would Szilagyi wait so long to come after you?" He clearly wasn't the forgive-and-forget type.

Another smile that made me think of blood-coated knives instead of good humor. "After I believed him dead, I hunted down and exterminated every member of Szilagyi's line, plus his friends and political allies. It *would* take centuries for him to build up enough support to mount a successful attack against me. If he came after me alone, he'd be slaughtered."

Now that Szilagyi had finally made his move, neither he nor Vlad would stop until one of them was *really* dead this time.

"At least he can't hear my thoughts when I link to him," I said, trying to look on the bright side of this bleak situation.

Vlad's gaze swung to me. "How?"

"Bones taught me that playing really annoying songs over and over in my head acted as a barrier against mind reading. I was supposed to use that on you, but then things changed."

"Remind me to kill Bones next time I see him," he bit off.

Being tricked by his enemy for so long had obviously pushed Vlad into new heights of rage. I didn't think the blazing in the hearth was accidental, and he would shred that armrest into sawdust with his increasingly vicious tapping. All of this should have made me head quietly toward the door, but I stayed where I was, mulling these developments.

"Shrapnel, notify the guards to pick up Leila's family and bring them here," Vlad said, shocking me.

The massive bald vampire nodded and left. I gaped at Vlad. "My family? Why?"

"Szilagyi asked you to betray me. You refused," he stated. "His next attempt to turn you to his side will involve taking the ones you love hostage. Hence, bring them here."

"He can't come after my family, he doesn't even know my real name. He keeps calling me Frankie," I sputtered.

Vlad's look was jaded. "He's already begun researching your identity. Even if your voltage meant you never used a credit card, everyone has a paper trail. That's why I've had guards watching your father and sister since the day you arrived."

"But how? *You* don't even know my last name, let alone my family's names!"

"Leila." No emotion colored his voice. "Marty gave me your full name, your father's name, your sister's name, and their locations within ten minutes of my speaking to him."

His words were like a punch to the stomach. Nausea rose, leaving a vile taste in my mouth. "You tortured it out of him."

"No, I told him if he didn't tell me what I wanted to know, I'd ask you next," was his implacable reply.

I flashed back to Marty's worried question when I'd first seen him. *You really okay, Frankie?* Vlad had used Marty's love for me against him, making him believe any reticence on his part would result in me getting the same brutal treatment he had.

I didn't need my psychic abilities to figure out why Vlad wanted to know all my family's details, either. They were his insurance against me changing my mind about helping him. He would've used them against me just as ruthlessly as he'd used me against Marty. Rage mixed with the bile inside me. No wonder Vlad knew what move Szilagyi would make next. The two of them thought exactly alike.

Vlad would've heard every word of my mental accusation, but he said nothing, and his silence was damning confirmation. I got up, walked over to where he sat, and then slapped him across the face as hard as I could. Maximus looked like he was going to have a stroke, but nothing changed in Vlad's expression except a bright red handprint that quickly faded.

I left the room without looking back, fury stiffening my spine, but my heart feeling like it had shattered within me. Marty had been right after all. The thought haunted me as I climbed the curving stone staircase. Once I'd finally reached my bedroom, I made sure to lock the door behind me.

Chapter 30

The sun had slipped halfway behind
the mountains when Maximus entered the library. It wasn't quite
six, but night fell quickly here—
and dragged on interminably when
anger and anxiety led to insomnia.
I'd spent much of the previous evening staring at
my doorknob, waiting to see if Vlad would attempt
to come in and apologize. That shouldn't be too
much to expect, former infamous medieval ruler or
not. But the handle on my door never moved. All
day, I'd told myself that was a good thing.

"Shrapnel called. They'll be here soon," Maximus stated.

The words brought no small measure of relief.
I was still furious with Vlad over *why* he'd kept
tabs on my family, but they'd be safer here than in
Szilagyi's hands. I might not be in the pom-pom-
waving mood, but I hadn't changed my Team Vlad
status. If not for Szilagyi dragging me into this
undead feud by ordering my kidnapping, I'd still be
enjoying a balmy winter with Marty in Gibsonton.
Not sitting in Romania wondering how my father
and sister would react to being dragged halfway

around the world—and unable to go home anytime soon.

But when I followed Maximus out of the library
and saw a familiar dark-haired figure at the end
of the hall, nerves competed with my simmering
anger. At once, I began to recite a montage of lyrics
to mask my thoughts. I'd slapped him last night
and avoided him all day, yet a small, absurd part of
me was still disappointed that Vlad hadn't sought
me out.

The closer I got, the more my discomfort grew.
His back was to me, hands clasped behind him,
showing that his cuffs had tiny black stones em-
broidered in them. Vlad's coat hung to his knees,
and the material looked so sleek, it must've been
cashmere. His pants were matching ebony, boots
peeking out from under the hem. When I drew
alongside him, a glance revealed that his collar had
the same subtly glittering embroidery as the cuffs,
but his charcoal shirt was understated enough
to make the outfit elegantly imposing instead of
ostentatious. His hair was slicked back, and the
severe style made his eyebrows look like curved
wings. It also showed off those etched cheekbones,
that darkly shadowed jaw, and those mesmerizing,
copper-colored eyes.

I suddenly felt very underdressed in my brown
slacks and beige turtleneck. Why hadn't I worn the
indigo dress instead, and would it have *killed* me to
put on some makeup?

Vlad's lips twitched. It occurred to me that
during my admiring evaluation, I'd forgotten to
keep blasting a song in my mind. I remedied my
mistake, but the lyrics to "Do You Really Want

to Hurt Me" seemed too close to home at the moment.

"Culture Club?" Now his mouth curled downward. "And you accuse me of practicing cruel and unusual punishment."

"That's not funny," I muttered, letting a swath of black hair fall over the scarred part of my face. It was more habit than self-consciousness, but when his gaze followed the movement, his mocking frown vanished.

"Every part of you is beautiful, Leila. One day, you'll come to believe that."

I looked away, cursing the tightening in my chest at the words and his low, resonant tone. Compliments didn't change what he'd done. *That* was what I really had to focus on.

Again, I'd stopped masking my thoughts, but Vlad didn't comment. He pulled out a long, flat box from inside his coat.

"For you."

I stared at it without reaching out. It looked like a jewelry box, and from its size, something big was inside. Was he one of those men who thought any awful deed could be overlooked if he forked over something sparkly?

My chin rose. "If I accept this, then it'll feel like I'm saying everything is okay between us, and it isn't. I shouldn't have hit you, so I'm wrong, too, but jewelry won't change . . . oh!"

Vlad had flipped open the box during my speech. What it contained made me wish I could stuff back my words with a pitchfork. Inside was a pair of long black gloves, one slightly thicker than the other. I touched them, blinking in amazement.

Specialized rubber from the feel of it, but the outside looked like leather, and they were no bigger
than normal gloves.

"The material is thin, but I'm assured that the
gloves can repel up to twelve thousand volts," Vlad
stated. The faintest hint of wickedness colored his
tone as he went on. "They don't, however, sparkle."

Somebody, please kill me now.

I was saved from more embarrassment over
my aggrandizing declaration when the front door
opened and a gust of cold air blew in. Shrapnel
bowed first to Vlad and then to me as he held the
door open for the people trailing behind him.

"Look at this huge fucking place!" a familiar
voice exclaimed. My sister, Gretchen, was the opposite of demure.

I snatched the gloves and put the right one on.
Vlad tucked the box back in his jacket and slid the
left one on for me since the thicker material made
it more awkward. Still, it was a thousand times less
bulky than the industrial glove Marty had gotten
me from a Florida Power & Light employee. No
one would look twice at these while the other led
to constant questions.

"Thank you," I murmured.

His hands lingered on mine, their heat apparent
even through the material. "You're welcome."

"Leila!"

My sister's voice yanked my attention back to
Gretchen. She managed to look around in awe
while also marching forward at an angry clip. Her
straight black hair was shorter than the last time
I'd seen her, but even though she'd been on a plane
for over a dozen hours, her makeup was perfect as

usual, accenting pretty features, full lips, and an upturned nose. Blue eyes a few shades darker than mine glared at me.

"What kind of cluster fuck have you gotten us into now?" she demanded.

"Hello to you, too, Gretchen," I said dryly.

Then my voice caught as I saw the man behind her. Hugh Dalton's hair had more salt than pepper now, but he still wore it cropped close to his head in the same style as when he'd been a lieutenant colonel. His blue-gray eyes took in Vlad's house with watchfulness versus admiration, and though he used a cane, his air of authority and tempered toughness remained the same.

I swallowed the lump that rocketed up my throat. "Hi, Dad."

I am the world's WORST liar, I thought an hour later. I'd tried to stall by urging my family to go to their rooms to unpack, but Gretchen was having none of that, and with less dramatics, neither was my father.

Vlad wasn't helping me come up with a cover story, either. No, he'd introduced himself as Vladislav Basarab without a moment's pause, though the significance of that name went over my family's heads. Shrapnel had offered them little explanation during his scoop-and-run procurement, so Vlad was leaving it up to me to tell my family a big whopping lie, or the truth.

I went with a big whopping lie, of course.

"You witnessed a mob murder and now you're in the Romanian witness protection program?" My father cast a pointed look around at the magnificent, two-story library. "Seems a lot different than the American version."

Wait until he saw the rest of the house. "Well, Romania is broken into communes and Vlad is um, like a mayor of several of them. Since I'm hiding from members of the European Mafia, the Romanian"—were they called something other than police here?—"*authorities* thought his house would be the safest place for me until, uh, they catch the bad guys," I finished lamely.

Vlad glanced away, but not before I saw his mouth twitch. Okay, it sounded like the load of bull it was, but I'd thought *he* would come up with something to tell them! Or at least give me more than a two-minute warning to make up a story myself.

Maybe he would've warned you earlier if you hadn't avoided him all day, an insidious little voice taunted.

Up yours, I snapped back at it.

Vlad coughed, something that didn't seem unusual to my father or sister, but made me narrow my gaze. Vampires didn't cough. Was he muffling a *laugh*?

"I'm sure Vlad can go into more detail if you have questions," I added in a frosty tone.

The grin he flashed me made me sure about the muffled laugh. "No, you're doing a splendid job."

My father frowned, adding to the new lines in his face that I didn't remember from the last time I'd seen him.

"How long are Gretchen and I expected to stay sequestered with you?" he asked with his usual directness.

The million-dollar question. I took a deep breath. "We're not sure. Maybe a couple weeks. Maybe a few months."

My sister rose to her full five feet four inches. "You can't expect me to put my life on hold that long!" she screeched. "I have a job, friends, plans—"

"Lower your voice," my father said tersely.

I'd never been able to get Gretchen to quiet down when she went on a verbal rampage, but decades of command hung in that single sentence. She stopped talking, yet the glare she shot me promised there was more where that came from.

My father turned his attention back to me. "What if we elect not to be sequestered with you? What then?"

"You'll be captured, tortured, and eventually killed by the people after your daughter," Vlad replied in a casual tone.

My mouth fell open at his bluntness. Gretchen let out a shocked gasp. Vlad looked at me and shrugged as if to say, *You wanted me to take over.*

My father gazed at Vlad with open calculation. I'd seen that hard stare cower countless people, but of course, it had no effect on Vlad. He stared back, that pleasant half smile never leaving his face.

"I still have top-level connections," my father stated. "Leila can be protected back in her own country."

Vlad's brow arched. "With her abilities? You know better than to expose her to your government or military. She'd never see the outside of a covert research facility again."

His derision when he said "research" was unmistakable. A muscle ticked in my father's jaw.

"So you know what she can do?"

Vlad and I were on opposite ends of the same couch, him relaxed, me stiff, but at that, he caught my hand and kissed it.

"I'm very well acquainted with her abilities."

Gretchen's eyes bugged while my father's expression darkened. Vlad couldn't have been clearer in his meaning.

"Ah, I'll take over from here," I said.

"How can you stand touching her?" my sister blurted, staring at our clasped hands. "Doesn't that hurt?"

I seized on the change of topic. "These gloves are specialized rubber. They block the current."

Gretchen's gaze traveled over Vlad, disbelief still stamped on her features. "Yeah, but how do you two do anything *else*, unless he has a special, current-repelling glove for his—"

"Gretchen!" my father cut her off.

My cheeks felt hot. *Don't say a word*, I thought to Vlad, seeing his chest tremble with suppressed laughter.

"He has a natural immunity," I gritted out.

They didn't know about vampires, and that was the explanation I'd given for how I could work with Marty. Considering the unusual abilities other circus performers had, immunity to electricity wasn't too much of a stretch.

Gretchen looked mollified, but my father's stern gaze told me he wasn't buying much of anything I'd said this past hour.

"I want to speak with whoever's in charge of your sequestering, Leila."

Vlad's smile was languid and challenging. "You are."

"Then I want to speak with someone *else*," my father replied curtly.

"I'm sure we can arrange that," I said at once. Vlad could get one of his people to play the part of Romanian WitSec, and if all else failed, mind control could be employed. I hated to do that, but my dad's life was more important.

After a moment of loaded silence, Vlad rose. He hadn't let go of my hand, so I got up with him, feeling the weight of my father's stare even as I pasted a false smile on my face.

"We'll talk more at dinner," I said. "Until then, I'm sure you want to unwind, unpack, and, um, freshen up."

"Shrapnel, please show our guests to their rooms," Vlad stated, his pleasant tone in stark contrast to the tension swirling in the air.

The large, mocha-skinned vampire appeared in the doorway. Gretchen stood, shaking her head at me.

"This is so messed up, Leila."

You don't even know the half of it, I thought.

Chapter 31

As soon as we were out of my family's sight, I pulled my hand from Vlad's and headed up to the fourth floor. Then I went straight into the paneled sitting area instead of my bedroom.

"If there's any chance of salvaging things between us—and I must be crazy to even *consider* that—you need to start off with a huge apology," I stated without preamble.

His arms folded across his chest. With that stunning jewel-encrusted coat adding to his already commanding presence, I felt like I'd somehow shrunk several feet, but I refused to be cowed. I stood straighter and began to tap my foot.

He glanced down. "Is that supposed to intimidate me?" he asked, his voice edged with satin-covered steel.

"It's supposed to show that I'm serious," I ground out.

When we'd entered the room, the fireplace hadn't been lit. Now flames shot up in the hearth like a bomb had detonated. I glanced at those, at Vlad, and crossed my own arms.

"*Now* who's trying to be intimidating?"

"Because of my actions, your family is safe from Szilagyi." The fire nearby blazed higher. "Yet you give ultimatums and demand that I beg your pardon?"

For so many years, I'd been an expert at keeping my temper at bay. Less than two weeks after meeting Vlad, and I felt as volatile as the currents running through my body.

"I get that you come from a time when using a person's family as blackmail was probably all the rage," I snapped, "but it's *not* cool to do in the twenty-first century! Seriously, how is this surprising to you?"

His brow arched. "We weren't lovers when I first put your family under surveillance."

"You're trying to get off on a technicality?" My voice rose in disbelief on the last word.

"Do you know the last time I let someone strike me without retaliation?"

"You're changing the subject," I muttered, but shame pierced me. Violence had no place in a relationship for any reason. I had no excuse for what I'd done and I knew it.

He stalked closer. "Aside from last night, there hasn't been a single instance. You've seen the scars on my body, but not all are from battles. Many were from when I was imprisoned as a boy and repeatedly beaten. In the centuries since, I've let few people touch me in friendship, fewer still as a lover, but none in anger without extracting my vengeance . . . yet you struck me, and I did nothing." His voice deepened. "If you don't find sufficient apology in that, then you don't know me at all."

Confusion added to the other emotions roiling inside me. Vlad's eyes were lit up with emerald, the ever-increasing fireplace flames an indication of his temper, but when he cupped my face, his touch was infinitely gentle. I leaned into his hand without thought, feeling the weirdest mixture of despair and elation. Logic said I should run screaming away from this relationship, but the truth was that I didn't want to.

"Swear to me on whatever you consider holy that you will never harm anyone I care about. If you can't do that, then this has to end, Vlad."

I might not want to let him go, but neither was I willing to take anyone else down with me in this potential quicksand.

His head bent, the rough silk of his stubble grazing my cheek. "Unless they try to harm me or mine, I swear it."

A vow with conditions, but everything had conditions with him. I closed my eyes as he pushed my turtleneck down, his lips sliding to my neck while his strong, scarred hand still cupped my face. The touch of his tongue sent delicious shivers through me and I moved closer, grasping his collar. He made a low, guttural sound and pulled me tighter against him, his other hand kneading my back while his mouth continued to sensually tease my neck.

Then a brush of teeth made me gasp. Fangs pressed against my throat, their hard, extended length adding friction that was both threatening and overtly carnal. The pressure of his mouth increased, tongue, lips, and fangs manipulating my most sensitive spots until my heart pounded and I rubbed against him with a need I couldn't articulate. Another rumbling noise came from him, so primal that my nipples scraped painfully against my bra and I was wet and aching with desire.

"Leila." His arms tightened around me, and his voice was darker. Predatory. "It's time."

I thought he meant sex, which I was on board with. But then his fangs slanted, their tips pressing against my neck instead of their length. My skin broke under those sharp points and a longer, harsher gasp escaped me as they penetrated deep.

That gasp turned into a moan at the sensations that spilled over me. Heat seemed to pour from his mouth, flashing through my veins to envelop my whole body. I felt fevered, dizzy, while the most unexpected surge of pleasure made my head fall back and my knees weaken. I knew vampire bites transmitted a venomlike substance, but I had no idea it felt stronger than morphine and more erotic than foreplay. My pulse throbbed under his mouth, and when Vlad drew in that first long suction, rapture shot from my neck to my loins with such intensity that my inner muscles clenched and I almost came.

Something like a growl sounded against my throat. Then his hand slid through my hair and drew my head farther back while another suction sent more pleasure cascading through me. Everything around me seemed to fall away, narrowing my world to nothing but the indescribable sensation of my blood emptying into Vlad. Strength abandoned me and I would have fallen had he not held me against him with that steely grip. Another suction made my panting break on a cry and I dug my nails into his back, clawing at him in growing

need. I wanted him inside me, and I ground my
hips against him in silent, explicit invitation.

Vlad's mouth was suddenly gone, leaving the
spot where he'd bitten me both icy and burning at
the same time.

"Do you *want* me to kill you?" he ground out.

I blinked in confusion, but then I heard Maximus's voice on the other side of the door.

"You'd kill me if I didn't interrupt you with this
information."

I hadn't even heard Maximus knock, but he
must have. Vlad still held me tight. From the emerald blazing in his gaze and that hard, thick flesh
pressed against my belly, he was close to telling
Maximus to go away or die bloody. But then he let
out a harsh sigh.

"Wait there."

Disappointment mixed with the lust that had
my loins throbbing. Vlad smoothed my hair back,
his mouth swooping down to give my neck a final,
lingering lick.

"It must be important or he wouldn't dare disturb me now," he murmured. Then he drew away
to look at me. "If it's not, I'll kill him and return
to you directly."

I would have laughed, except I wasn't sure if he
was kidding. "I understand."

My body didn't. It ached with denied need while
my neck continued to pulse with icy hot vibrations.
I touched it, feeling the twin holes. Vlad's eyes followed the movement and emerald took over his
gaze again.

"I love seeing my marks in your flesh."

If he'd looked smug while saying it, I would have

been piqued, but his expression showed unadulter-ated possessiveness instead. Must be a vampire thing.

A grin bared his teeth. "It's very much a vampire thing." He gave me a hard kiss that took away the breath I'd just started to get back under control. I blamed blood loss on the fact that I had to sit down when he finally let me go.

"I'll be back as soon as I can," he said. Then he flung open the door. "Maximus," he greeted the stony-faced blond vampire on the other side. "This had better be good."

The door shut behind them and I closed my eyes, taking several deep breaths. Less than a minute later, the door opened.

"Leila."

Vlad's foreboding tone made my remaining desire vanish, and I stood so fast that I nearly stumbled.

"What's wrong?"

He came over and took my arm. "You need to come with me."

Chapter 32

 I walked between Vlad and Maximus down the narrow stone staircase. Every fifty feet or so, we came to a landing where we passed through a metal, guarded doorway that led to another set of descending steps. This part of the house didn't have heat, so my breath came in white plumes. Despite Vlad giving me his coat, I couldn't stop shivering. It also didn't have electricity, so if not for the torches he flamed into light, I would have been blind in the stygian darkness. I knew it was my imagination, but the walls of the tunnel seemed to shimmer with despairing essences, adding to my sense of dread. The dungeon was the last place I wanted to go to, but it was where we were headed.

The last guarded door opened into a cavernous area that was pitch black until Vlad lit more torches with his power. The first thing I saw was several sets of manacles embedded in a huge stone pillar in the center of the area. When we approached it, I saw that these manacles were unusually thick, with silver spikes lining them that faced inward. From their varying heights and sizes, I calculated their purpose.

Side ones were for the wrists. Bar between them, the neck. Lower, wide bar for the waist, the two below that, the thighs, and the ones closest to the floor, ankles. The pillar faced the thankfully empty cells cut into the rock across from us. Knowing Vlad, their positioning was so that any prisoners could see whatever was done to the unlucky person restrained here. Between the pillar and the cells were three deep holes, and from the dark stains lining them, I guessed that they were normally occupied by thick wooden poles. The outdoor area must not be the only place where Vlad got his impalement on.

"I regret that this is necessary," Vlad stated, grasping the wrist manacles.

His words echoed in the subterranean surroundings, ominous and eerie as they bounced back. I wished this wasn't necessary, too, but I said nothing as I took my gloves off, tucking them into his coat. Then I walked over, leaned back against that looming rock wall, and felt the weight of icy, unforgiving metal as Vlad set the clamps against my hand.

I have no idea how long I screamed, but my throat was burning by the time I regained control enough to distinguish reality from other people's memories. My face was also wet from tears, and shudders wracked me so violently that the ache in my limbs wasn't due to phantom pains, but from being so lost in the horrific memories that I'd managed to hurt myself with my reaction—something that had never happened before.

Of course, in all the recollections I'd relived, I had never experienced anything like *this*. When I realized that I was sagged in Vlad's arms, my first reaction was revulsion so deep that a roar tore from my wounded throat.

"*Getawaydonttouchme!*"

He released me so abruptly that I fell onto the floor. Instinct made me curl my right hand to my side instead of using it to break my fall. I sprawled into a heap, but the action meant I didn't pick up any new memories from stained stone ground, which was the most important thing.

"Should I help?" Maximus asked in a carefully neutral tone.

I doubted the question was directed at me, but I answered anyway. "No. Give me a minute."

My voice was still raw. I sat on the floor, trying to paste together my fractured emotions while hugging myself for warmth. That was a mistake I wouldn't have made had I been thinking clearly. As soon as my right hand came in contact with Vlad's coat, another memory assailed me.

I stood naked in front of a closet on the far side of my bedroom. With the press of a button, row upon row of clothes whirled by, some casual, some formal, and a few so ornate they were meant only for ceremonial events. I stroked my jaw as I considered my choices. I couldn't meet her family wearing just anything. She deserved better than that. Finally, I selected a long coat inlaid with black sapphires at the collars and cuffs.

This would do. Perhaps the gloves would also help to soothe her ire. Their completion came not a moment too soon.

That image faded, replaced by Vlad looming over me in this oppressive dungeon instead of gloriously naked in his bedroom. I stared up at him, the memory of his actions shocking me for a different reason this time.

"You dressed up to meet my family?" The unexpectedly thoughtful gesture made me choke on a laugh. "*How* can you be the same person that did all those other things? You're not just versatile and complex—it's like you're a schizophrenic!"

Vlad knelt next to me, an emerald sheen encompassing his eyes like a cat's when light shone upon them.

"We are all more than the sum of our sins," he said in an even voice. "You know that better than most people, Leila."

Then he held out his hand. I stared at it, what I'd experienced through the multiple essences contained in those manacles making horror flit over me. Then other images covered those, *my* memories of Vlad, so different in comparison. Very slowly, I placed my hand in his and let him help me up. I walked back to the manacles, repressing a shudder. *The second time is always easier*, I reminded myself. Vlad had ordered my family pulled in, but Maximus had been unable to reach Marty. He might be fine or he might need help, and the only way to find out was to follow the essence trail Marty had left in these restraints the day Vlad had questioned him.

Before I grasped the wrist manacles again, I fingered the edge of Vlad's coat and gave him a faint smile.

"Nice choice. You looked great in this."

His brow arched. "Of course I did."

His indefatigable arrogance made me shake my head, but it also gave me the last bit of strength I needed to grab the metal clamps again. That same swarm of horrendous images bombarded my mind, but as expected, they were fainter, allowing me to fight through them and find the essence thread I was looking for. Once I did, I concentrated until everything else fell away.

To my dread, the new surroundings I found myself looking at didn't appear much better than the ones I was actually in. Instead of dark stone walls, concrete was all around me, the few splashes of color a wooden door in the corner and blood staining the front of Marty's shirt.

Mihaly Szilagyi stood in front of him, wearing another nondescript outfit and holding a knife dripping with red. The silver-haired vampire who'd snapped my legs and left me to die was there, too, restraining Marty while chewing an unlit cigarette and looking bored.

I dropped the link with a snarl that came from a part of me I hadn't known existed.

"I found Marty. Szilagyi's got him."

"No," Vlad said again.

I paced in front of the fireplace. Despite him turning it into an inferno that was barely contained by the gilded grate, I still felt chilled to the bone.

"I have the right to talk to the bastard who kidnapped my friend," I snapped. "Since we don't have his phone number, linking to him through my abilities is the only option."

Vlad settled back into the crimson Louis XV

chair, an elbow propped on the armrest, chin balanced on his hand. He looked completely relaxed except for his eyes, which focused on me with unrelenting intensity.

"You link to Szilagyi, and his response will be to torture your friend to a level designated to break you. That's why he took Martin. He wants you to see what he does to him, but if you're not looking, then he won't spare the effort."

My hair swung with my furious strides. "Marty was already cut up pretty good, so Szilagyi isn't waiting for anyone!"

"That's for information" was his pitiless reply, "but Martin can't relay anything of real import, so his primary effectiveness lies in your affection. Once Szilagyi realizes he can't use him to force you to betray me, Martin's usefulness ends, so if you want to keep your friend alive and in the best possible condition, you *won't* link to Szilagyi."

"Why doesn't he find another psychic?" I muttered. "I'm not the only one: psychics work with police all the time."

"A regular psychic isn't enough. You can track people in the present *and* get accurate glimpses of the future. I've only met two other people with that ability. One is dead, and the other is having what you might call technical difficulties with his power."

My fists clenched, currents pulsing so strongly inside me that I half expected the nearest light socket to short-circuit.

"You wouldn't abandon one of your people to this fate, so don't expect me to respond any differently, Vlad."

"You were at that club less than two hours before those vampires attacked," he stated. "When you spied upon Szilagyi, he was fully clothed while resting under several blankets. He made sure you saw him in nothing but a nondescript concrete room, and a nondescript concrete room is where he has Martin."

"What does this have to do with anything?" I demanded.

"It means that he's not far," he replied, tone implying it was obvious. "Szilagyi gave the silver-haired vampire orders to kill or retrieve you *after* they saw surveillance footage of you at the club, so that puts him at less than two hours away. He hasn't left Romania since or he wouldn't be so concerned with you seeing details of where he's hiding, and I doubt it's a modern or even refurbished house because most of those have heat, yet he used blankets when vampires don't easily get cold."

He ticked off the items as he spoke. Put together, they made sense, and I cursed myself for not seeing it, too.

"I have my people scouring all abandoned or seldom used buildings within a two-hundred-mile radius," Vlad continued. "It's a large area, but soon we'll either find Szilagyi or force him to run. Once he surfaces, then you, my beautiful psychic, can link to him and see exactly where he is."

It was a logical plan that tightened the noose around Szilagyi's neck, yet left Marty to the whims of fate. Maybe Szilagyi would kill him before he ran. Maybe he wouldn't. Problem was, I didn't have a better idea. That didn't mean I was settling for coin-flipping odds on my friend, however.

"If I come up with a way to stick it to Szilagyi *and* save Marty, promise me you'll act on it."

Vlad's gaze was hard yet steady. "I don't want him to die since it would hurt you and he was acting under my orders when he was captured. So if you find a way that doesn't pose more danger to my people, you have my word that it will be done."

Chapter 33

 I walked through the huge hall, catching glimpses of a few vampires in their discreet yet vigilant positions as I passed. Vlad told me he had some things to attend to before dinner, but I think he sensed that I wanted to be alone. My emotions had been put through the wringer and today still wasn't over. Soon, I had to sit across from my family and keep up the witness protection charade. If their lives hadn't been upended in a spectacular way because of me, I would have pled a headache and stayed in my room, but I couldn't be so selfish.

"Leila," a familiar voice hissed.

I blinked, seeing my father come out from around the back of the staircase as if he'd been hiding behind it.

"What are you doing?" I wondered.

He walked over, his limp more pronounced from his haste. The effects from the roadside bomb that precipitated his early retirement would stay with him forever.

"I've been looking for you," he stated while his gaze darted around. "No one would tell me where you were, either. They just said I'd see you at dinner."

After decades of being in command, my dad would *love* that sort of evasiveness. He started toward the back of the staircase and gestured for me to follow. I did with a sigh, making a mental note to tell Vlad to have his people be a little more forthcoming than their normal, stonewalling selves.

"Sorry about that," I began. "Vlad's staff is used to—"

"You have no idea the danger you're in," my father cut me off, voice still barely above a whisper.

"Um, sure, the European Mafia are scary people—"

"Not them."

He must not have thought I was moving fast enough because he tugged me behind the staircase. My borrowed coat muted the effects of the voltage, but a wince still crossed his face.

"It's *him*," he said, gesturing to Vlad's coat. "That man isn't who he says he is. Vladislav Basarab is an alias, and a twisted one. I know you must care for him, but when I ran his name through my contacts, you wouldn't believe what I found."

Struck by the same exhausted, overstressed irrationalism that led some people to cackle at funerals, I laughed. I couldn't help it. Maybe this was the last straw for my sanity.

"I can imagine your *face* when they told you that was the real name of Dracula!" I snorted, tears leaking out. "That's what you get for snooping instead of being sequestered from the outside world like you're *supposed* to under witness protection."

His expression was like a thundercloud now. "This isn't a joke, Leila. The man who goes by the name Vladislav Basarab is so heavily involved in organized crime that my contacts advised me not to investigate him further or I might disappear. Does *that* sound funny to you?"

Organized crime. That was one way to describe it, if you didn't know that vampire hierarchy predated most current laws.

"Dad," I said, getting control of myself, "Vlad isn't who you need to worry about. He won't hurt you, Gretchen, or me, but you do need to stop investigating him. None of your contacts would be able to dig up anything close to the truth, anyway."

"Then tell me the tru . . ."

His voice trailed off, and his gaze narrowed. "Why are there blood specks on your collar?"

Before I realized what he intended, he'd yanked my turtleneck down.

"What is *this*?" he spat, staring at the holes in my neck.

I didn't have the chance to reply. Shrapnel appeared, lifting my father off the ground with one meaty arm.

"What are you doing?" I asked, aghast.

"He grabbed for your throat," Shrapnel said in explanation, my father's furious struggles not even causing him to twitch.

"Leila, run!" my dad said hoarsely.

"Oh my God, what is *happen*ing?" Gretchen screeched, rounding the bottom of the staircase.

If a bridge had suddenly materialized, I would've jumped off it. "Let him down," I told Shrapnel, who released my father with a muttered "Fine, but if he lunges for your throat again—"

"He won't," I said shortly. "Gretchen, stop screaming. Dad, I don't need to run. Vlad's people are crazy protective of me and you might not see them, but trust me, they're around."

My father stared at me like I was a stranger. "What have you gotten involved in?" he asked, so quiet that I could barely hear him above Gretchen's litany of "Oh God, oh God."

"Your neck, his alias, this castle." My dad's tone hardened. "Is that the trouble you're in? You saw some sick form of role-playing among rich foreigners that went too far?"

"And now I'm struck with déjà vu," an ironic voice said behind me. "You may go, Shrapnel. I'll handle this."

Shrapnel bowed to Vlad and vanished. I was used to people disappearing with vampiric speed, but my sister blanched and my dad's brows drew together like they'd been yanked by a string.

"How the fuck did he do that?" he demanded harshly.

I had two choices: Tell the truth, or have Vlad mesmerize my dad and sister into believing a lie. Nothing less than mind control would work now that my dad had seen holes in my neck and the two of them watched a bulky guard seemingly disappear.

Vlad moved next to me, his hand resting on my back. "I'll honor whatever decision you make, but the truth is always better than a lie, even when it's the more difficult path."

I looked at my father's granite expression and

my sister's frightened one, and sighed. "They'll tell people."

Vlad flashed a charming smile at my father. "No they won't. He's smart enough to realize that repeating such information is futile. The only people who'd believe him are others of my kind, and they don't suffer whistleblowers or fools. As for her"—a nod indicated Gretchen—"she'll do as he tells her."

My sister bristled. "I'm twenty-two years old. No one tells me what to do!"

"Gretchen, be quiet," my dad growled.

She glared at him but didn't say anything else. My lips twitched despite the seriousness of the situation. Vlad's instincts were correct—she'd never go against a direct order from our father. Hugh Dalton had always intimidated her.

"Tell me the truth about what's going on," my dad ordered.

I, however, had never been intimidated by him. But I did want to try and repair my relationship with my family, and if our reconciliation wasn't built on honesty, then it wouldn't be real.

"Show him, Vlad," I said.

His gaze changed from copper to bright, glowing green, and his smile bared teeth that now had two sharp fangs. A muscle ticked in my father's jaw but his expression didn't change.

"Fancy contacts and novelty teeth don't impress me."

"I didn't think they would," Vlad replied in a silky voice. "But that happens before I do this."

He levitated into the air, hovering several feet off the ground. Then flames erupted from his hands, first eerie blue, then orange, yellow, and red. They climbed up his arms, licked the edges of his long brown hair, and while their heat was palpable, not a stitch of fabric or a single hair on him burned.

"I am Vladislav Basarab Dracul, born 1431 as a mortal, but reborn in 1462 as a vampire," Vlad stated, staring into my father's eyes. "And I am but one out of millions of vampires, ghouls, ghosts, and demons that live in secret among you."

Piling the drama on a little thick, aren't you? I thought. Then a thud made my gaze swing to the right.

My sister had fainted.

Vlad opened the wine and poured the deep red liquid to the brim before handing me the glass. I accepted it like it was a lifeline, taking a large, graceless gulp. On the plus side, my father no longer thought I was mixed up in a rich, role-playing cult. In the negative column, he was probably on the phone with the Pentagon right now, helping to organize a full-scale attack against any creature that didn't have a pulse.

Vlad gave me a look of sardonic amusement as he poured his own glass. "High-level officials all over the world already know other species exist, but as long as we don't interfere in their affairs, they're happy to pretend that we're not real."

In truth, I was less worried about my father telling anyone than I was about him and Gretchen getting over their horror that the undead existed— and that I was dating one of them. Now that I was thrown together with my family, I realized how much I'd missed them. We'd all made mistakes, but maybe we could learn to work through them enough to have some sort of relationship.

If Gretchen ever stopped screaming, that was.

"What about your other girlfriends?" I muttered, plopping onto the bed. "Did their families eventually settle down?"

He sat next to me with a fluid, powerful grace that only someone with control over every muscle in their body could exhibit. If I'd moved like that when I was thirteen, I would've been a shoe-in for a gold medal.

"Depends," he said, surprising me by answering what had mostly been a rhetorical question. "Five of them were vampires themselves. Out of the humans, the last one's family did come to accept it, the two before her didn't tell their families, the one before that didn't have any living family, and the first . . . her family incited others in their village to burn my house down while shouting, 'Death to the wampyre!'"

I laughed before the underlying significance made my breath catch. "You're almost six hundred years old, but you've only had ten girlfriends before me?"

"Ten lovers, two wives, and a few dozen anonymous encounters when loneliness got the better of my standards."

Wow. Vlad said he was selective about who he slept with, but some part of me must not have believed him.

"The woman by the river. Which one was she?" I asked, holding his darkly burnished gaze.

He set his wine on the floor. "My first wife. She bore me a son, and a few years later while I was fighting the Turks, I met Tenoch. He showed me what he was, turned me, and then killed himself shortly after he saw me through the initial blood craze. I returned home intending to reveal what I'd become to my wife, but my actions on the battlefield had upset her." His mouth twisted. "She thought I'd become too brutal. It seemed an inopportune time to tell her that I was no longer even human."

"I bet," I said softly.

"I had to avoid her to keep my secret." Another humorless smile. "I went off on another military excursion and we were ambushed shortly before dawn. Vampires may not die in sunlight, but new vampires are exhausted by it for the first few months. While I was fighting, the sunlight felled me and my men thought I was dead—little wonder since I no longer breathed. Word was sent to my wife, who thought the Turks were on their way to capture her. I'd told her of my treatment under the Ottoman Empire as a boy, and she decided she'd rather die than face the same brutality. She threw herself from the roof of our home into the river below, and that is where I found her after I awoke and returned to tell her I was alive."

His voice was matter-of-fact, but I knew the guilt he still carried over her death. I covered his hand with mine.

"I'm sorry."

"Don't be. It was a long time ago."

He took my wineglass, setting it on the floor next to his. Then he pulled off my gloves. Once my hands were bare, he unbuttoned his shirt, staring at me while the green in his eyes grew until it swallowed up that rich copper shade.

"All last night and today, I've wanted your hands on me." The words were roughened by lust as he yanked his shirt off, revealing that muscled chest with its pattern of scars and those mouthwatering abs. "I'm not waiting any longer."

I stared at him and licked my lips. Sounded good to me.

Chapter 34

For the second day in a row, Gretchen and my dad declined to join us for lunch. I doubted they'd join us for dinner tonight, either. Hell, they'd pretty much confined themselves to their rooms. I'd give them another day before I tried to talk to them. Finding out that humans weren't the dominant species on the planet was a big pill to swallow. Finding that out while being kept under an infamous vampire's roof was an even bigger pill. At least Gretchen had quit her incessant screaming. Had to be grateful for the little things.

Another thing I was grateful for was that Szilagyi wasn't carving into Marty anymore. I linked through the manacles to check on him several times a day, and while Szilagyi still had him restrained in that nondescript concrete room, he seemed to mostly ignore Marty. Vlad must've been right. Szilagyi was keeping Marty so he could use torturing him as a way to make me give in to his demands, but as long as I linked to Marty instead of the puppet master, he never knew when I was watching.

Eventually, Szilagyi would figure out why I hadn't tapped into him again. For now, he believed I didn't know he had Marty, but he was clever. He'd piece it together, and once he did, it would be open season on my friend. I could only hope we'd find him before that.

I'd tried to distract myself by digging into the sweetest, flakiest baklava I'd ever tasted. Then Maximus appeared. If his lack of bowing wasn't sufficient to indicate that something was wrong, one glance at his furious expression would've been enough.

"Lachlan's group was attacked while searching the old abbey near Reghin," he announced. "He and Ben were killed. The others are requesting assistance."

Vlad's chair upended from how fast he rose, and fire erupted from his hands. "This is the second time Szilagyi's men have attacked on my territory. It will be the last."

I stood, too, but in shock. "Ben, as in my friend Ben?"

Maximus shot me a single pitying glance. "Yes."

Denial made me argumentative. "That doesn't make sense. Why would *Ben* be out searching for Szilagyi? He's human!"

"He was training to become a vampire. Observing my men while they were on a scouting mission was good experience for him," Vlad replied shortly.

Was. Past tense. Somehow that drove the reality home more than Maximus's words. Ben, the cute, curly-haired boy who'd helped save my life by keeping his cool in a crisis, was dead. My lunch turned to rocks in my stomach.

Vlad wasn't suffering from denial over this news. "Maximus, you're coming with me," he stated. "Leila, don't leave the house for any reason. I'll return soon."

He gave me a brief, fierce kiss before striding away. If I hadn't gotten so used to touching him, that would've been that. I would've kept my right hand glued to my side and I never would've seen him again. But that hand grazed him during our kiss, and while he walked away, images flashed across my mind in full color yet hazy clarity.

I strode through a crumbling abbey located in the cleft of a mountain that seemed to crouch over it. My knives were splattered with crimson and the angry scent of smoke emanated from me. The fight was over, but I wasn't leaving until I'd searched every inch of these ruins. Szilagyi might have left a clue to his whereabouts. If not, I had other avenues to pursue.

"Take that one back to the house," I ordered, flashing a genial smile at the prisoner struggling in Maximus's arms. "We'll see what information he has."

Before Maximus could reply, a tremendous shudder shook the abbey, followed by the flash of flames and a deafening roar. Szilagyi rigged this place to explode was my first thought, followed instantly by Doesn't the fool remember that I'm immune to fire? But then the earth opened up in great cracking chasms, dragging me and the others down while the roof collapsed on top of us.

When the roaring and shaking increased, I realized the rest of Szilagyi's trap. He hadn't only set explosives in and under the abbey—he'd deto-

*nated the mountain above it, too. Rage and disbe-
lief filled me. No. I couldn't die like this.*

*I tried to pull myself out, but the earth shook so
violently I could find no purchase and it was too
congested to fly. Then multiple tons of rock landed
upon me as the mountain rained down, pinning
me with gargantuan pressure before tearing my
body apart from their weight and velocity.*

I came out of the vision with pain still arcing
through every limb. That didn't stop me from running out of the dining room and down the hall.
At the end of that long, gothic expanse, the front
doors were open and Vlad was between them, the
sunlit backdrop of a beautiful winter day highlighting his frame in ethereal white.

"Stop!" I shouted as loud as I could.

"He rigged the abbey *and* the mountain?"

A short laugh escaped Vlad. I didn't see anything funny about it. In fact, I was still shaking
from reliving his death.

"Yes. This whole attack is designed to bring you
there and then kill you."

He stroked his jaw. Sunshine played across half
his face while darkness etched the side turned away
from the windows. He was a kaleidoscope of light
and shadows, much like the startling contrasts of
his personality, and while he'd never looked more
vibrant or fierce, I still had to keep from running
my hands over him to reassure myself that he was
whole—and to make sure that I'd truly changed
his future from that horrible fate.

"Szilagyi knows I'd come to assist my men. He

must've planned this for weeks to have sufficient charges to bring down the mountain."

I let out a shaky laugh. "Gotta love an evil mastermind."

Vlad came over to me. He'd sat me down in the library when I kept screaming about how he'd die if he left. In hindsight, I should've been calmer in my warning. If he thought I was having an antiquated case of feminine hysterics over him going into regular danger, he might have ignored me and gone anyway.

He knelt in front of my chair, a smile flitting across his lips. "You're not prone to hysterics of any kind. That's why I listened when you said to stop."

Then he rose, going to the door. "Maximus!"

The blond vampire appeared at once. From his hard expression, he'd overheard everything.

"Take Shrapnel and four others to the abbey," Vlad stated. "Only one of you is to enter at a time to secure prisoners or collect our dead, and be conspicuous about who. You're being watched, but Szilagyi won't detonate the charges if he sees that I'm not there. He can only bring down the mountain once."

Maximus bowed to Vlad, but he stared at me while he did it, and the emotion in his gaze was unsettling. Then he left, and when Vlad turned back to me, his expression was harshly amused.

"I never thought a woman would come between us, but you might. If Maximus wasn't loyal to the last drop of blood in his body, I'd kill him for how he looks at you."

His tone was casual, but once again, I didn't

know if he was using a figure of speech or being serious.

"He's just grateful that you're not going to die today."

A brow rose. "You think this is the only time he's stared at you that way?"

I hadn't known that, but it didn't change anything. "You can't kill someone for how he *looks* at me. That's crazy."

I thought I heard, "I can if he keeps it up," but I wasn't sure, and his next words startled me into forgetting that.

"I'll see you in a few hours. I don't want to be far behind Maximus and the others."

"You're still going?" I blurted, astounded.

His smile was coldly anticipatory. "Not inside, but someone is watching that abbey in order to detonate those charges. With luck, it will be Szilagyi himself."

I wouldn't link to the puppet master to find out; if he was there, Szilagyi would sense that I was spying on him and leave. Instead, I grasped Vlad's arm with my right hand. If I saw another image of his death, I wasn't letting him leave this room no matter what he said.

Nothing. I let out a huge sigh of relief.

"Go ahead."

He stroked my cheek, that deadly little smile never leaving his face.

"Don't fear. Szilagyi needed to bring a mountain on me to kill me because I'm too powerful to fall in a normal ambush."

Then he was gone, my hair rustling with the speed of his exit. Vlad had the devil's own ego, but according to myth, pride was how Lucifer fell. His arrogance could turn out to be his Achilles' heel if Szilagyi exploited it the right way.

My teeth ground together. That wouldn't happen. Vlad would search for him in his way, and I'd do the same in mine. So far the memories locked inside those bones from the club hadn't yielded more information, but I'd keep sifting through them. With luck, one of them would lead to Szilagyi's location, or to whoever might be helping him. Vlad said he thought that some of his "allies" really wanted him dead. He'd been seeking out items for me to touch the night of the club fire, but since we'd discovered the identity of the puppet master, combing through people he knew to determine friend from foe had been back-burnered.

Still, *someone* had snatched Marty off the streets, and Szilagyi had been tucked in his concrete box at the time. It could've been the young-looking vampire with the prematurely silver hair, but as Vlad had said, Szilagyi had waited centuries to make his move because he needed enough people supporting him first. If Szilagyi was close to us as Vlad surmised, maybe his secret cadre of allies were, too . . .

As sudden as the bolt of electricity that had changed my life, I realized how we could find Szilagyi without spending weeks on painstaking searches of abandoned structures or poring through memories contained in his people's bones. All we'd have to do was to give the puppet master what he wanted.

Me.

Chapter 35

I'd been waiting in the indoor garden, and I jumped up as soon as I heard the front door slam accompanied by the mutter of voices. But close as I was to the entrance, I still only caught a glimpse of a red-soaked Shrapnel and Maximus restraining an equally bloody stranger before they disappeared toward the entrance to the underground stone staircase. More vampires I didn't recognize appeared and disappeared just as quickly, one of them cradling a body with achingly familiar curly brown hair.

Ben. Tears pricked my eyes that I fought back. I'd grieve for him properly later. Right now, I had to trap the vampire responsible for his death.

"I'll be there shortly," Vlad said in a tone I never wanted to hear directed at me. Then he strode toward me, smelling strongly of smoke and charred meat, but as usual, without a singe mark on him. The only things that marred his gunmetal-colored shirt and black pants were smears of red that required no explanation.

"Vlad—" I began.

"After your vision, I wanted you to see for yourself that I'm safe," he cut me off in a much gentler tone, "but I must join Maximus and Shrapnel now. We only managed to take one of Szilagyi's men alive and I intend to question him myself."

He'd already turned away, moving with that inhuman speed toward the entrance of the staircase that led to the dungeon, when my voice chased after him.

"I doubt he knows where he is. Szilagyi considered anyone at that abbey expendable since he intended to flatten it with the mountain. Besides, I know how to find him *tonight*."

That stopped him cold. He whirled to face me, green sparking in his coppery gaze.

"How?" A single word heavy with surprise and lethal intent.

"You're not going to like it, but hear me out."

His brow went up at that. Then he walked over in a leisurely way that somehow looked more dangerous than his supersonic bursts of speed.

"Continue."

I glanced around. I didn't see any of the dozen or so guards he had on this floor, but they were there. Maybe I should've waited until we had more privacy.

"I trust everyone in this house implicitly, so speak," Vlad stated, overhearing that in my mind.

"Let me go into town by myself. I'll pretend to run away, then link to Szilagyi and tell him I want to switch sides. He'll snatch me up, take me to where he is, and then I'll link to you and you can come and fry him."

Vlad said nothing. Time stretched until the silence was painful. I couldn't tell what he was thinking from his expression. It was so bland, he might have been daydreaming.

"Even if he didn't have his men kill you on sight, Szilagyi won't let you discover where he is," he finally replied. "He'd make sure you were unconscious when you were transported to his location. Before you arrived, he'd have you stripped of any objects, clothes included, that you could link through in order to contact me. Then, because he wouldn't trust you, he'd torture you until he was satisfied that every word you told him was the truth. In short, it's a brave but stupid idea."

I bristled. I might not be the world's most famous vampire like some arrogant people I knew, but I was *not* stupid.

"How do you think I connected to you when I was trapped at the club?" I snapped. "I hadn't seen you that day. Your essence wasn't on a single piece of my clothing, yet I still managed to link to you. Szilagyi could have me stripped naked without a single clue as to where I was, and in ten minutes, I could still be transmitting my location to you."

"I thought you'd brought something I touched with you," he muttered, his gaze narrowing. "How did you do it?"

I walked the last few paces that separated us, taking his hand and not flinching at the stains that coated it.

"You're in my skin," I said. "The day before, you'd traced my mouth with your hand and almost kissed me, so I followed the essence you imprinted on my lips back to you."

His eyes glowed, emerald against bronze, as

he brought my hand up and kissed it. The gloves I'd put on meant I didn't feel that silky brush of flesh, but I imagined that I could still feel his heat through the current-repelling material.

"He's no fool. He'll restrain you to keep you from touching anything, my dark-haired beauty. Even your lips."

"Then you'll imprint some of your essence onto my hand," I replied steadily. "You're probably doing that right now."

That fathomless stare bore into mine. "But how will you know where you are to tell me?"

"By following essence trails left in that room. Someone's bound to know where they are. Even if I can't pull a location from that, I can link to whoever ties me up and follow that person. Szilagyi won't know what I'm doing. You told me you can't hear my thoughts when I access my power. The rest of the time, it'll be the worst of the eighties songs in my head."

"He'll know you're using your power, and be suspicious as to why." He dropped my hand. "At best, he'll torture you until you can't block him from your thoughts and he learns what you intend to do. The answer is no."

"I'm not her, Vlad."

I said it knowing full well that I was tearing open his deepest scar, but I didn't let that stop me. He was merciless and unapologetic when he knew he was right. I'd be the same way.

"I *wouldn't* rather die than fall into your enemy's hands," I continued. "Even if everything you fear happens, I can take it. I've relived every terrible thing that people—human and otherwise—do to each other, and though it broke me once, I came back stronger. Szilagyi kidnapped me, tried to kill me, did kill my friend Ben, and is now holding my dearest friend hostage. I want revenge, and I want Marty safely back."

"I don't fucking believe it," a feminine voice gasped.

I swung around. Gretchen was about fifty paces behind me in the hall, and from the way her mouth hung open in a classic expression of disbelief, she'd overheard everything.

"What is wrong with you?" she went on, now marching toward us. "You'd think getting electrocuted, cutting your wrist, and dating a vampire would be close enough to death for anyone, but no! *You've* got to offer yourself up like a present to some freaky vampire who'll probably kill you!"

Of all the times for my sister to come out of her room. "Gretchen, now's not—"

"Not what, a good time?" she finished angrily. "It never is with you, Leila! But since you're about to try and get killed *again*, I'm not waiting. So here's a news flash: You're not the only one whose life went to shit when Mom died. And if Dad going emotionally catatonic afterward wasn't bad enough, you started shoving me away as soon as you came out of that coma."

"Shoving you away?" My voice rose as long-buried wounds rocketed to the surface. "I was a little busy trying to cope with getting Mom killed and electrocuting everyone while reliving their darkest secrets, remember?"

"Know what I remember?" While I'd gotten louder, Gretchen's voice became soft. "Coming home from school to find you in a bathtub full of blood. Calling 911 while holding your wrist together and praying I wouldn't have to bury someone else I loved, and I remember that as soon as you got better, you *left*."

If she'd screamed it at me, it would've been easier, but the quiet despair in her voice cut me deeper than that knife had back then. How could I explain the darkness I'd felt trapped in? Or the conviction I'd had afterward that if I didn't get away from her, I'd destroy her life more than I already had?

I couldn't explain, and in hindsight, it didn't matter.

"I was wrong, Gretchen," I said, blinking back tears. "I couldn't see past my own pain so I let it swallow me up. By the time I fought through it, you wanted nothing to do with me and Dad was wrapped up in his job again. Marty was all I had. That might have been my doing, but I abandoned you once when I shouldn't have. I'm not making that mistake with Marty now."

Then I went over and touched her cheek, my new gloves making it possible to do so without hurting her. She swatted my hand away, but her blue eyes were shiny, and redness peeked through her artfully applied makeup.

"I'm not trying to get killed, I just want this over with," I said softly. "Szilagyi wants me for my abilities. I'll let him think he's got me, and then Vlad will bring the pain."

She looked behind me to the vampire I still hadn't convinced yet. Her chin lifted.

"I'm supposed to trust *Dracula* with your life?"

"Not Dracula," I said with a faint smile as I turned around. "Vlad Tepesh, former *voivode* of Wallachia and the most arrogant, deadly, frightening man I've ever met."

His lips curled with disdainful amusement. "Compliments won't sway me any more than the word *please*, Leila."

"You take those as compliments?" Gretchen was incredulous.

"Of course." His smile bared his fangs. "She named all of my best qualities." Then that unrelenting gaze landed on me.

"I'll consider this as a possible option for later, but for now, the answer is still no."

"You promised," I said angrily, ignoring the look of surprised approval Gretchen shot toward Vlad. "You said if I came up with a plan to rescue Marty that didn't put your people in too much danger, you'd act on it. Well, here's the plan!"

"It endangers *you* too much" was his implacable reply. "As my lover, you're also considered one of my people."

"But not as valuable," I countered, a hurt I hadn't known I carried causing me to say the next part. "You've admitted that you'll never love me, so if something goes wrong, it's not that hard for you to find another girlfriend. Marty *does* love me, and he's the best friend I've got. I refuse to abandon him."

Vlad's eyes turned flat green and he stood so still that it made looking at him almost painful. Not a breath or twitch disturbed his beautiful, inflexible frame. Even his gaze didn't waver by the slightest degree. No one alive could hold himself so immobile, and it was as if he showed me the unbridgeable distance between us with that icily rigid posture.

"My people will continue to scour the area," he stated after a silence that sliced like knives across my emotions. "Starting tomorrow, you will also visit nearby prominent vampires' houses looking for a trace of Szilagyi's essence. Someone has to be assisting him. Once we find out who, that will lead us to your beloved friend."

Then he walked away, throwing one last scalding comment over his shoulder.

"If you need something else tonight, you'll find me in the dungeon, doing what I do best."

Chapter 36

I was glad Vlad was occupied with his gruesome task. It gave me time to mull our latest spat without worrying that he was clued into my thoughts since his "due diligence" policy meant the prisoner would receive all his attention. To help take the edge off, I took a bath and drank three glasses of wine while I quietly acknowledged the reason behind my unexpected venom toward him tonight. It wasn't just frustration because he refused to implement my plan. It was because I'd done the stupidest thing possible—started to fall in love with a man who would never love me.

Sure, Vlad might care for me in his fashion, but he'd never allow himself to be emotionally vulnerable enough to love. With his usual brutal honesty, he'd stated that up front. I thought I could deal with it, but somewhere along the lines, this complicated, mesmerizing, often terrifying man had gotten so deeply beneath my skin that he'd pierced my heart. Now, I wasn't so sure that having most, but not all, of him would be enough, and the hell of it was, I *still* didn't want to let him go.

Maybe I wasn't the only one with psychic abilities, I thought. Unless something drastic changed, Marty would be dead on in his prediction that Vlad would break my heart.

The last thing I felt like doing was sleep, but I'd need to be clearheaded tomorrow if I was using my powers to hunt for Szilagyi. A couple hours of restless tossing and turning later, I'd just started to drift off when sharp raps at the door startled me. Vlad wouldn't knock, and Maximus was busy helping him play hide-the-hot-poker on Szilagyi's captured henchman.

"Leila." My father's voice, followed by another series of raps. "Let me in. We need to talk."

Gretchen, I thought with a mental groan. She must've told Dad about what she overheard earlier. Why hadn't I asked Vlad to glare her into keeping her mouth shut?

I got up, putting a robe over my silk nightgown before I opened the door. My father came inside, his rapid but thorough glance taking in the area that was a smaller, paler green, and more feminine version of Vlad's bedroom.

"Where is he?" he asked without preamble.

"Torturing the hell out of an enemy combatant he captured tonight," I replied with equal abruptness.

"And this is the man you're risking your life for?"

Hugh Dalton had the kind of hardened, self-possessed stare that some vampires a hundred years older hadn't manage to perfect, and he turned it on me with full force. It bounced off.

"No, I'm risking it for myself, Marty, and a nice boy who helped save me recently and then got killed by the vampire I'm trying to take down," I said coolly.

He spun in a half circle and paced a few steps away, his limp making the strides shorter and less graceful than his former militarily precise movements.

"It's fine to hate me," he stated, jaw clenching as he shot a pain-filled look my way. "I failed your mother and I should have been there for you after the accident. I . . . part of me blamed you at first. You must know that after touching me, but deep down, there was never a question as to who was really responsible for her leaving and subsequent death. Me. So please, even though Marty was a better father to you than I, don't expose yourself to more vampires trying to save him. Keep punishing me, I deserve it. But don't endanger yourself more than you already have."

The truth we'd both known for years was finally spoken between us, and now that the words hung in the air, I felt a weight inside me ease. I'd told Vlad that talking about my father's deepest sin was too painful, but what I didn't realize was that the wound had only festered by ignoring it. Memories I hadn't allowed myself to recall sprang to my mind like clips from a movie reel: The four of us collecting seashells along the Virginia shoreline when my dad was stationed near D.C. How Gretchen, only eight, had fallen giggling into the sand while I taught her cartwheels. My dad sweeping us up and spinning us in circles until we screamed with delight while my mom laughingly chided him to put us down before we got dizzy.

The happy family we'd once been had broken

into pieces, but broken things could still heal. I was proof of that. *We are all more than the sum of our sins*, Vlad had said. If I wanted to lay down the burden I still carried over my darkest deed, then I had to forgive my father for his.

"We both failed her," I said, voice roughened from the pain of remembrance. "But if Mom were here, she'd tell us to get over it already. She'd say that nothing was more important than our family sticking together, and I—I want to listen to her now like I didn't back then."

He grabbed me, pulling me against him despite the current that made him shudder. His cane dropped to the floor as he put both arms around me, tucking my head into his shoulder as he'd done when I was a little girl. I embraced him back, keeping my right hand to my side since I hadn't gone to bed wearing my gloves. It had been so long since I'd hugged my dad, breathed in that blend of Old Spice and aftershave, yet somehow, the years of estrangement seemed to melt into mere months.

Then I gently pushed him away and gestured at his ruined leg. "A bomb blew your convoy apart and crippled your knee, but you still crawled toward the survivors and kept providing cover fire." Watery smile. "I'm going with Vlad to help look for the vampire who captured Marty, but it's not because I think he was a better father to me than you. It's because I'm the daughter of a man who refused to abandon the people he felt responsible for even when he was outgunned, bleeding, and only able to crawl."

"God, you're as stubborn as your mother," he said in a voice that cracked from emotion.

I laughed even though my vision blurred from tears. Guilt had made memories of my mom too painful to dwell on, but now it felt good to recall the various aspects of her personality.

"She *was* stubborn, wasn't she?"

My father opened his mouth to reply, but then Vlad entered the room. He didn't seem surprised to see my father. I guess he would've heard us talking as he approached.

Dad retrieved his cane and straightened to his full six-foot height. Then he stared at Vlad with an intensity that would've made a lesser man squirm.

"I don't care who or what you are. You fail to protect her while using her as a homing device on your enemy, and I'll find a way to kill you."

Tough as Hugh Dalton still was, it was the equivalent of a house cat threatening a Bengal tiger. To his credit, Vlad didn't laugh or crack one of his charmingly lethal smiles.

"Oh, I always protect what's mine," he replied, and his tone made me think he was speaking to me, too.

My dad glanced at me, sighed in a way that said he strongly disapproved of this relationship, and left, his salt-and-pepper head erect even if the rest of his body was no longer straight. I closed the door behind him but waited before turning around, not sure if I'd finished one confrontation only to have another.

"Done already?" I asked neutrally.

"I am. The others aren't" was his reply. A slithering noise followed, and then seconds later, the hiss of water.

I turned around. His clothes and shoes were in

a pile on the floor and he was in the shower. He hadn't bothered to turn the light on, but the door was open and he'd chosen to shower in my room. Not his. For Vlad, that was as much an offer to join him as a formal invitation.

I shouldn't. The smart move would be to go back to bed and sleep on all the concerns I had about this relationship, but I went into the bathroom instead, flipping on the light. The glass doors encasing the shower concealed nothing from my gaze.

Vlad's head was directly under the spray, dark brown hair appearing longer with the water sluicing through it. Red rivulets turned to pink and then ran clear as the blood that had soaked through his clothes washed away. From his taut nipples, the water was cold, but faint steam rose as it hit him. His body was even more tempting with that glistening wetness highlighting every ripple, hollow, and bulge. Long, thickly muscled legs set off the twin mounds of an ass that practically dared you not to stare at it. I did until he took a bar of soap and began rubbing lather over himself. White suds clung to sinewy arms, draped across broad shoulders, gathered in the hollow of a sculpted chest, slid down the enticing dark trail on his stomach, and then crowned in the crisp hair of his groin.

My gaze stayed there, and when he lathered flesh that grew and thickened under his hand, a distinct throb began in my loins. Vlad's seething masculinity was matched only by his incredible power, and though both were way out of my league, I was drawn to him like the proverbial moth to a flame. Without thought, I slipped out of my robe and then my nightgown.

When I met his gaze, it was bright green and predatory, making a shiver run through me that had nothing to do with being naked in a chilly room. I'd never had someone stare at me the way he did. As if he already owned me body and soul, and I was the only one who hadn't realized that yet. Moving like I was in a dream, I entered the shower, gasping when he pulled me to him. The water was icy, but his flesh was scalding, and the shock of burning and freezing at the same time was heightened by the intensity of his kiss. His mouth was molten bliss, tongue a sinuous brand; large hands igniting desire everywhere they roamed. My nails dug into the muscled expanse of his back, and he let out a low laugh at the current that jolted into him.

"I love how excitement sharpens your power." Growled as his mouth trailed down to my neck. "When you're about to come, your whole body vibrates. Most incredible thing I've ever felt."

Then he sucked the spot he'd pierced three days ago. The punctures had healed, but shards of erotic sensation coalesced under his mouth as if reminding me how good his fangs felt buried there. I'd gripped his head and stood on tiptoe to press him closer before I realized what I'd done.

Another chuckle, more darkly possessive than amused. "I told you you'd crave my bite." Then the graze of sharp teeth. "Is this what you want?"

It was, and between the taunting strokes of his fangs and his ruthlessly knowing hands, I could barely stay upright. Desire melted my bones to candle wax, and the wetness between my legs was from more than the shower spray, but the sensual triumph in his tone stirred something primal in me. Yes, he'd made me crave his bite, his kiss, and other things I could never have from him, but I refused to be the only one drowning in need.

I sank to my knees, grasping his hardened flesh with my left hand. I'd never done this before, but I'd seen it through the eyes of other people and it seemed basic enough. I closed my mouth over the tip of his shaft, running my tongue along heated flesh that was smoother than velvet, yet hard as marble. Something between a groan and a hiss sounded above me, and then his hand brushed my cheek.

"Don't stop."

The words were a command; his tone wasn't. It resonated with the intensity of a plea, probably the closest I'd ever come to hearing Vlad say please. Inwardly, I smiled. Who had what the other person wanted *now*?

His laughter ended on a harsh note as I took him deeper, tasting the faint, not unpleasant tang of soap. My teeth pressed against him from his girth, tongue curving along that rigid flesh as I encased him until I had to stop despite there being more. The cold water made me shiver, but Vlad's warm thighs pressed against my breasts, his scorching hands twisted in my hair, and my mouth was filled with his pulsing, hot length, making those parts of me deliciously burn. Always extremes with Vlad, but right now, I wouldn't have it any other way.

I withdrew my mouth with the same slowness he'd used the first time we made love, things low in me clenching with the memory. Then I encased him again to the accompaniment of another rasping groan. He sounded the same way when he was inside me, and my body responded. My breasts felt heavier, my nipples puckered to hypersensitivity, and my loins swelled while wetness slicked my inner thighs. That arousal made me move my head a little faster, draw on him harder. His grip on my hair tightened while that faint tang of soap changed to something salty.

"Yes. Like that."

His voice was almost guttural, and the next thing he muttered wasn't in English. I increased the pace and pressure, and the space between those harsh moans became shorter while he swelled even bigger in my mouth. His hips rocked against me, that firm grip on my head exciting because it was reminiscent of how tightly I clutched him when he went down on me. I wanted him to feel that same out-of-control passion so I pressed closer, sucked harder, moaning myself as his thighs rubbed my breasts to tease my nipples. Saliva escaped to coat the parts I couldn't fit as I moved even faster, my thighs clenching as the throbbing between my legs became unbearably intense.

Suddenly, I was off my knees and in his arms. The tile chilled my back as he yanked my legs around his waist and pressed me against the shower wall. Then his mouth crushed onto mine, muffling my groan at the feel of him against that aching part of me. A deep thrust made every nerve ending flare with blinding pleasure, tearing something very close to a scream from me. I was so wet that he slid in to the hilt, and when he began to withdraw, I shoved against him in wordless demand for more.

I felt him smile wide enough that for an instant,

I kissed only his teeth. Then he arched forward so strongly that his pelvis ground against my clitoris, the friction sending more rapture spiraling through me. I whimpered into his mouth, rocking against him, my thighs tightening on his waist and my arms lashed around his neck. Each cleave of his flesh amplified the pleasure, contracting invisible strings inside me until I felt like my body thrummed from ecstasy. Kissing him was a drug I never wanted free from, but when I began to get light-headed, I broke away to gulp in air.

He untangled my right hand from around his neck, bringing it to his mouth. "Look at me, Leila."

I hadn't been aware of closing my eyes, but at some point, I must have. I slit them open, my breath catching. Vlad's hair plastered to his shoulders in wet, dark sections, his muscles bunched with every moan-inducing thrust, and his eyes blazed so brightly that it was like looking at the sun. That stare held me more securely than his arm under my hips as he turned my hand over and then bit into the fleshy mound beneath my thumb.

The sound that came from me was almost animalistic. That was how he made me feel—feral, uninhibited—and as heat slid down my arm to slowly spread through the rest of me, those feelings grew. I needed more of his bite, his touch, his body, and especially the fierce emotion in his gaze as he swallowed my blood, and I needed it now.

That was why I whimpered in protest when, all too soon, he withdrew his fangs and released my hand.

"Your turn," he said throatily.

Then he bit into his wrist deep enough to leave

a gash before holding it to my mouth. Still lost in that primordial state, I swallowed without hesitation, not minding the harsh coppery taste because it was *his* blood. I licked until every drop was gone and the wound closed on itself. Once it did, he bit his wrist again. This time, I was the one who pulled it to my lips, sucking strongly as I stared at him.

The smile he flashed me was lust at its most savage. His movements became harder, faster, turning my moans into sharp cries. When his wound closed a second time, I let his wrist go and yanked his head down to mine. His tongue invaded my mouth with the same sensual brutality as his thrusts, and I met both with equal fervor. If he hadn't positioned his hands behind my head and hips, the tile behind me might have cracked from how fiercely he drove into me, but I didn't care. His blood slid like fire through my veins, filling me with even more wildness. Nothing existed except this moment, and as my whole body shuddered from the overload of ecstasy, I didn't even notice the cold anymore. All I felt was heat, inside and out.

Chapter 37

I'd assumed Vlad would accompany me on every scouting mission, but he didn't. Sometimes, he sent me to one vampire's house while he went to another and brought back items for me to touch. It took me days to figure out why. He was sending me to allies least likely to betray him, taking on the riskier vampires himself. In that way, he kept his promise to broaden the search for Marty while still protecting me from situations he considered too dangerous.

It was annoying and touching at the same time, adding further chaos to my already tumultuous emotions. If Vlad was the heartless creature he made himself out to be, he'd utilize me to his best advantage by throwing me into the most perilous situations. But he didn't. Which was the real Vlad? The one whose heart was forever out of reach, or the man who seemed to prize my safety more than the quickest path to vengeance?

I pondered that as the black SUV I was in came to a stop outside a set of tall iron gates. Maximus drove, Shrapnel rode shotgun, and I was alone in the backseat. Another SUV filled with six ad-

ditional guards followed closely behind us. We
were fifteen minutes from Oradea, Romania, but
to look around, you wouldn't guess that a bustling
city was nearby. This gate was tucked inside thick
woods, the long gravel road leading to it nearly invisible from the turnoff—assuming you found the
secluded road leading to *that*. The owner of this
property either liked his privacy or he hated having
unexpected visitors, which was exactly what the
three of us were.

Maximus rolled down his window and pressed
a button on the metal console that jutted out a
few feet from the ground. I couldn't hear a camera
zooming in on his rugged features, but I had no
doubt that his image was being transmitted.

"*Vlad Tepesh küldöttei Gabriel Tolvai—hoz
jöttek*," he stated.

I only recognized the name. Gabriel Tolvai, an
ally of Vlad's that, as per usual, he *didn't* suspect
of being in league with Szilagyi. Still, it was one
more name to cross off a list, even if Tolvai lived in
a secluded area where the closest neighbors seemed
to be of the animal variety.

The tall gates slid open and we drove through
them. After we traveled the length of a football
field, Maximus pulled up to a stately, two-story
white house with ochre-colored trim. The old
world architecture looked like an aesthetic choice
rather than the home's actual age, and while the
house was large, it was still less than a fourth the
size of Vlad's home.

Two bearded guards carrying automatic weapons stood by what looked like the main entrance.
Since this was a vampire residence, I guessed the big

guns were filled with silver bullets instead of lead. Maximus and Shrapnel didn't seem concerned. When we got out of the car, they didn't even look at the guards who held open the double doors for us, so I mimicked their aloof demeanor. Our other armed escort got out but stayed by the vehicles, their presence as threatening as it was silent. In my usual pattern, once I crossed the threshold into Tolvai's house, I began to recite the worst songs the eighties had to offer. No way would I risk running into another mind reader unprepared.

A slender boy with russet-colored hair walked down the hall toward us. He wore jeans, sneakers, and a black jacket slung over an Ed Hardy T-shirt. He didn't even look old enough to drink in the States, so I was surprised when Maximus and Shrapnel inclined their heads at him.

"Greetings from our sire, Tolvai," Maximus said formally.

Tolvai responded with a burst of dialog that I didn't understand a word of. It wasn't Romanian—I'd gotten better at recognizing certain words in that language—but my confusion was cut short when Shrapnel held up a hand.

"Vlad requests that you speak English in front of his guest so she understands everything that is being said."

"Is that right?" Tolvai replied, the words richly accented.

Amber eyes swept over me. Once I stared into them, I didn't know how I'd ever mistaken Tolvai for someone younger than me. The weight of centuries reflected in those jewel-colored eyes, and the way his gaze raked me from facial scar to shoes said that a human was less than worthless to him.

"If Vlad wishes, I shall repeat myself," Tolvai said, smiling at me the way a great white shark would at a plump seal. "What has happened that Vlad sent his most senior guards to my house without even a phone call to inform me of their coming?"

"Recently, four vampires set fire to one of Vlad's businesses in southern Suceava," Maximus stated. "Three of the perpetrators were killed, but one escaped. Vlad is asking all of his allies to assist him in finding this last arsonist."

The barest smile touched Tolvai's lips. "Of course I will offer my assistance. Any attack on a vampire's territory must be swiftly avenged lest his enemies take it as a sign of weakness."

I was surprised by the veiled taunt. Tolvai hadn't been on Vlad's suspect list, but maybe he should reconsider. Shrapnel also didn't seem to appreciate the subtext. His glare could have burned holes into Tolvai's deceptively young-looking features, but the vampire didn't show the slightest amount of concern. In fact, when his gaze dipped dismissively to me again, either he was loyal—albeit sarcastic—or word of what I could do hadn't spread to him yet.

Both were put to the test when Shrapnel said in a mild tone, "Then you won't mind if Leila touches a few things in your home."

Tolvai's expression registered confusion, but not alarm. "*Miért?* But why?" he amended in English.

"Because Vlad asks you to," was Maximus's reply.

Anyone could discern the challenge wrapped in

the large vampire's silky tone. Tolvai's lips tightened, and if it weren't for those ancient eyes, he'd have resembled a teenager about to have a full-on temper tantrum. For several tense moments, I wondered if he'd refuse. But then he swept out his hand.

"If Vlad wishes, then she may do so. But to quote the American saying, if she breaks anything, she buys it."

I glanced at Maximus and Shrapnel as I took off my right glove. "I'll let you know if I find anything."

"Anything like what?" Tolvai asked sharply. "Do you suggest that I am involved with this arsonist?"

"Of course not." Butter wouldn't have melted in Shrapnel's cool reply. "But wouldn't you want to know if one of your people went behind your back and broke truce with Vlad?"

I walked farther down the hall, letting the vampires handle this power contest themselves. After a tense silence, Tolvai bit out, "Vlad and I will have words about this." Then he swept past me in a blur, disappearing up the staircase. If I were a vampire, I imagined the scent of his anger at having his home searched would have clogged my nostrils.

I glanced back at Maximus and Shrapnel, shrugged, and then continued on my way. They knew by now that I concentrated better if they didn't hover over me. Tolvai's entrance hall wasn't nearly as impressive as Vlad's, but I liked the pastel palette more than Vlad's tendency toward darker, gothic colors. I detoured at the first room, an elegant lounge with a white marble fireplace and ceilings three times as high as I was tall.

Once inside, I ignored the fancy figurines or other objets d'art. Years of training myself on what *not* to touch made it easy to choose the most essence-heavy objects. Despite their high traffic level, light switches and lamps were out of the question, but that left doorknobs, handles of any kind, drawers, armrests, pens, glasses, and the like. After I handled various objects that showed images of feeding, sex, and some harsh discipline of Tolvai's staff, I moved on to the next room. Then the next one. Maximus and Shrapnel stayed in the hallway, allowing me my space while the constant collision of memories versus reality made me feel like I was on a vivid acid trip.

I had just stroked a sunshine-colored couch in the fourth room when the lounge dissolved, turning into bare concrete walls with a single wooden door. Two vampires I recognized were inside. One was nailed to the wall with silver, the other typing on an iPad while seated on a bed of furs.

Szilagyi cocked his head and then rose. I'd been mentally singing as a defense against any mind readers in Tolvai's house, and the lyrics had announced my invisible presence before I could disconnect.

"My little psychic spy, I wondered when you would return," Szilagyi purred. Then he walked over to Marty and a knife appeared in his hand as if by magic. "You've missed some of the fun, but not all of it."

You don't need to hurt him, I thought, willing to say anything to stop what I knew was about to happen. *I, ah, already want to switch sides.*

Szilagyi gave me a smile so hard that it could

cause ice to fracture. "If that's true, then why are you blocking your thoughts behind that song . . . Leila?"

I ignored his use of my real name. As Vlad said, it was only a matter of time until Szilagyi picked up my paper trail.

There could be other mind readers here, I improvised. *If so, they can't pick up all my thoughts under the music, but I'm risking my life contacting you and that should show I'm serious.*

Szilagyi didn't know I'd connected to him accidentally, but his essence on the armrest had been so strong, it had acted like an instant messaging system.

"Ah." Szilagyi appeared to mull that. Then, "Why did you abandon your loyalty to Tepesh? You seemed very staunch in it the last time we spoke."

I cast about for any reason he might believe. *Things changed since then. You told me Vlad was faking nice, and you were right.*

The best lies were steeped in truth, Marty had once told me. I seized on that and continued, hiding my thoughts behind those endlessly repeating lyrics.

Vlad even seduced me to get me emotionally attached to him, but since the first day he brought me to his house, he's had people monitoring my family. When you kidnapped Marty, he grabbed them to use as ammunition against me. Still, joke's on him because my family and I have been estranged for years. Marty's the only one I care about. That's why I snuck something of yours with me and contacted you as soon as I got here.

"And where is here, Leila?" Szilagyi asked smoothly.

My lies had worked too well, and now they'd trapped me. I paused. Szilagyi ran a hand along Marty's face in a mockery of a caress. Marty said nothing, but he gave the faintest shake of his head. Even after everything Szilagyi had done to him—and was about to do—he didn't want me to tell Szilagyi. He truly was the most loyal friend I had.

Despite this, I couldn't betray Vlad, not to mention get Maximus and Shrapnel killed by answering Szilagyi because they wouldn't let him take me without a fight. *I can't tell you*, I thought while my stomach felt like it twisted into knots.

Szilagyi clucked his tongue. "How unfortunate." Then his knife flashed out. Marty doubled over as much as his restraints allowed. Something thick and red hit the ground.

Stop! I mentally roared.

"I will when you tell me where you are," Szilagyi countered. His knife kept flashing. More gore splattered to the floor and Marty screamed in a way that would haunt my nightmares.

I can't! I replied with another mental bellow. *Maximus and Shrapnel are with me. If you come, they'll kill me before they allow you to take me.*

"Maximus *and* Shrapnel?" That made Szilagyi pause, but not in fear. In obvious delight. Clearly I'd just added a cherry to the already yummy sundae of my situation.

Yes, and if they realize they're outnumbered, they'll kill me, I repeated, seeking a reason that would dissuade him. *I'm no good to you dead, so give me a little time. Vlad's sending me all over the*

*place, as you may have heard. I'll contact you as
soon as circumstances are better.*

Szilagyi spun away from Marty to stare at what
would have been eye level to me if I'd actually been
there.

"All right," he said.

I was so surprised by his capitulation that my
mind briefly went blank. "But if you're lying to
me," he went on, "your friend will experience such
pain that hell will be a relief once I finally kill him."

My lack of belief in heaven or hell didn't prevent
me from shuddering at the threat. *I'm not lying.
I'll contact you as soon as I'm under less heavy
guard. Vlad's already getting lax by letting me go
out without him.*

Fear for Marty made every mental syllable ring
with the illusion of truth. After a long moment,
Szilagyi gave me another frosty smile.

"You have a week to contact me with a location
to collect you. Otherwise, your friend will suffer
for your betrayal."

Got it, I thought, stuffing down my doubts over
how I'd pull that off.

His dark brown stare seemed to reach into my
soul. "Then I'll hear from you soon, Leila."

I dropped the link and sank to my knees, still
blasting away songs from an era where rockers
had longer hair than their girlfriends. That awful
gray room was replaced by shades of pale blue,
yellow, and peach, the tall windows letting in the
radiance of a sunny winter's day. Fear that I'd
just condemned Marty to a terrible death battled
with determination. *You can do this,* I chanted to
myself. Someone at Tolvai's had a connection to

Szilagyi. We'd find out who, Vlad would interrogate the hell out of him, and we'd find Szilagyi's location and save Marty in time. I kept repeating it until I forced myself to believe it.

The attack came less than twenty minutes later.

Chapter 38

I was still searching Tolvai's house to see if I could determine who he'd been in collusion with when the first window shattered. I knew better than to assume anything benign caused it, so I ran to look for Maximus and Shrapnel. In the seconds it took me to see them in the entrance hallway, the house was under a full-scale assault.

Glass exploded inward as vampires crashed through multiple windows, converging on the two men in the hallway. More violent sounds came from outside, too, and gunfire made me instinctively hit the floor. Once there, I froze, not sure if I should try to help, or if I'd only get in their way. My decision was taken away when suddenly I was snatched up from behind, my right wrist held in an iron grip. Whoever grabbed me cursed from the voltage he absorbed, but I couldn't hit him with my full power. I couldn't even connect to Vlad and tell him of the attack because my hand was immobilized.

Then a voice hissed in heavily accented English,

"Quit struggling! Szilagyi has ordered me to protect you."

Tolvai. It wasn't one of his people who were in league with Szilagyi. It was *him*. No wonder Szilagyi had capitulated so easily at my refusal to tell him where I was. Tolvai hadn't stormed off in ire over his house being searched, but to message Szilagyi about his unexpected visitors. That's how he'd known where to attack. When I first saw Szilagyi typing away on his iPad, he'd probably been ordering the assault.

Tolvai hustled me up the stairs and into an upper bedroom closet. Meanwhile, the battle sounds continued. From the shouts and how the walls and floors shook, Szilagyi had attacked with overwhelming force. Maximus, Shrapnel, and the other guards wouldn't have a chance. Tears burned my eyes, but I refused to face my enemy crying. I waited, hoping Tolvai's grip on my wrist would let up enough for me to do *some*thing, but it never did.

When the shouts and tremors finally stopped, the silence drowned me in a tidal wave of dread. Were Maximus and Shrapnel still alive? Then a man's voice called out, of course not in English. Tolvai responded in the same language, and he sounded relieved.

"What?" I asked.

He didn't reply, which was no surprise, but he did move away as though being in close proximity to me had been distasteful. Before I could snap a current at him or connect to Vlad, an ominously familiar person appeared in front of me.

"Hello again," purred the silver-haired vampire who'd left me to die in a burning club.

I didn't see his fist. Only felt the explosion of pain that darkness quickly snuffed out.

I had no idea how long I was out, but I awoke with a chemical taste in my mouth and ropes digging into my wrists and ankles. No shocker there, but my head wasn't pounding, which did surprise me until I remembered how much of Vlad's blood I'd been drinking recently. That would accelerate my healing. It wouldn't help with the biting cold temperature, however. Immediately, my teeth began to chatter, but before another thought could cross my mind, I began to recite the lyrics to Right Said Fred's "I'm Too Sexy." Not an eighties song, but sufficiently irritating on endless repeat.

When I risked opening my eyes, I didn't see gray concrete walls, Szilagyi, or Marty. Instead, I was in a wooden stall, the straw-covered ground smelling strongly of horses, and I was naked except for a scratchy blanket tucked around me.

I wasn't, however, alone.

The silver-haired vampire lounged on top of the high stall door, balanced effortlessly on the narrow strip of wood. He stared down at me with a little smirk that would've made me shiver even if I wasn't already doing so from the cold.

"Expecting someone else?" he asked in a smug tone.

I allowed a single *Oh crap* to slip through my thoughts before I buried that under lyrics declaring that I was too sexy for my shirt—not that I was wearing one at the moment. Just because Szilagyi wasn't in sight didn't mean he wasn't close by, tuning in to my head.

"In fact, I was," I said, and my reply would've been smooth if not for my teeth chattering. "Where's Szilagyi?"

Silver Hair jumped down, sticking the landing perfectly, of course. He was dressed for the cold in a long suede jacket over a cream sweater, and the material of his chocolate-colored pants looked like corduroy. But what drew my gaze were his gloves. He wore the same oversized, industrial ones I'd used before Vlad got me the normal-looking pair. They weren't the only things in Silver Hair's hands, either. He also carried a wooden mallet and a knife that looked like it was made from ivory.

My previous *Oh crap* upgraded to an *Oh shiiiit!*

"You told Szilagyi you've had a change of heart about joining his side, but he's not convinced," the vampire replied cheerfully. "Until he is, he's not letting you near him in case you try to summon Vlad and ambush him."

I schooled my features not to show fear, but I felt like my stomach had dropped to my knees.

"How am I supposed to summon Vlad if I don't have anything of his to link through? And more importantly, how can I convince Szilagyi of my sincerity if I'm nowhere *near* him?"

The vampire's grin widened, and his flipped his weapons in the air before catching them. "That's where I come in."

It was the answer I'd expected—and dreaded. He'd even made sure to pick torture items made of wood and bone instead of the more highly conductive steel, and his gloves would provide protection against any currents that did slip through. Despair knotted in me. I'd wanted to give myself to Szilagyi to trap him, but Vlad had vetoed that plan. He'd said Szilagyi wouldn't believe me and would torture me into telling the truth. Looked like he was right.

"You leave her alone!" a familiar voice called out.

"Marty?" I asked in astonishment.

I looked around, but although I was in one of many stalls, the walls were so high that I couldn't see into any of them.

"Yeah, I brought him," Silver Hair said. "I doubt you're tough, but you surprised me once before. So even if you can hack what I do to you, I bet you'll break at what I do to *him*."

"Why don't you light up your peepers and use vampire hypnotism to ask if I'm a double agent?" I snapped, trying a different tactic.

He laughed. "Because Marty tells me that due to your condition, you're given regular doses of vampire blood." He tapped the corner of his eye. "Means you're immune to these."

I knew that, which was why I'd hoped to trick him with my answers, but my gamble that Marty hadn't told them of my need to imbibe vampire blood had backfired. All of my gambles had backfired, from the look of things. Tremors kept wracking me from the freezing temperature, and the macabre thought came that it would make my blood run slower when Silver Hair cut me.

My gloves were gone, wrists tied to two separate wooden posts, but I could still touch my right hand with my fingers. As unobtrusively as possible, I slid them over my palm. Vlad's thread jumped out like a flare embedded beneath my thumb, but no one else's. Silver Hair must've used his own current-

repelling gloves when he transported and then restrained me.

The bad news kept coming. I'd assured Vlad
that even tied up and naked, I could direct him
to my location, but I'd counted on Szilagyi taking
me to where *he* was. Not having Silver Hair tie me
up in a stable where the only essences I could pull
from the wood beneath my hand were from horses.

Silver Hair yanked the blanket off. The stables
weren't windy, but it still felt like the cold punched
me all over. I thought I'd been freezing before, but
without the slight retention of body heat from the
blanket, I shook so hard that the rope around my
wrists and ankles began to cut into my skin.

Either Silver Hair liked seeing everything jiggle
or he really enjoyed his pre-torture interlude. His
cornflower-blue eyes became flecked with emerald
as he perused me.

"Where oh where shall I start?" he wondered
aloud.

Marty began to yell again, cursing and promising revenge if Silver Hair hurt me. It only seemed
to amuse the vampire. My despondency grew until
it felt like it was choking me. I could contact Vlad,
but all I'd be able to tell him was that I was in a
stable. I didn't even know if I was still in Romania,
or how long I'd been unconscious to give him any
sort of a search grid.

*This is what you get for thinking you could out-
smart someone centuries older than you*, an insidious inner voice taunted. *For all your big talk, you
and your friend are going to die, and there's nothing you can do about it but scream.*

FUCK you! I thought, something steely rising in me. That dark inner voice had been responsible for my worst mistakes, like tattling about my father's affair out of spite instead of love, cutting my wrist, and walking away from my family after I healed. I refused to let it direct my actions now. Yes, all my plans had gone to shit, but I'd make new ones. I might indeed die, but it would be fighting every step of the way.

"Wh-wh-what's your name?" I asked, teeth chattering so hard that it made me stutter.

He snorted. "Trying to stall? That won't work with me."

"N-n-not trying to stall, but if y-y-you're going to t-torture me, we sh-sh-should at least be on a first n-name basis."

He laughed. Under other circumstances, I would've said someone with his pleasant features, vivid blue eyes, and runner's build was attractive, but nobody pulled off cute when they were about to carve into you as if you were a juicy steak.

"I was born Aron Razvan, but for the past three centuries, I've called myself . . . eh, the English translation would be Rend."

It came as no surprise that his chosen nickname implied violence. No wannabe badass would choose a moniker like Petal.

"Leila D-Dalton," I managed. If I shook any harder from the cold, I might dislocate something.

Another jovial smile. "Well, Leila, this will hurt, but if I find that you're not trying to trick Szilagyi, then after I heal you, I'll send you to him." His smile faded, and green covered his gaze until not a speck of blue remained. "But if you are trying to fuck us, you *will* regret it."

Then that pale ivory knife slashed across my shoulder, signaling that Rend was done talking.

Chapter 39

 Over the past twelve years, I'd gotten familiar enough with pain to classify it in stages of mild, moderate, acute, intense, excruciating, and freeing. That last one might sound strange, but if you've been pushed past every other milestone and were still alive, the final one—the one that inevitably leads to the sweet nothingness of death—is a relief.

This was the third time I'd entered the "freeing" stage with Rend. Like the other two instances, soon he'd use one of many irrigation syringes he'd prefilled with his blood and force-feed it to me, healing the damage he'd done before I ruined his plans by dying. But right now, hovering over the precipice between life and death, I experienced a moment of clarity.

All I had to do was hang on until he switched to torturing Marty. He hadn't made me confess my true loyalties yet, and he was getting irritated. Soon he'd seek to break me through my love for my friend, but Rend didn't know that every crimson drop he forced me to swallow did more than heal my body—it fueled my power. I felt it growing, surging against my skin, burning inside with a seething intensity that would have killed me if not for all the vampire blood I kept swallowing. It was all I could do to contain the rivers of electricity that tried to push their way out of my hand. If Rend hadn't been so careful to touch me only with his nonconductive weapons, plastic syringes, and thick rubber gloves, he might have sensed the danger. As it was, his precautions would be the death of him.

Touching him might not be enough, after all. I'd see his worst sin, but perhaps not where he'd been before he grabbed me from Tolvai's. The only way I'd definitely find where I was—and hopefully where Szilagyi was—would be through Rend's eyes.

Or, more accurately, through the memories in his bones.

I felt darkness overwhelming me when he cursed in something that sounded like a cross between Latin and Romanian. Then, he shoved a needleless syringe in my mouth and I tasted his cold blood again. That liquid seemed to turn to fire after it slid down my throat and hit my bloodstream. My body convulsed while it healed, leaving me shaking from the surge of power and the agony of countless nerve endings knitting back together.

"Either you're telling the truth, or you're strong as fuck," Rend muttered in English this time. "Let's find out."

By the time I blinked enough to clear my vision, I saw the stable door was open. Directly across from my stall, in another open stable, was Marty. He wasn't tied to the posts with rope like I was, but speared through in multiple places with silver.

From how pale he was, he hadn't fed in several days, and his blood barely pooled around the stab wounds.

Silver poisoning, starvation, and draining of blood were the most efficient ways to negate a vampire's strength. Rend was no amateur, as he'd proved. But what simultaneously broke my heart and filled me with feral purpose was seeing the crimson streaks on Marty's cheeks. He'd cried while listening to Rend torture me, so much that his tears had turned from pink to red.

"I hope Vlad rips your guts out and burns them in front of you," Marty snarled at Rend.

The vampire laughed. "I've watched him do that to someone, you know. The smell is horrible."

Marty spat when Rend came nearer. "If you were ever that close to him, then he should have killed you."

His back was to me, so I couldn't see Rend's expression, but his tone turned colder than the air around us.

"Oh, he did worse than kill me. He cut me off from his line mere months after turning me, all because I broke some of his endless, stupid rules. For decades, I was every vampire's bitch until Szilagyi found me and took me in, but enough about the past." He took those rubber gloves off and tossed them aside. "Your turn."

Rend's body briefly blocked Marty from view as he squatted down until he was nearly the same level as Marty's four-foot, one-inch frame. Then he took a silver knife from an open satchel on the ground and waved it in a taunting manner.

"You mentioned ripping guts out. Sounds like

a good place to start. Speak up if you have something to tell me, Leila."

"Don't worry about me, kid," Marty rasped, and though his voice was hoarse, the words were firm. "I'll be okay."

"No, you won't," Rend replied with obvious relish.

Yes, he will, I thought savagely, and released the energy roiling beneath my skin.

Ozone scented the air, replacing the smell of horses. The rope around my right wrist fell away as a sizzling strand of white cut through it. Rend cocked his head at the crackling sound, glancing over his shoulder at me.

I aimed everything I had at him, channeling it in a rush of power that made my hand feel like it exploded when electricity burst from it. A glowing lash ripped across Rend's upper body, shooting out from me so fast, he still had that quizzical expression when he glanced down at where it hit him.

"That hurt," Rend said clearly.

Then everything north of his collarbones pitched over into the hay. The rest of his body remained crouched in front of Marty, that silver knife still gripped in his hand. The open area of gore where his head, neck, and shoulder used to be revealed Marty's stunned face above it. He stared at Rend's body—both parts of it—and then at me, mouth opening and closing wordlessly as if he'd been the one who was decapitated. The long current of white coming from my hand fizzled and then disappeared with another whiff of ozone.

"He s-s-o had that c-coming," I said through madly chattering teeth. Exultation filled me, but it didn't stamp out my lingering fury. I had to suppress the urge to summon another bolt and keep whipping Rend's remains until he resembled the hay beneath him. That frothing energy continued to pulse inside me, fueled by pain, rage, and about a pint of vampire blood.

"He's not alone," Marty hissed.

Later, it would bother me that I was happy by this news. I cut through the rest of my ropes in time to be standing naked but unrestrained when a Mediterranean-looking man suddenly appeared in the space between me and Marty's stalls.

My hand flashed out, those currents seeking the wild rush of another release. A line of blazing white arced from my skin, cracking across the man's neck. Just like with Rend, his head hit the ground before the rest of his body.

"One more," Marty whispered, still staring at me in shock.

I wanted to put on one of the dead vampire's clothes—and shoes!—but footsteps were already coming down the stable's narrow hallway. I snatched up the discarded horse blanket and darted out of the stall, hoping whoever was coming hadn't noticed the dead man's legs sticking out of Marty's stall.

From the preternaturally fast way the blond man turned and headed in the opposite direction, he had. I ran after him, extending my right hand and willing all those remaining currents out of me. But my level of power had decreased after two deadly releases. The lash that snapped across the blond vampire brought him to his knees, but it was too low and didn't cut all the way through him. I hesitated. For all intents and purposes, I was unarmed and he was undead. That meant I didn't stand a chance.

Then I forced that thought back with recklessness born of desperation. He *couldn't* get away and warn Szilagyi. If Maximus and Shrapnel were still alive, that would result in their death sentences. Low voltage or no, I had to stop him.

The vampire pushed himself upright, and it was a toss-up as to which he looked more astonished over—the gash that had cut halfway through his torso, or me charging at him while clutching a dirty blanket. Then it was my turn to be shocked as, instead of attacking, he staggered and began to run *away* from me.

I chased him, all the vampire blood I'd drunk plus his still-healing wound making me able to keep up. He ran out of the stables and into a snow-covered field. The sun was setting, but it was still light enough for me to see the cell phone he took out of his pants. Panicked, I snapped my hand at it. White flashed through the air, hitting the phone as if driven by missile lock. It blasted apart and he shot a wild look over his shoulder at me before accelerating his pace.

The distance grew between us. For all my increased abilities, I was still human and he was still *not*. In seconds, he'd be too far ahead for me to see. Even if that didn't happen, I had to get warm or I'd die. The snow felt like razors on my bare feet and despite the blanket, I shook so hard that I began to stumble. In a last-ditch effort, I aimed my right hand at his head and shoved all the waning energy I had toward it.

Red exploded as if I'd hit him with a paint gun pellet. The vampire staggered, turning in my direction. That's when I saw that the back of his head was missing. Despite everything I'd seen over the years, let alone experienced today, I gagged, but I didn't slow down. He fell over, thick dark blobs staining the snow, yet he wasn't dead. His hands swatted at his head in an uncoordinated manner, as if some thread of consciousness urged him to stuff his brains back inside the ruins of his skull.

I reached him in the next minute. He still looked dazed, but part of his head had already begun to heal. Soon he'd be fully recovered—and *pissed*. I fell to the ground next to him, avoiding most of his wild swipes as I began to search him. My teeth chattered until I tasted blood and my hand shook so badly that it took a few tries to get inside his coat. His eyes were open but unfocused, the sounds he made horrible animalistic grunts. Even when a few of his blows landed, I continued to tear at his clothes. Two hands would've been more thorough, but I couldn't afford to lose any time reliving his sins.

Something stabbed me in his inner coat pocket. At the same moment, those smoky brown eyes focused on me with terrifying clarity. Without even looking to see what metal the weapon was, I yanked it out and shoved it into his heart, twisting with all of my might.

Chapter 40

 I trudged into the stables wearing clothes and shoes several sizes too big. I'd even put on the vampire's shirt despite its bloody rip in the chest. I was too cold to be picky.

Marty would've heard me coming, but until I appeared in the entrance of his stall, I don't think he'd allowed himself to really believe that I was okay. He stared me as I dropped to my knees in front of him. Two fat red tears rolled down his cheeks.

"You made it, kid."

I began ripping the knives out with hands that still shook, my own tears falling onto my cheeks. Their fleeting warmth was welcome. I didn't know if I'd ever feel free of the cold that seemed to have turned my bones to icicles within me.

"You made it, too," I said huskily.

The truth of those words made more tears fall, blurring my vision as I yanked out the last of the knives. Once Marty was free, he grabbed me in a hug so tight, it would have been painful if not for how happy I was to be held by him again.

Then he pushed me back. "We gotta hurry, kid.

Now that Szilagyi *and* Vlad are after us, we need to disappear."

I blinked, thinking hypothermia must be messing with my ability to comprehend. "What do you mean, we need to disappear?"

He sighed. "I heard Rend say that you agreed to betray Vlad to Szilagyi, so he'll come after you with everything he's got. With luck, they'll keep each other occupied long enough for us to leave Europe—"

"I didn't betray him, Marty," I interrupted. "Rend was right. I lied to Szilagyi. In fact, I need to search through Rend's bones to find out where he is and then contact Vlad with the information."

"Vlad let you get captured?" Marty shook his head in disgust. "I warned you that he was ruthless. Vlad doesn't care about what happens to you as long as he gets what he's after."

"That's not true," I said sharply. "We were searching some vampire's house when Maximus, Shrapnel, and I got ambushed, but you are right about one thing. I *did* offer to let Szilagyi capture me in order to lead Vlad to him. He refused."

Marty's expression said that he couldn't believe I was the same person he'd known for years. Maybe I wasn't. The old Leila had a tendency to hide from her problems while suppressing her unwanted powers. This Leila was running toward them while milking her abilities for all they were worth.

"How long do you think we have until Szilagyi realizes there's a problem?" I asked, moving to the next issue.

"Not long. He stayed in frequent contact with

Rend," he muttered, still giving me that who-are-you look.

I stood. "Then I better get started with Rend's bones. If Maximus and Shrapnel are still alive, they won't be for long after Szilagyi realizes Rend and the others are dead. Or he'll move and we'll have to hunt for his location all over again—"

"I know where he is."

My mouth fell open long enough for my teeth to stop chattering. "You know where Szilagyi is *right now*?"

"Of course. They didn't worry about blindfolding me when they brought me to him. They never intended to let me live."

I bent and hugged him even harder this time before tweaking his bushy brown sideburns in delight. "You are beautiful, you know that? Wait while I link to Vlad and tell him."

"Or you could use Rend's cell phone," he pointed out.

Marty nodded at the satchel a few feet away. Sure enough, next to several silver knives and other gruesome-looking instruments was a cell phone.

"Use his gloves to make the call," Marty went on, baring his fangs in a fierce grin. "He won't need them anymore."

I stripped the gloves off Rend's now-shriveled hands and wiped the remains of my blood onto his stylish suede coat. Then I grabbed the cell phone . . . and paused.

"Do you know Vlad's number?"

Marty recited it, and ended up punching in the numbers himself because I kept messing them up with the thick gloves. Vlad answered on the second ring.

"Who is this?" No niceties, just a demand. That was my guy.

"It's me. We were attacked at Tolvai's. I'm with Marty now, but Szilagyi isn't here, obviously, or I wouldn't be calling you on a cell. Marty knows where he is, though, and—"

"Where are *you*, Leila?" Vlad interrupted, his tone rough.

I'd thought it would take days to feel like I'd thawed out inside, but hearing him ask where I was before his centuries-old enemy's location made a warm glow spread through me.

"Actually, I don't know. Marty, do you know where we are?"

He shrugged. "They had me in the trunk with you when they brought me here. But if the phone has GPS, you can hit map and then location to find out where we are."

"Leila." Vlad's voice lost its roughness and became the too-pleasant one he used right before he torched someone. "If you're acting of your own free will, then link to me right now."

"Huh?" He only wanted to talk the psychic way?

"Do it," he ordered, and then the call ended.

Maybe he was worried that Rend's cell could somehow be monitored. I took my former torturer's glove off and stroked the skin beneath my thumb. Like before, Vlad's thread leapt out at me. I followed it backward, the wood and straw interior of the stables turning into a cream, peach, and sunshine-colored room that would have been elegant except for the shattered windows, overturned furniture, bloodstains, and multiple char marks. Vlad stood in the center, flames coating his arms, holding up a large blackened hunk of . . . something.

Okay, so where are you? I thought at him. That pastel decor sure wasn't in any room of *his* house.

The answer hit me even as he spoke. Everything was so trashed, I hadn't recognized it right away.

"I'm at Tolvai's." Vlad shook the blackened hump he held aloft. "He was just telling me how stunned he was by the attack and how he had no idea where you, Maximus, or Shrapnel were."

That charbroiled *thing* was Tolvai?

"Can you hold off on, ah, questioning him?" I said, out loud this time. "I've seen enough gross things for one day."

Vlad dropped the crispy vampire and slammed a booted foot onto him, holding him down. "Are you being coerced into giving me a false location? Is Szilagyi attempting to ambush me?"

Realization dawned. He couldn't read my mind through the cell, and I'd never contacted him via a phone call before.

I used my thoughts to reply this time. *No, I'm not being coerced. When I accidentally linked to Szilagyi at Tolvai's, I told him I'd switched sides so he wouldn't hurt Marty. He didn't believe that, and after the attack, he had a vampire named Rend—someone you disowned a long time ago, apparently—take me and Marty somewhere to torture us into discovering if I was sincere. Long story short, Rend and the other vampires are dead now.*

"It's been seven hours," he burst, grinding his heel into Tolvai with brutal force. "I've not heard a word from you in all that time. Why, if you were being tortured, did you not link to me?"

I closed my eyes, once again answering with my thoughts even if they were starker than I would've put into words.

I was unconscious at least half that time. When I awoke, I thought I might die, so I didn't want you to overhear that when there was nothing you could do about it.

He didn't speak, but the flames covering his arms slowly extinguished until only the faint wisp of smoke remained.

"Active the GPS in that phone," he said at last.

Marty handed it to me. Seemed he'd done that while I was having my mental conversation. I dropped the link long enough to read our location and then followed his thread back to relay it.

"Western Romania, in a village called Leurda near the Motru River. Look for a horse stable with a dead vampire outside it."

"I'll send people immediately," he stated.

Tolvai began speaking in that other language. Either he was crying or his vocal cords hadn't healed all the way, because his voice was nothing like the imperious one I remembered.

"If that's not a confession, he's lying," I said to Vlad. "He told Szilagyi where we were, and guarded me during the attack until Rend got me."

"Oh?" Vlad's foot dropped like a wrecking ball. A charred piece of . . . something broke off Tolvai to skid across the room.

"I—I don't know if anyone else made it," I said,

guilt over Maximus, Shrapnel, and the others causing me to stutter this time.

Vlad looked up and sighed. "You succeeded in
finding my enemy. My men were prepared to die
for that, but God willing, some of them are still
alive. If they are, I will find and free them. Now,
have Martin tell you where Szilagyi is."

"Where's Szilagyi, Marty?" I asked.

"Castle Poenari, tunneled into the rock under
the tower."

I repeated the information, surprised to see
Vlad's face darken. Flames shot back up his arms
and an invisible wind blew his hair in brownish-
black swirls around him.

"What's wrong? Is that a friend's house?" How
crappy if another ally been in collusion with Szilagyi.

"No." Vlad's tone dripped acid. "It's *my* former
home."

While the smell indicated that the stable recently
contained horses, all the stalls were empty, to Marty's dismay. Since he'd been drained and hadn't
been allowed to feed in a week, he truly was hungry
enough to eat a horse, making me glad none of the
beautiful animals were here.

We weren't in the stables anymore, though. We
were about a quarter mile away in Rend's car, the
heater turned on full blast. He'd parked it inside a
nearby tree line, still giving us a clear view of the
stables so that we'd see when Vlad's people showed
up. It was also a safer place to wait if unwelcome
vampires arrived. After searching Rend's incom-
ing and outgoing cell log, it looked like he checked

in around every four hours, but what if he'd been
expected to report to Szilagyi sooner about his
"progress" with me? I intended to search through
his bones to see if I could find that out, and find
out whether or not Maximus, Shrapnel, and any
others survived the fight. First, Marty explained to
me that Castle Poenari was the home Vlad rebuilt
during his initial reign as Prince of Wallachia—
and the same place where his wife killed herself.

As if those memories wouldn't be enough to
keep him away, the ruins of Castle Poenari were
also another Dracula tourist attraction. Much as I
hated Szilagyi, I had to admire his cleverness. Of
all the ruins Vlad had his people searching, they
probably avoided ones where the Dracula legend
was hawked like snake oil because they shared
Vlad's loathing of that. Plus, who would've expected Szilagyi to make his underground nest in
the former home of the vampire he was trying to
kill? Twisted didn't even begin to cover it.

"I am so Googling 'Vlad Dracul' once this is all
over," I stated. "Wikipedia knows more about his
past than I do."

Marty grunted. "You won't like what you find."
Then his look became jaded. "Especially since
you're sleeping with him."

My cheek heated but I didn't glance away. "Szilagyi told you that?"

"No, my nose did. When we were in the trunk
together, I could smell him on you even over the
chloroform Rend dosed you with. They did, too.
That's probably why they didn't believe that you'd
really betrayed him."

"They knew before," I replied, shrugging. "I told

Szilagyi that Vlad seduced me to further cement me to his side."

"Wouldn't surprise me a bit," Marty muttered.

I stiffened. "It should because it's not true. Look, I don't blame you for disliking Vlad. He impaled you and coerced you—both unforgivable. Still, there's another side to him."

"Sure," Marty replied flatly. "The side that burns people to death."

I opened my mouth to reply, and then paused. Now wasn't the time to defend my relationship with Vlad. I'd have to continue this conversation later.

"Give me the skull."

He passed it over and I took my glove off, grimacing. In true death, Rend had shriveled so much that he looked mummified, but enough bits of skin and hair clung to the skull to make touching it unappealing. Still, I ran my right hand over it. As expected, Rend's worst sin made his torturing me look innocent by comparison. The next memory was his death—always a standout event for people—and I felt dark satisfaction seeing it replay before me. Then came countless images as his life passed in front of my eyes with incomprehensible speed.

Discovering Maximus, Shrapnel, and the other guards' fates plus finding out if Rend was supposed to check in sooner than normal with Szilagyi would be like looking for specific snowflakes in an avalanche, but I had to try. Everything I needed to know had happened earlier today. I'd start at Rend's last memory and then work my way backward, if possible. I rubbed his skull, trying to will forth the image of his death. It flickered in front of me before fading, replaced by another unintelligible mess. I tried again, concentrating, and the dark blue interior of the car abruptly fell away.

A cord of pure white lashed out, slicing through Rend's shoulders as easily as a sword through water ... Me, streaked with blood, writhing under the point of an ivory knife ... Marty's anguish as silver knives drove into his flesh ... Me and Marty in a trunk, him restrained with silver, me with rope ... A large hall decorated in pastel hues, its opulence marred by glass, blood, and multiple bodies on the ground ... Two vampires being forced into a van, both of them pierced with silver harpoons. One was bald and dark-skinned, the other pale with shoulder-length blond hair ...

"They're alive!" I shouted, so excited I dropped the link.

"You can tell that already?" Marty asked in disbelief.

He had a point. I'd spent days unsuccessfully trying to glean more details from the bones of the vampires who'd attacked the club. Why were Rend's memories so much easier to navigate? Only one thing had changed since then. Like a magnifying glass could amplify a ray of sunshine, drinking large quantities of vampire blood must kick my psychic abilities into hyper drive. I'd already seen what it did to my voltage, but I hadn't expected it to affect my other powers. I didn't want to dwell on the ramifications of that because it brought up possibilities I wasn't ready to consider. Instead, I touched Rend's skull again, focusing my energy on that last image I'd seen of Maximus and Shrapnel.

It took two tries, but once I found it, I centered my
attention on seeing what came before that . . . and
before that . . .

I let out a gasp that had Marty demanding,
"What, what?" while shaking me.

I dropped the link—and the skull—to grasp
Marty's hand.

"We need to go to Castle Poenari."

Chapter 41

"Watch it, for God's sake! You'll get us killed!"

"No, I'll get *me* killed. You're already dead," I corrected.

Okay, so I'd almost sideswiped another car, but for my first time driving, I was doing pretty well. I hit the gas, ignoring the glare Marty shot my way. Yes, I was speeding, but we were in a hurry. Besides, he had a lead foot, too.

"I'll be all the way dead when Vlad realizes what you're doing and blames me for not stopping you," Marty said gruffly.

I had to use Rend's cell so Vlad couldn't read my thoughts when I called him an hour ago. I told him I'd glimpsed something from Rend's bones that made me think it was best to leave immediately instead of waiting for his people to get us, and that I'd see him later at the castle. Both things were true. I just hadn't mentioned what I'd glimpsed or *which* castle I'd meet him at. If I had, he would have ordered his men to drag me back to his home using any force necessary, and that wouldn't do.

As I'd told him before, I wanted revenge against Szilagyi, too. Right now, I was on my way to get it.

"No, he promised never to hurt anyone I cared about unless that person attacked him or his people. You're doing neither."

"I bet he'll make an exception," he muttered as I fishtailed a little on my turn off the highway. The road must be icy. Couldn't be me taking the turn too fast.

Rend's gloves combined with Marty not having his usual modifications to reach the pedals meant that I had to drive. I'd avoided learning in the past because I could never get a license with my electricity issues, but having people's lives on the line made for great motivation.

"You'll get pulled over," Marty warned when I roared past the other traffic.

"Then you'll mesmerize the cop into letting me go. You're not going to talk me out of this, so quit trying."

"I should make you drop me off at an airport and take the first flight back to Florida," he grumbled under his breath.

I flashed a look at him before turning my attention back to the road. "You want me to do this without you? Say the word."

"Over my dead body" was his instant reply, followed by a muttered "It's the off season for performing, anyway. Slow down or you'll miss the turn."

I slowed, taking the street that led to Castle Poenari. Once we were off the main road, streetlights became scarce until it seemed like the darkness had swallowed us. The narrow lane, tall trees, and steep terrain all seemed to advise against going forward, but I kept my foot on the gas. The ominous atmosphere worked to our benefit. By day, Castle Poenari would be populated by tourists, but this late at night, I doubted anyone would be there except Szilagyi and his men, burrowed in rooms they'd dug out before Bram Stoker penned the first words of *Dracula*.

"Tell me when we've gotten close enough."

We couldn't drive right up to the castle. For one, the cliff it was located on meant that visitors had to walk over a thousand steps up the mountain to reach it. For another, we didn't want to announce our presence to Szilagyi. Yet.

After about thirty minutes, Marty said, "Pull over." I did—right into a ditch, from the way the front end tipped.

"It's not my fault," I protested before he could say anything. "I couldn't see what was there with all the snow!"

I thought I heard him grumble "Women drivers" under his breath. Then he met my gaze and his eyes turned green.

"You ready, kid?"

"Yeah," I said, soft but emphatic.

Without another word, he took one of Rend's knives and cut his palm, holding it out to me. Equally quiet, I grasped it and swallowed the dark crimson liquid. As soon as I did, that weak pulse of power inside me began to flare.

We made only one stop on our way here; a gas station where I used the money in Rend's wallet to fill the tank and Marty refilled another way from two employees and a motorist. None of them remembered it afterward and Marty's cheeks were downright ruddy once he was done. He knew he'd need extra for me.

Marty cut his palm twice more. I knew I'd had enough when that harsh taste began to sweeten and my skin itched from the currents pulsating through me. My weariness vanished, replaced with an exhilarating mixture of nerves and purpose.

I pulled my right glove off and then wiped my mouth. Barely any red stained my hand when I looked at it.

"Let's do this," I said, and left the warm interior of the car for the cold, snowy darkness.

Castle Poenari sat at the top of a cliff, as silent and imposing as a great stone dragon. From my vantage point, it looked as though its steep walls sprouted from the sheer rock face by magic. Only one narrow road wound its way through the valley. Reaching the castle required a vertical climb where one wrong step could have disastrous results. Building it before the time of bulldozers or machinery must have been an undertaking of unimaginable proportions. Even with most of it in ruins, what remained still held the power to impress . . . and intimidate.

This was where Vlad had lived before he was a vampire. He'd overseen the castle's restoration and fought in the vast forest surrounding it when he'd been as fragile as any mortal man. Of course, even back then his fierceness had been legendary. Maybe that was what had intrigued the vampire Tenoch enough to find him and change him. I'd never know. Vlad said that Tenoch had killed himself soon afterward. I hoped it wasn't from regret over making Vlad as close to immortal as a person could be.

Far below the house was the Arges River. This was where Vlad had pulled his wife's lifeless body from centuries ago, that event changing him as decisively as becoming a vampire had. But I wasn't here on a sightseeing trip, or even to trace my hand over stones that contained more knowledge about Vlad than all the historical or fictional books written about him combined. I was here because between the river and his former house, hidden by trees and jagged rocks, was the entrance to an escape tunnel.

They say revenge is a dish best served cold. If so, Szilagyi had spent centuries piling on the ice before he'd acted, and he made sure to have a way out if Vlad ever did discover his underground nest. Rend's memories also showed that only a handful of Szilagyi's men knew the tunnel existed. Because of this, he wouldn't have multiple vampires guarding it.

Marty and I crept around the side of the mountain. I should've been nearly blind with the dense woods blocking out most of the moonlight, but I wasn't. Vampire blood sharpened my strength and senses, making me able to pick my way through the rough terrain while seeing, hearing, and smelling things with clarity I'd never before experienced. Through Rend's memories, I knew where to go as if he'd drawn me a map. I led the way, Marty following close behind. We didn't have much time. All was quiet now, but Vlad was coming, and he'd tear this whole mountain down to get to Szilagyi if that's what it took.

That was fine, as long as I did what I came for first.

Marty sniffed deeply. "Rend was here, I can smell him," he whispered.

I inhaled, too, but the forest was so rich with scents that my newly sensitive nose couldn't determine a particular person's olfactory calling card.

"Anyone else?" I whispered back, glancing at him.

"Yeah. Both of them came through here, too."

He meant Maximus and Shrapnel, the only ones I'd seen who had survived the attack. After all, Szilagyi couldn't hustle two harpooned vampires into his lair in full view of Castle Poenari's tourists, and he would've been too impatient to wait until dark to start interrogating them.

I started upward again, waving Marty forward. After another fifteen minutes of climbing, I held my hand up in the universal gesture for stop. Then I crouched down, squinting.

There. The huge broken boulder marked the entrance to the tunnel. I couldn't see it from the thick bushes and felled tree trunk, but that was the point. If it could be easily seen, it wouldn't be effective.

I glanced upward toward the castle that trees and the steepness blocked from my view. Everything was still quiet, good. I should only need ten minutes to—

Multiple *booms!* sounded in almost simultaneous succession. The mountain trembled and rocks began to cascade downward. A slew of curses ran through my head. Clearly Vlad was going for a shock-and-awe entrance, but my goal had been to get to Maximus and Shrapnel *before* Szilagyi knew he was under attack. As soon as he realized Vlad had found him, he'd probably kill any hostages before making a run for it through the tunnel.

I dashed forward, abandoning any attempt at being stealthy. With the barrage above, it didn't matter anymore. The bushes in front of the tunnel were thick and thorny, but I shoved past them, my heavy clothes helping to limit the scratches. Then I ducked under the huge broken boulder, careful not to hit my head on the rock ledge immediately beneath it. Once clear of that, I turned left into the tunnel as if I'd been here a hundred times.

It was pitch black, making me grateful that my enhanced vision meant I wasn't stumbling around blindly. Something happening above made the tunnel shudder as if in the throes of an earthquake. That was my cue to start running. What, had Vlad flown in carrying a huge wrecking ball with him?

After I went about a hundred yards, I saw the glow of green ahead. A male voice called out in Romanian, but I didn't reply. I kept coming, and when I rounded a curve, a skinny man with black hair and a beard stood in the tunnel. He looked to be in his forties, but those glowing eyes proved that he wasn't human.

"Sorry," I said coolly. "I don't speak Romanian."

He looked me over in surprise, taking in my too-big clothes and shoes. He didn't seem afraid, though. Idiot. Did he think I was a lost hiker who'd accidentally stumbled across the tunnel?

"You need to get out of my way," I said, flexing my right hand. I didn't want to waste my power on him. I only had so much juice and it was ear-marked for other things.

"Who in hell are you?" he asked with a thick accent.

"Know the difference between dying nobly and dying because you're stupid?" I replied, ignoring his question. "Nothing, you're dead either way. Hear that racket? That's Vlad Tepesh attacking, so if I were you, I'd run instead of staying to fight."

"Fight you? You're human, I kill you," he sneered, but another shudder followed by a *boom!* made him glance around nervously.

"If I was easy to kill, I wouldn't be talking to you."

He still didn't move. This was taking too much time, not to mention giving Szilagyi an opportunity to hear everything. I held out my right hand. He just stared at it, cocking his head.

I was about to unleash a current when a blur of motion shot by me. It barreled into the vampire, knocking him backward. Amidst the mad whirl of limbs and flashing silver knives, I caught a glimpse of a four-foot body crowned by bushy brown hair. Marty, not willing to hang back and let me deal with it. *God, please don't let the other vampire be faster than him!* I couldn't risk letting a deadly lash of energy fly, either. Not when it could cut through Marty instead of Szilagyi's guard. All I could do was wait, hand at the ready in case another guard heard the disturbance and came to investigate.

After a few seconds that shredded my nerves, the guard fell back, Marty on top of him. His hand gripped a knife handle half as long as his thick forearm, the blade buried deeply into the guard's chest. Then he jumped off, executing a low bow.

"And the crowd goes wild," he said smugly.

"Could you just let me handle it next time?" I hissed to cover how worried I'd been.

Marty rolled his eyes. "Please. I was fighting to the death before your grandparents were born. Now, let's finish this."

He jogged deeper into the tunnel. I hurried after him, only then realizing that in my moment of panic, I'd said a prayer to a god I didn't believe in. Strange.

When we reached a fork in the tunnel, I paused. Rend hadn't been the one to take Maximus and Shrapnel here, so I hadn't seen which way to go through his memories. If I made the wrong choice, I could be dooming them. No matter how quietly I moved through the tunnels, unless Szilagyi was so busy focusing on Vlad's attack, I was now close enough that he'd hear my thoughts and know why I was here.

No time for indecisiveness. I went right and Marty followed, silver knives gripped in each hand. As I ran, I also stroked underneath my thumb, seeking Vlad's essence. I couldn't wait despite him being busy with the attack. He had to know about the tunnel. Szilagyi couldn't be allowed to escape.

I'd intended to relay a quick message and then disconnect—not just because time was of the essence, but also to limit his fury with me once he discovered where I was—but when the tunnel fell away and I saw Vlad as though I hovered above him, I stared in disbelief. A pile of stone, brick, and rubble surrounded him that once had been the tower rising imperiously into the mountainous horizon. No, he hadn't brought a wrecking ball with him, as I wondered upon hearing the noise and feeling the tremors. *He* was the wrecking ball.

Vlad tore through layers of rock and earth with nothing more than his bare hands, flinging huge chunks aside in a maelstrom of destruction. Fire blazed over every inch of him, making him look more like Dante's version of a demon than a vampire. The light coming from him allowed me to see even as he tore deeper into the earth, ferociously annihilating everything in the way between him and his enemy. The mountain shuddered as if it could feel pain over the force of Vlad's assault, parting deeper and deeper beneath his merciless barrage. For a second while watching him, I was so stunned that I forgot to breathe.

"What are you doing here?" I thought I heard him shout, but the continuous smashing of rock and stone was thunderous.

Not sure if he could hear me, I mentally yelled my reply. *There's an escape tunnel on the lower east side of the mountain about three hundred yards from the river. Send people to guard it. Maximus and Shrapnel are still alive. I'm going to get them.*

Then I did disconnect, whatever he would've said lost as the tunnel rushed back around me. Marty had carried me while I was in my trance, and now we were in front of a large crevasse that looked to me like the open throat of a stone monster. Inside it, barely visible in the light of Marty's glowing green eyes, were Maximus and Shrapnel.

Marty jumped into the depths with me still

in his arms. I grunted at the hard jolt when we landed. The pit had to be fifty feet deep. Then I sprang away from him, my right hand extended and ready to shoot a cutting whip through anything that moved.

Nothing did. Maybe Vlad's attack had cleared out the guards who were interrogating Maximus and Shrapnel. I thought I'd have to kill whoever was in here, but aside from the two vampires restrained to the wall in sickening ways, the pit was empty.

"Leila." Maximus's voice was unrecognizable from the silver harpoon still embedded in his throat, and he was so covered in dried blood that it took me a moment to realize that was all he had on. "What are you doing here?"

I let out a harsh imitation of a laugh. "Oh, you know. I was in the neighborhood."

Chapter 42

Marty began to rip out the knives and harpoons that he could reach, muttering something to Shrapnel about karma. I wasn't strong enough to pull out the restraints like he was, but I wasn't helpless. Cold satisfaction filled me as I cut through their harpoons and manacles with a laserlike beam of electricity, allowing the weight of their bodies to do the rest of the work. *No, not helpless at all.*

Szilagyi had thought I was when he brought me into this fight back when he had Jackal kidnap me. Ever since, I'd been nothing but a pawn to him. Now that pawn had killed three of his people, led Vlad to his hideout, and freed two men who'd risked their lives trying to protect me from Szilagyi's latest attack. I only wished I could see the puppet master's face when he realized that all his carefully laid plans had come crashing down around him.

"Leila," a male voice with a distinct accent said from behind me. "We meet at last."

I didn't need to look to know who it was. *Be careful what you wish for!* rang through my mind.

Why hadn't I waited until I was *out* of the mountain to gloat about my victory?

I turned. As expected, there was Szilagyi, wearing the same sort of nondescript sweater and thick cotton pants that he had the first time I saw him. But what really held my attention were his two guns; one pointed at me, one at Marty.

"Do I really need to say don't move?" he asked pleasantly.

The current spiking from my hand died away. He'd blast a hole through me before I could even twitch, and from the malevolent gleam in his dark brown eyes, I didn't know why he hadn't already.

"You may want to consider running for your life," I said, speaking calmly the way one did to an unpredictable animal.

His generous mouth curled in derision. "Why? I know who's here, and you already told him about my tunnel, didn't you? So I can't escape." He cocked the guns. "But neither can you."

I didn't say any of the cliché things that sprang to my mind, like *You don't want to do this* (yes he did), or *We can talk* (we were way past the talking stage). Instead, a grim part of me wondered if I had enough vampire blood in me to snap out an electric lash while dying from a gunshot wound. If he pulled that trigger, I intended to find out.

Screams rang out from above, so anguished that I winced in instinctive sympathy even though they must've come from Szilagyi's remaining guards. Then a large form appeared in front of me like a shadow come to life. It happened so fast that it took a moment to realize what I was looking at— the back of a vampire, dressed all in black, his hands lit up with orange and blue flames that cast an eerie glow over the inside of the pit.

"Hello, Vlad," Szilagyi said, and to his credit, he didn't sound afraid. "I must admit, I'm surprised. You chose to protect her instead of strike out at me. How unexpectedly soft of you."

I had the option of cringing behind my boy-friend's back or hurrying to get Maximus and Shrapnel out of their restraints. It was a no-brainer. I backed away slowly, but once I reached them, I whirled and yanked, cut, or pried away the last of the silver pinning Maximus and Shrapnel to the stone walls. I glanced over at Szilagyi several times while I worked, but he didn't move, and those two guns were now pointed at Vlad.

"Why would I kill you quickly when I can take you with me and spread out your torment over years?" Vlad replied in a caressing voice. "I owe you for so many things. My captivity after I became a vampire, smearing my name, your be-trayal of Romania to her enemies, your murder of my son, all my people you've killed, and finally, your abuse of Leila."

Then his voice deepened, and those flames licked up his arms. "Though she seems to have recklessly set out on her own quest for vengeance, hasn't she?"

Vlad glanced at me during that last sentence, and despite the seriousness of the situation, I cringed. That single brief look said loud and clear how furious he was over me coming here, but if he'd waited *ten more minutes* before attacking, I could've snuck Maximus and Shrapnel out without Szilagyi even knowing it!

Szilagyi let out a short laugh as he overheard that. "You might indeed have done so. You've shown yourself to be amazingly resourceful, as your presence here and the smell of Rend's blood on your clothes proves."

Maximus and Shrapnel, now free, flanked Vlad on either side. They were weaponless, but they still managed to exude a palpable form of menace. Maybe it was because of how their bodies were covered with dried blood and nothing else. Marty stayed by me, his hand sliding toward the knife still strapped to his belt. Vlad's glance flicked to Maximus, Shrapnel, and Marty in lightning-fast succession before returning to Szilagyi.

"Leave."

The single word was weighted down with immutable command. Maximus and Shrapnel turned to go, but Marty hesitated. At that, the coffee-skinned vampire picked him up and then leapt out, one meaty hand silencing his protests. Maximus moved as if to grab me, but I snapped a warning whip of electricity at him.

"Don't even think of it. I'm leaving with Vlad or not at all."

He glanced at Vlad, who gave me another you're-so-in-for-it glare before jerking his head up. Maximus disappeared out of the pit with a soundless jump and I returned my attention to the standoff between the two remaining vampires.

Vlad smiled at Szilagyi, and that simple baring of teeth managed to be terrifying in its charm. "Now you have only me to contend with, my old enemy. Do you know why? Because I wanted you to remember over the course of the next several agonizing years that you couldn't best me even when I stood alone." His gaze dropped to the guns and he let out a short laugh. "Unless you actually believe shooting me will work?"

"No," Szilagyi said, surprising me as he dropped the guns. Those distinguished features twisted into a mask of hatred. "I know those won't stop you. Our sire willed something extra into you when he changed you. A remaining part of Cain's legacy of power. I knew it the first time I saw how unnaturally strong and gifted you were. Tenoch must have already set his plans for death in motion when he changed you and knew he wouldn't need it anymore."

I didn't know what Szilagyi meant, but Vlad did. His smile widened, changing from icily pleasant to genuinely amused.

"Here I'd thought only Mencheres suspected that. Very perceptive of you, but it makes me wonder why you're not begging for your life if you realize there is no way you can defeat me."

Something ancient and vicious lurked in Szilagyi's whiskey-colored gaze. "Begging would only please you, but I know what won't. You care for her; I can smell it. You may think you've won, old *friend*, but I'll make you remember what it's like to lose someone precious, and how fitting that you'll lose her here."

I watched something slip from his sleeve, no bigger than a cigarette lighter, but I didn't do anything. Maybe because I'd seen too many movies where the villain monologues all of his evil plans before attempting to act on them. Szilagyi didn't say a word. He simply pressed a button on it and the world exploded.

Well, not *the* world, but the one around me, anyway.

Vlad's reaction saved me from being killed right then. Rocks blasted out with tremendous force, but his body formed a shield that protected my front while his arms covered as much of my back as they could. My head was stuffed into his chest, his chin holding it down and covering the top of it. The backs of my legs felt shredded from the flying shards, but with the ground dissolving beneath us, that was the least of my problems.

Then Vlad's grip tightened and suddenly nothing was beneath my feet. Were we flying? Being sucked down with the crumbling mountain? I shouldn't have turned to the side to look, but I did—and saw an ocean of fire coming straight at us.

I'd relived death-by-explosion before, so I knew what seemed to take several seconds actually happened in an instant. Vlad vaulted us up, escaping most of the stone and brick minefield, but the fire was too fast. It rushed upward, matching his speed easily. I squeezed my eyes shut again, bracing for the inevitable agony. If I was lucky, death would take me quickly. At least I knew Vlad would survive the flames. Szilagyi had detonated another mountain, but this one wouldn't claim him. It would only take me, and while that sucked, I wasn't the type to want company in death.

Then those roaring flames enveloped me. I felt it in the pressure that covered every inch of me, but though the wind from the inferno whipped my hair around, the only heat I felt came from the vampire who held me so tight, it was hard to breathe.

Had my body gone into shock, numbing me from the pain? Possible, but it had never happened so fast before. I risked another glance—and saw flames all around me, even rippling above me, but though the smoke turned the few breaths I managed into ragged coughs, it was almost as if the fire skipped over me. Not even my clothes or hair were singed.

It was so unbelievable that my mind refused to accept it. I *had* to be burning. Any second now I'd feel that excruciating pain slam into me and smell the horrifying odor of my own flesh cooking. But even as I waited, Vlad slanted us sideways and increased his speed. The smoke and flames were now to our left, giving me an unrestricted view of Castle Poenari as it smoldered and crumbled into the mountain below it.

Finally Vlad set us at the bottom of that mountain, far enough away from the rock slides that smeared the formerly pristine snow with ugly streaks of gray and black. It took several seconds for my legs to stop shaking enough for me to stand on my own, and even then, I couldn't bring myself to release the grip I had around his neck.

"How?" I managed, my mind filling in the rest of what I couldn't verbally articulate. *How did I not burn to death?* Nothing should have survived that fire except the vampire still holding me upright.

Vlad loosened my grip enough to stare down at me. "My aura saved you."

At my blank look, he went on. "You did notice

that my clothes never burn when I call forth flames. My power recognizes anything contained within my aura as part of me and thus won't consume it. Other fire travels right over my aura as if repelled by it, so I coated you in it to make the flames pass over you."

I was so stunned that I couldn't speak. He'd actually managed to make me *fireproof*? How long would it last?

His mouth twisted into a musing smile. "I don't know. I've never done this before. Perhaps it will wear off in as little as an hour, perhaps it will last weeks."

It took me a few moments to process the subtext behind that statement because I was still overwhelmed by what had just happened.

"If you've never done this before, how did you know it would work?"

His expression changed into the arrogant one I knew so well. "Because it had to. I wasn't about to let you die."

I shook my head with a sort of bemused amazement. I'd worried that his ego might be the death of him, but as it turned out, it had saved my life. Of course he wouldn't hesitate before trying something that had never been done before. He was Vlad Tepesh. How could he fail?

Another rumbling sound made me look upward toward what used to be Castle Poenari. A huge smoking hole was all that was left of the tower, and almost all of those imposing high walls had crumbled into the forest below. The structure I'd so recently thought of as a stone dragon now looked like a ragged skeleton.

"Oh, Vlad," I said softly. "Your home. It's . . . gone."

His hands settled onto my shoulder, their heat searing through the layers of clothing I'd stolen from my now dead captors.

"It hasn't been my home for centuries. I'm not sorry that it's gone. Its place in my life is long over."

Above the noise from the rock slides, trees falling, and other destructive sounds, I heard shouts. Vlad and I turned, and though I couldn't see who it was in the distance, he smiled.

"Maximus, Shrapnel, and Martin seem to have survived the explosion. They must have gone out the tunnel."

Then he looked at me and his smile faded. "Why did you wait to tell me about that?" Hints of anger colored his voice.

"Because you would've sent someone else to free them," I replied, the topic helping me to regain my shattered composure. "I can't do anything about the guards who were killed, but Maximus and Shrapnel were captured while protecting me, so it was only fair that I was the one to get them out. I didn't even want Marty to come along, but he insisted."

"Such a reckless, foolish risk," he muttered, but when he brushed my hair, his touch was gentle despite his hardened tone.

I smiled, holding up my hand. "Reckless, maybe. Foolish, no. You were right. This *is* a formidable weapon."

He clasped it, absorbing the current it contained without a flicker in his expression.

"Yes, but you are still only human."

I laughed, the sound of it drowned out by the crunch of rocks as the mountain continued to shudder as though in the throes of birth pangs.

"So was Van Helsing, yet in every movie, he beat the vampire in the end. Never underestimate the power of humanity."

Epilogue

 Dawn broke with a veil of fog, tinting everything with a haze like the glimpses I occasionally caught of the future. Vlad had sent me and Marty back home while he and several guards searched the ruins under Castle Poenari. He wanted to make sure none of Szilagyi's people who survived the explosion escaped, and he wanted his enemy's bones, either as proof that he was dead, or as a trophy, or both.

After a brief reunion with Gretchen and my dad to assure them that I was fine after my captivity, I pleaded exhaustion and went to my room. I *was* tired, but I couldn't sleep for many reasons. One of those was because of what happened at the stable. It didn't bother me that I'd killed Rend and the other guards. Given the right circumstances, most people were capable of taking a life, and this had been a kill-or-be-killed situation. But what I hadn't anticipated was how I'd enjoyed it.

Surviving against deadly foes accounted for some of the exhilaration I'd felt, but not all of it. I could use the excuse that Vlad's ruthlessness was rubbing off, but deep down, I knew this cold-bloodedness was all mine. Vlad had even pointed out the darkness in me before our relationship began. I'd thought he was referring to everything I'd seen from my abilities. Now I realized he meant what lurked within me, and it had probably been there since before the accident.

As disturbing as that realization was, what really kept me awake had nothing to do with my unexpected harsh streak. The sun burned off most of the morning fog by the time I heard Vlad's booted stride down the hallway. He came into my room, threw his dirt-smeared coat onto the floor, and was in the process of kicking off his boots when what I was doing made him pause.

I sat in front of the mahogany fireplace, my right hand inside the orange and blue flames. They leapt between my fingers and curled around my wrist, but not one of them directly touched my skin. Instead, they skipped over me as if I wore an invisible glove, and while their warmth was pleasant, it wasn't scorching as it should have been with my proximity.

"Ah, so my aura is still embedded in you," Vlad commented, not sounding concerned. He resumed his boot removal.

I withdrew my hand, looking at its unblemished state with a mixture of wonder and dismay. "Did you find Szilagyi's bones?"

"No." Boots off, he came over, kneeling beside me. "Don't worry. If he managed to survive, it will take a day at least for him to dig his way out. My men have the area surrounded, and now you, my beauty, can link to him and see if he'd dead, or see what hole he's attempting to crawl out of."

I stared at him for a long moment. The dirt and soot made him look fiercer, darkening that sexy stubble along his jaw and making his cheekbones more prominent. His lips were parted, showing a glimpse of white teeth that could tease and terrorize with equal skill. Firelight added a hint of gold to his copper-colored eyes, and those encircling rings of emerald grew as his brows drew together in a frown.

"What's wrong? You smell distraught."

I glanced at the fire. If not for Vlad willing his aura into me, I would have died from flames last night, but my survival had come at a price neither one of us had anticipated.

"I already tried looking for Szilagyi," I said, glancing back at Vlad. "There's nothing to link to anymore."

He started to smile. "Then he truly is dead."

I savored his expression because it might be the last time he looked at me this way. Then I forced myself to continue.

"I don't know. It's not just Szilagyi's essence that I can't link to anymore. It's everyone's."

I stroked the ornately carved wood around the fireplace for emphasis. "I'm not picking up impressions from what I touch anymore. Coating me with your aura did more than make me fireproof, Vlad. It also covered my abilities like some sort of supernatural glove and nothing gets in."

Very slowly, he rose, his expression changing from satisfaction to absolute inscrutability. Neither of us spoke the words that seemed to scream in the silence. *What if this wasn't temporary?* It might be a cure for the psychometric abilities I'd to be rid of, but they were also the main reason Vlad had been drawn to me in the first place. If their loss *was* permanent, I'd gained some of the normalcy I longed for, but it might cost me the man I was falling in love with.

And his enemy might still be out there. The explosion should have killed Szilagyi, but he'd cheated death before, and a bone-deep pessimism warned me that we hadn't seen the last of him.

"Don't worry," Vlad said, repeating his earlier words with less conviction this time. "I'll double the guards at Poenari. Either my men will find Szilagyi alive, or, once your powers return, you can verify that he is truly dead."

I didn't dispute his belief that I'd get my abilities back. Right now, we were both guessing on that count.

"Reading my thoughts again?" I asked dryly.

He flashed me a tight smile. "Always."

Then he put his boots back on, leaving his coat where it lay. "I'll notify my men to double the watch, and now I intend to take one more sweep of the area before I rest."

He kissed me, and when we drew apart, something I couldn't name flickered over his face as he stroked my right hand. But all he said was, "Get some sleep, Leila. I'll return soon."

After he left, I realized he'd taken the time to reassure me over Szilagyi, but hadn't said a word about my thought that I was falling in love with him. Was he avoiding that topic because he was incapable of love—something I now doubted—or because my power loss had indeed made him reevaluate our relationship?

In the very near future, I'd put both possibilities to the test. I didn't want to lose Vlad, but I wouldn't start running from my problems again. I'd confront them despite their potential cost, and with or without any additional abilities.

"Get ready, Vlad," I whispered into the empty room. "This is far from over."

Watch for the return of Vlad and Leila
in the next Night Prince novel,
available in Spring 2013.

In the meantime,
see how the adventures
of Cat and Bones all started.

Keep reading for a peek
into the Night Huntress world . . .
from the very beginning!

All available from Avon Books

HALFWAY TO THE GRAVE

Half-vampire Catherine Crawfield is going after the undead with a vengeance . . . until she's captured by Bones, a vampire bounty hunter, and is forced into an unholy partnership. She's amazed she doesn't end up as his dinner—are there actually good vampires? And Bones is turning out to be as tempting as any man with a heartbeat.

"*Halfway to the Grave* has breathless action, a roller-coaster plot . . . and a love story that will leave you screaming for more. I devoured it in a single sitting."

ILONA ANDREWS

"Beautiful ladies should never drink alone," a voice said next to me.

Turning to give a rebuff, I stopped short when I saw my admirer was as dead as Elvis. Blond hair about four shades darker than the other one's, with turquoise-colored eyes. Hell's bells, it was my lucky night.

"I hate to drink alone, in fact."

He smiled, showing lovely squared teeth. *All the better to bite you with, my dear.*

"Are you here by yourself?"

"Do you want me to be?" Coyly, I fluttered my lashes at him. This one wasn't going to get away, by God.

"I very much want you to be." His voice was lower now, his smile deeper. God, but they had great intonation. Most of them could double as phone-sex operators.

"Well, then I was. Except now I'm with you."

I let my head tilt to the side in a flirtatious manner that also bared my neck. His eyes followed the movement, and he licked his lips. *Oh good, a hungry one.*

"What's your name, lovely lady?"

"Cat Raven." An abbreviation of Catherine, and the hair color of the first man who tried to kill me. See? Sentimental.

His smile broadened. "Such an unusual name."

His name was Kevin. He was twenty-eight and an architect, or so he claimed. Kevin was recently engaged, but his fiancée had dumped him and now he just wanted to find a nice girl and settle down. Listening to this, I managed not to choke on my drink in amusement. What a load of crap. Next he'd be pulling out pictures of a house with a white picket fence. Of course, he couldn't let me call a cab, and how inconsiderate that my fictitious friends left without me. How kind of him to drive me home, and oh, by the way, he had something to show me. Well, that made two of us.

Experience had taught me it was much easier to dispose of a car that hadn't been the scene of a killing. Therefore, I managed to open the passenger door of his Volkswagen and run screaming out of it with feigned horror when he made his move. He'd picked a deserted area, most of them did, so I didn't worry about a Good Samaritan hearing my cries.

He followed me with measured steps, delighted with my sloppy staggering. Pretending to trip, I whimpered for effect as he loomed over me. His face had transformed to reflect his true nature. A sinister smile revealed upper fangs where none had been before, and his previously blue eyes now glowed with a terrible green light.

I scrabbled around, concealing my hand slipping into my pocket. "Don't hurt me!"

He knelt, grasping the back of my neck.

"It will only hurt for a moment."

Just then, I struck. My hand whipped out in a practiced movement and the weapon it held pierced his heart. I twisted repeatedly until his mouth went slack and the light faded from his eyes. With a last wrenching shove, I pushed him off and wiped my bloody hands on my pants.

"You were right." I was out of breath from my exertions. "It only hurt for a moment."

ONE FOOT IN THE GRAVE

Cat Crawfield is now a special agent, working for the government to rid the world of the rogue undead. But when she's targeted for assassination she turns to her ex, the sexy and dangerous vampire Bones to help her.

"Witty dialogue, a strong heroine,
a delicious hero, and enough action
to make a reader forget to sleep."

MELISSA MARR

"Hallo, Kitten."

I was so preoccupied with my breakdown that I didn't hear Bones come in. His voice was as smooth as I'd remembered, that English accent just as enticing. I snapped my head up, and in the midst of my carefully constructed life crashing around me, found the most absurd thing to worry about.

"God, Bones, this is the ladies' room! What if someone sees?"

He laughed, a low, seductive ripple of the air. Noah had kissed me with less effect.

"Still a prude? Don't fret—I locked the door behind me."

If that was supposed to ease my tension, it had the opposite result. I sprang to my feet, but there was nowhere to run. He blocked the only exit.

"Look at you, luv. Can't say I prefer the brown hair, but as for the rest of you . . . you're luscious."

Bones traced the inside of his lower lip with his tongue as his eyes slid all over me. Their heat seemed to rub my skin. When he took a step closer, I flattened back against the wall.

"Stay where you are."

He leaned nonchalantly against the countertop. "What are you all lathered about? Think I'm here to kill you?"

"No. If you were going to kill me, you wouldn't

have bothered with the altar ambush. You obviously know what name I'm going under, so you would have just gone for me one night when I came home."

He whistled appreciatively. "That's right, pet. You haven't forgotten how I work. Do you know I was offered a contract on the mysterious Red Reaper at least three times before? One bloke had half-a-million bounty for your dead body."

Well, not a surprise. After all, Lazarus had tried to cash a check on my ass for the same reason. "What did you say, since you've just confirmed you're not here for that?"

Bones straightened, and the bantering went out of him. "Oh, I said yes, of course. Then I hunted the sods down and played ball with their heads. The calls quit coming after that."

I swallowed at the image he described. Knowing him, it was exactly what he'd done.

"So, then, why *are* you here?"

He smiled and came nearer, ignoring my previous order.

AT GRAVE'S END

Caught in the crosshairs of a vengeful vampire, Cat is about to learn the true meaning of bad blood—just as she and Bones need to stop a lethal magic from being unleashed. Will Cat be able to fully embrace her vampire instincts to save them all from a fate worse than the grave?

"A can't-put-down masterpiece that's sexy-hot and a thrill-ride on every page. I'm officially addicted to the series. Marry me, Bones!"

GENA SHOWALTER

I was sitting at my desk, staring off into space, when my cell phone rang. A glance at it showed my mother's number, and I hesitated. I so wasn't in the mood to deal with her. But it was unusual for her to be up this late, so I answered.

"Hi Mom."

"Catherine." She paused. I waited, tapping my finger on my desk. Then she spoke words that had me almost falling out of my chair. "I've decided to come to your wedding."

I actually glanced at my phone again to see if I'd been mistaken and it was someone else who'd called me.

"Are you drunk?" I got out when I could speak.

She sighed. "I wish you wouldn't marry that vampire, but I'm tired of him coming between us."

Aliens replaced her with a pod person, I found myself thinking. *That's the only explanation.*

"So . . . you're coming to my wedding?" I couldn't help but repeat.

"That's what I said, isn't it?" she replied with some of her usual annoyance.

"Um. Great." Hell if I knew what to say. I was floored.

"I don't suppose you'd want any of my help planning it?" my mother asked, sounding both defiant and uncertain.

If my jaw hung any lower, it would fall off. "I'd love some," I managed.

"Good. Can you make it for dinner later?"

I was about to say, *Sorry, there was no way*, when I paused. Tate didn't even want me watching the video of him dealing with his bloodlust. Bones was leaving this afternoon to pick Annette up from the airport. I could swing by my mom's when he went to get Annette, and then meet him back here afterward.

"How about a late lunch instead of dinner? Say, around four o'clock?"

"That's fine, Catherine." She paused again, seeming to want to say something more. I half expected her to yell, *April Fool's!* but it was November, so that would be way early. "I'll see you at four."

When Bones came into my office at dawn, since Dave was taking the next twelve-hour shift with Tate, I was still dumbfounded. First Tate turning into a vampire, then my mother softening over my marrying one. Today really was a day to remember.

Bones offered to drop me off on his way to the airport, then pick me up on his way back to the compound, but I declined. I didn't want to be without a car if my mother's mood turned foul—always a possibility—or risk ruining our first decent mother-daughter chat by Bones showing up with a strange vampire. There were only so many sets of fangs I thought my mother could handle at the same time, and Annette got on my nerves even on the best of days.

Besides, I could just see me explaining who Annette was to my mother. *Mom, this is Annette. Back in the seventeen hundreds when Bones was a gigolo, she used to pay him to fuck her, but after more than two hundred years of banging him, now they're just good friends.*

Yeah, I'd introduce Annette to my mother— right after I performed a lobotomy on myself.

"I still can't believe she wants to talk about the wedding," I marveled to Bones as I climbed into my car.

He gave me a serious look. "She'll never abandon her relationship with you. You could marry Satan himself and that still wouldn't get rid of her. She loves you, Kitten, though she does a right poor job of showing it most days." Then he gave me a wicked grin. "Shall I ring your cell in an hour, so you can pretend there's an emergency if she gets natty with you?"

"What if there *is* an emergency with Tate?" I wondered. "Maybe I shouldn't leave."

"Your bloke's fine. Nothing can harm him now short of a silver stake through the heart. Go see your mum. Ring me if you need me to come bite her."

There really was nothing for me to do at the compound. Tate would be a few more days at least in lockdown, and we didn't have any jobs scheduled, for obvious reasons. This was as good a time as any to see if my mom meant what she said about wanting to end our estrangement.

"Keep your cell handy," I joked to Bones. Then I pulled away.

My mother lived thirty minutes from the compound. She was still in Richmond, but in a more rural area. Her quaint neighborhood was reminiscent of where we grew up in Ohio, without being too far away from Don if things got hairy. I pulled up to her house, parked, and noticed that her shutters needed a fresh coat of paint. Did they look like that the last time I was here? God, how long *had* it been since I'd come to see her?

As soon as I got out of the car, however, I froze. Shock crept up my spine, and it had nothing to do with the realization that I hadn't been here since Bones came back into my life months ago.

From the feel of the energy leaking off the house, my mother wasn't alone inside, but whoever was with her didn't have a heartbeat. I started to slide my hand toward my purse, where I always had some silver knives tucked away, when a cold laugh made me stop.

"I wouldn't do that if I were you, little girl," a voice I hated said from behind me.

My mother's front door opened. She was framed in it, with a dark-haired vampire who looked vaguely familiar cradling her neck almost lovingly in his hands.

And I didn't need to turn around to know the vampire at my back was my father.

DESTINED FOR AN EARLY GRAVE

They've fought against the rogue undead, battled a vengeful Master vampire and pledged their devotion with a blood bond. Now it's time for Cat and Bones to go on a vacation. But Cat is having terrifying dreams of a vampire named Gregor who's more powerful than Bones . . . and has ties to her past that even Cat herself doesn't know about.

"Frost's dazzling blend of urban fantasy action and passionate relationships make her a true phenomenon."

Romantic Times BOOKreviews

"Who is Gregor, why am I dreaming about him, and why is he called the Dreamsnatcher?"

"More importantly, why has he surfaced now to seek *her* out?" Bones's voice was cold as ice. "Gregor hasn't been seen or heard from in over a decade. I thought he might be dead."

"He's not dead," Mencheres said a trifle grimly. "Like me, Gregor has visions of the future. He intended to alter the future based on one of these visions. When I found out about it, I imprisoned him as punishment."

"And what does he want with *my wife*?"

Bones emphasized the words while arching a brow at me, as if daring me to argue. I didn't.

"He saw Cat in one of his visions and decided he had to have her," Mencheres stated in a flat tone. "Then he discovered she'd be blood-bound to you. Around the time of Cat's sixteenth birthday, Gregor intended to find her and take her away. His plan was very simple—if Cat had never met you, then she'd be his, not yours."

"Bloody sneaking bastard," Bones ground out, even as my jaw dropped. "I'll congratulate him on his cleverness—while I'm ripping silver through his heart."

"Don't underestimate Gregor," Mencheres said. "He managed to escape my prison a month ago, and I still don't know how. Gregor seems to be more interested in Cat than in getting revenge against me. She's the only person I know whom Gregor's contacted through dreams since he's been out."

Why do these crazy vampires keep trying to collect me? My being one of the only known half-breeds had been more of a pain than it was worth. Gregor wasn't the first vampire who thought it would be neat to keep me as some sort of exotic toy, but he did win points for cooking up the most original plan to do it.

"And you locked Gregor up for a dozen years just to keep him from altering my future with Bones?" I asked, my skepticism plain. "Why? You didn't do much to stop Bones's sire, Ian, when he tried the same thing."

Mencheres's steel-colored eyes flicked from me to Bones. "There was more at stake," he said at last. "If you'd never met Bones, he might have stayed under Ian's rule longer, not taking Mastership of his own line, and then not being co-Master of mine when I needed him. I couldn't risk that."

So it hadn't been about preserving true love at all. Figures. Vampires seldom did anything with purely altruistic motives.

"What happens if Gregor touches me in my dreams?" I asked, moving on. "What then?"

Bones answered me, and the burning intensity in his gaze could have seared my face.

"If Gregor takes ahold of you in your dreams, when you wake, you'll be wherever he is. That's why he's called the Dreamsnatcher. He can steal people away in their dreams."

THIS SIDE OF THE GRAVE

Cat and Bones have fought for their lives as well as their relationship. Just as they've triumphed over the latest battle, Cat's new and unexpected abilities are making them a target. And help from a dangerous "ally" may prove more treacherous than they've ever imagined.

"Cat and Bones are combustible together."

CHARLAINE HARRIS

The vampire pulled on the chains restraining him to the cave wall. His eyes were bright green, their glow illuminating the darkness surrounding us.

"Do you really think these will hold me?" he asked, an English accent caressing the challenge.

"Sure do," I replied. Those manacles were installed and tested by a Master vampire, so they were strong enough. I should know. I'd once been stuck in them myself.

The vampire's smile revealed fangs in his white upper teeth. They hadn't been there several minutes ago, when he'd still looked human to the untrained eye.

"Right, then. What do you want, now that you have me helpless?"

He didn't sound like he felt helpless in the least. I pursed my lips and considered the question, letting my gaze sweep over him. Nothing interrupted my view, either, since he was naked. I'd long ago learned that weapons could be stored in various clothing items, but bare skin hid nothing.

Except now, it was also very distracting. The vampire's body was a pale, beautiful expanse of muscle, bone, and lean, elegant lines, all topped off by a gorgeous face with cheekbones so finely chiseled they could cut butter. Clothed or unclothed, the vampire was stunning, something he was obviously aware of. Those glowing green eyes looked into mine with a knowing stare.

"Need me to repeat the question?" he asked with a hint of wickedness.

I strove for nonchalance. "Who do you work for?"

His grin widened, letting me know my aloof act wasn't as convincing as I'd meant it to be. He even stretched as much as the chains allowed, his muscles rippling like waves on a pond.

"No one."

"Liar." I pulled out a silver knife and traced its tip lightly down his chest, not breaking his skin, just leaving a faint pink line that faded in seconds. Vampires might be able to heal with lightning quickness, but silver through the heart was lethal. Only a few inches of bone and muscle stood between this vampire's heart and my blade.

He glanced at the path my knife had traced. "Is that supposed to frighten me?"

I pretended to consider the question. "Well, I've cut a bloody swath through the undead world ever since I was sixteen. Even earned myself the nickname of the Red Reaper, so if I've got a knife next to your heart, then *yes*, you should be afraid."

His expression was still amused. "Right nasty wench you sound like, but I wager I could get free and have you on your back before you could stop me."

Cocky bastard. "Talk is cheap. Prove it."

His legs flashed out, knocking me off-balance. I

sprang forward at once, but a hard, cool body flattened me to the cave floor in the next instant. An iron grip closed around my wrist, preventing me from raising the knife.

"Always pride before a fall," he murmured in satisfaction.

ONE GRAVE AT A TIME

Cat's "gift" from New Orleans's voodoo queen just keeps on giving, and now a personal favor has led to doing battle against a villainous spirit. But how do you send a killer to the grave when he's already dead?

"Every time I think I know all there is to know about Cat and Bones, Ms. Frost creates new layers of depth. . . . Prepare yourself for blood and gore galore, interspersed with tons of dark, witty humor, fierce fighting, and one-of-a-kind romance."

Joyfully Reviewed

"We summon you into our presence. Heed our call, Heinrich Kramer. Come to us now. We summon through the veil the spirit of Heinrich Kramer—"

Dexter let out a sharp noise that was part whine, part bark. Tyler quit speaking. I tensed, feeling the grate of invisible icicles across my skin again. Bones's gaze narrowed at a point over my right shoulder. Slowly, I turned my head in that direction.

All I saw was a swirl of darkness before the Ouija board flew across the room—and the point of the little wooden planchette buried in Tyler's throat.

I sprang up and tried to grab Tyler, only to be knocked backward like I'd been hit with a sledgehammer. Stunned, it took me a second to register that I was pinned to the wall by *the desk*, that dark cloud on the other side of it.

The ghost had successfully managed to use the desk as a weapon against me. If it hadn't been still jabbed in my stomach, I wouldn't even have believed it.

Bones threw the desk aside before I could, flinging it so hard that it split down the center when it hit the other wall. Dexter barked and jumped around, trying to bite the charcoal-colored cloud that was forming into the shape of a tall man.

Tyler made a horrible gurgling noise, clutching his throat. Blood leaked out between his fingers.

"Bones, fix him. I'll deal with this asshole."

Dexter's barks drowned out the sounds Tyler made as Bones slashed his palm with his fangs, then slapped it over Tyler's mouth, ripping out the planchette at the same time.

Pieces of the desk suddenly became missiles that pelted the three of us. Bones spun around to take their brunt, shielding Tyler, while I jumped to cover the dog. A pained yelp let me know at least one had nailed Dexter before I got to him. Tyler's gurgles became wrenching coughs.

"Boy, did you make a colossal fucking mistake," I snarled, grabbing a piece of the ruined desk. Then I stood up, still blocking the dog from any more objects the ghost could lob at him. He'd materialized enough for me to see white hair swirling around a craggy, wrinkled face. The ghost hadn't been young when he died, but the shoulders underneath his dark tunic weren't bowed from age. They were squared in arrogance, and the green eyes boring into mine held nothing but contempt.

"*Hure,*" the ghost muttered before thrusting his hand into my neck and squeezing like he was about to choke me. I felt a stronger than normal pins-and-needles sensation but didn't flinch. If this schmuck thought to terrify me with a cheap parlor trick like that, wait until he saw *my* first abracadabra.

"Heinrich Kramer?" I asked almost as an afterthought. Didn't matter if it wasn't him, he would regret what he did, but I wanted to know whose ass I was about to kick.

NEW YORK TIMES AND
USA TODAY BESTSELLING AUTHOR

JEANIENE FROST

FIRST DROP OF CRIMSON

978-0-06-158322-3

The night is not safe for mortals. Denise MacGregor knows all too well what lurks in the shadows and now a demon shapeshifter has marked her as prey. Her survival depends on Spade, an immortal who lusts for a taste of her, but is duty-bound to protect her—even if it means destroying his own kind.

ETERNAL KISS OF DARKNESS

978-0-06-178316-6

Chicago private investigator Kira Graceling finds herself in a world she's only imagined in her worst nightmares. At the center is Mencheres, a breathtaking Master vampire who Kira braved death to rescue. With danger closing in, Mencheres must choose either the woman he craves or embracing the darkest magic to defeat an enemy bent on his eternal destruction.

ONE GRAVE AT A TIME

978-0-06-178319-7

Cat Crawfield wants nothing more than a little downtime with her vampire husband, Bones. Unfortunately, they must risk all to battle a villainous spirit and send him back to the other side of eternity.

JFR1 0312

*G*ive in to your Impulses!

These unforgettable stories only take a second to buy and give you hours of reading pleasure!

Go to *www.AvonImpulse.com* and see what we have to offer.

Available wherever e-books are sold.

IMP 0811